HUSK

WANDERER OF WORLDS

5

CONLON / STRANGE

OTHER BOOKS BY THE AUTHORS

ACKNOWLEDGEMENTS

We wish to acknowledge the people who helped bring this book to fruition; those who listened to passages read out loud and pointed out the parts that snagged, those who received the first version and emailed us their comments or questions and, of course, those who buy our books and read them with relish. The support they give us in our endeavour is invaluable as we aim to write a new kind of story—incomparable to most out there but able to hold its own on the shelf or maybe even on the screen one day (big or small, we wouldn't mind!). Specifically, thank you to David Strange who quietly supports the Wanderer books by letting his wife write them all day, and to David Woodward who enthusiastically supports the Wanderer books by being a sounding board to his fiancée. We must also extend an appreciative thank you to our wonderful beta readers who are always keen for the next instalment; Kylie Crase, Nicole Hary, Jodie Lane, Fiona Moran (who writes as Fiona Emily) and Sue Strathdee. Much love.

For David, Katy and Carole

For Rosie, whose lovely characters didn't deserve to be treated that way by mine.

CONTENTS

The Story So Far

At sixteen years of age, Daeson leaves his farm and accidentally Wanders out of his homeworld. He awakens in the city of Gredann on the world of Trent—a world controlled by Authorities. He falls in with a group of criminals, managed by the sophisticated Omerri Backhouse, who seduces and manipulates him for two years. While he is with her, he helps her by using his dual abilities—he is a Healer and is also able to tell when someone is lying.

Synjan works for the crime-lord Ellis, who keeps a tight rein on her. Even though Omerri and Ellis have a minor partnership and Synjan knows everyone on both payrolls, she is kept apart from Daeson. When a mission goes sour and Synjan is shot, she is taken to Daeson for a life-saving Heal. Soon after, Daeson leaves Omerri, his eyes finally open to his lover's ruthlessness and selfishness. Omerri sends Synjan to bring him back because she's a Wanderer Navigator and can find anyone. Instead, Synjan leads Daeson to the Portal and travels with him to the next world.

Ellis sends Hunter Hawke Donovan after them—a man he has had tentative contact with since Hawke was a boy. Hawke was a Wanderer Shielder stolen out of his world and abandoned to the Authorities. The organisation made him their ward and put him in a boarding school. As a teen, he was offered the choice of working for Ellis but Hawke signed up with the Authorities instead. Ellis and Hawke have a mutual friend—Kegan Frederickson—who is also in the Authorities. He trained Hawke to defend himself. He is also connected to Synjan, training her at Ellis' behest. As Hawke's mentor and friend, Kegan was able to influence Hawke to go on a mission to track and return Synjan, even though Hawke was assigned on leave. When Hawke's superior—his father figure, Division General Cayden—discovers what's going on, he promises to help Hawke on his 'personal quest', though he is curious about what the details are.

Ellis, too impatient to wait for results, recruits his secondary Wanderer Navigator, a young man called Fyfe. Together, they Wander into the world of J'Bdyamn where they are absorbed by a hostile tribe and its psychotic leader. After escaping the natives with the help of a woman named Paki, they begin the arduous task of travelling to the Wanderer Portal—almost halfway around the world. It will take them months to reach it.

Meanwhile, Daeson and Synjan are distancing themselves from the life they left behind, moving quickly through the world of Femme, where they learn they are being pursued by a Hunter. After waking up on Earth, they move with the panic of being pursued. Synjan returns to old habits and steals what is required for their travels, kidnapping a woman—Peri—to drive them to the Portal. Synjan and Daeson connect hands, expecting to vanish out of the car but the car and their victim are brought with them into the next world, where they crash.

1

Prophecy

H E'D FOUND HER.

Hunter Hawke Donovan was unable to stop his smile from broadening as he watched the monitor. It showed footage of Synjan dashing through a large indoor market with stolen merchandise in hand. For a panicked woman on the run, she moved with a precision that her partner didn't match. She ducked around groups of people while he smacked into them, holding out a hand of apology as he lumbered on. He didn't behave like the criminal type. She did, darting through the mall with a style and purpose he attributed to Ellis' influence; her work for his underground organisation would have trained her to appraise a crowd and move swiftly through her surroundings. Or could it be her Navigator talent helping her?

The cameras didn't show what happened in the carpark. The angle was wrong so he couldn't watch her hotwire a car. He knew she'd taken a red SUV because of the police report.

He identified a tendril of admiration for her and it pissed him off. Any other Wanderer running around stealing shit and causing trouble would earn his disdain and outright hatred. He considered her special because of his own vanity; she'd taken the parallel life he'd refused and he saw his reflection in her. It shouldn't change his core beliefs... but were they core beliefs? Had he simply conditioned himself to hate every Wanderer that left chaos in their wake because of what had happened to him as a kid?

He focussed on the monitor, rewinding and playing it back, grateful for Synjan's ignorance of the ever-present security cameras. She came from a world without digital eyes and mobile phones that could record her every move. It wouldn't be long before the local authorities caught and arrested her, then he could leave London and fly out to Australia to pick her up. On the trip back to Ellis, he could find out everything he wanted to know.

"Have they been arrested yet?" Hawke asked of a male officer moving past his desk with papers in hand.

"What? I'm not from this division, sir."

"Why the fuck are you in this room, then? This is a closed-door operation!" Hawke yelled, wanting as few people to know about Synjan and her Healer accomplice as possible—not that anybody knew Daeson was a Healer. If that news got out, the whole organisation would be after him. He didn't want to deal with that kind of competition.

"I, uh..."

The officer looked at the two long rows of desks occupied by Authorities in crisp dark blue uniforms. No help there. Colonel Collins had stepped out to take a meeting so

Hawke was leading the charge. His commandeered team were a study in professionalism, typing and clicking at their computers, absorbed by their search for Hawke's Wanderer pair.

They were busy coordinating with the Authority office in Australia, located in the country's capital, Canberra. It was how Hawke had got his hands on the mall footage so quickly. After the recent spree in a city called Brisbane, Hawke tasked the team with finding out what happened next. It was harder to get news from local enforcements in a different country. Luckily, Australia was a British colony.

Hawke stood to put more force into his command. "Get out of here!"

The officer glared at him, unused to being yelled at by some random guy in civilian clothes. His cheeks flared pink and a sneer twitched his top lip.

"I have a flare report for the Colonel."

The news shocked Hawke into silence. The pit of his stomach hollowed out.

"When did the flare occur?"

"This information is for—"

"WHEN?"

"An hour ago."

Hawke sank to his chair. "Is there any more footage?" he asked nobody in particular.

"Working on it," one of the soldiers said from the closest desk. Maybe she was a civilian, she was the only one not wearing a uniform.

The footage was irrelevant, if it existed. He already knew Synjan had Wandered. That was why she'd robbed the shop and stolen the car—her escape route had been very close. Clever. Not clever enough to avoid calling attention to herself but she had no way of understanding how security-conscious this world was.

How the fuck was he going to catch them? Synjan and Daeson had left Earth an hour ago and he still had over seventeen hours of his designated wait before Collins would clear him to leave.

Portal travel put a strain on people. Civilians couldn't use the portal twice in a month. It was recommended Authorities not go more than once a week. Hunters could take it down to a forty-eight-hour wait. Twenty-four hours was the compulsory minimum requirement. Hawke had neglected this rule a few times. Instead of the usual unpleasant taste in his mouth, he'd felt queasy—he'd only ever thrown up once, when he'd pushed himself hard chasing a pair of particularly fast Wanderers some years ago. He'd shot one of them but the other had got away. The second one had been travelling light and must've been a Navigator. He'd lost the trail soon after.

The officer whom Hawke had accosted had already moved on. Hawke spoke to the female maybe-civilian who'd answered him last.

"Where's the portal-fax?"

"Corner of the room. Behind you, your eight o'clock." She didn't look up from her typing. The lack of uniform and no use of 'sir' or other officious language confirmed she was a civvy—unless she had a special rank like him. He liked her straightforward answers but was concerned about her presence. Who was she? One of Kegsy's people or maybe a spy? Someone to check up on him? She focussed on her task, gave blunt answers and attended to the people in her surroundings. He didn't want to confront her and prove he had less information than she did.

Hawke got up and found the portal-fax. There was a memo pad and pen near it that he used to scribble a quick message on. He faxed it through to Hunter HQ at Red Rock, attention Division General Irian Cayden.

After a tedious forty-minute wait—most of which he spent pacing—he got a fax back with his request approved. He was surprised to see the General's assistant-in-chief's scrawling signature. He could sign for the office so the approval would stick but it meant Cayden wasn't at HQ like he'd said he would be... like Hawke hadn't quite believed he would be. But where had he gone?

It wasn't something Hawke could chew on right now. Grabbing the fax out of the machine, he took great pleasure in interrupting Colonel Collins' important meeting so he could thrust the paperwork under his nose.

Ten minutes later, Hawke rode the elevator down to the portal. His new messenger bag was filled with travelling supplies and seated firmly on his shoulder. He'd signed out a semi-automatic pistol and hip holster to take on his journey, knowing that Synjan would be armed and not wanting to face her without a gun of his own. The next world, Alpha Five, was a civilised place with planned urban spaces. The Authorities were building it from scratch because there had been no inhabitants on it and it was a stable world with very few natural disasters. There were only pockets of civilisation under Authority control. He'd go to the most commonly-accessed portal at the Zed Plateau—

No.

The elevator doors opened but he didn't immediately step out. He lingered so long that they tried to shut on him. He shoved his hand between them and pushed one door back, forcing both to churn open. The noise attracted the attention of the pair of armed soldiers standing guard. He didn't miss the way their eyes were drawn to his weapon, assessing his threat. Neither of them were alarmed enough to comment or act.

Hawke went to the portal programmer's desk and stared at the balding spot on the top of his head until the man looked up.

"World of Alpha Five. List my options."

"Options? There's only Zed Plateau," the programmer replied.

"There's more than one fucking base."

"Aren't you a Hunter? The last Wanderer sighting was at Zed and the other portals are just training grounds."

Hawke made a gesture and the programmer peered at his screen and pressed a few keys.

"Okaaaay, so other than Zed Plateau you've got Greystone Marsh, Skattle Ocean and the Hjaaloken."

"Yahl... what the fuck?"

"Hjaaloken. It's a base in the desert, near a few outpost constructs used for weapons training."

Hawke stared at the programmer, thinking that a training base in the desert sounded awful. On the flipside, a marsh or an ocean would be no better.

"Which one is the farthest away from Zed?"

"Hjaaloken."

Of course. Synjan had evaded him effortlessly thus far and the only clue he had to catch up with her was from a dubious source—a Clairvoyant that he still wasn't sure had helped him. His faith in Woy had swung from one extreme to the other since meeting her. She'd told him not to go to Zed and he had three options left to him. How useful.

"Sir?"

Hawke swore internally and hoped his instincts were good.

"Send me to the desert and let them know I'm coming," he said.

Twenty minutes later he lay back in the portal chair, an oxygen mask over his mouth and nose, sending him to sleep.

From a distance, Hawke could hear people yelling about a crash-cart. It was like a dream, but he was familiar enough with portal travel to know that he was in the groggy stage of waking. His chest had something heavy pressing on it and he found it hard to draw breath. A rancid smell filled his nostrils.

The weight on his chest lifted and he inhaled deeply. It was like ice travelling down his throat. His eyes watered with the sensation of choking. Blurry figures raced to him as he struggled to get out of the portal-chair—he didn't know what the fuss was but the acidic taste lurking in the back of his throat had him suspecting he'd thrown up. He managed to heave himself out of the chair, but his frail legs refused to hold him.

He passed out before he hit the floor.

2

Injuries And Responsibilities

THE FIRST THING Daeson became aware of was the stifling heat. It didn't compare to the jungles of J'Bdyamn, but returned him to a distant memory— to the time he'd ventured into the smithy's workshop and been savaged by air heated in the furnace. He fumbled in darkness broken only by the subtle glow of flame when he heard the growl of a large animal. It sounded furious, ready to attack. His brain struggled to make sense of it, he should be hearing the whickering of horses outside, not the rumble of a bear!

Panicked, he forced his eyes open but didn't understand what he was seeing. There was no angry dog or bear in sight. He tried picking himself up but he was in a box of some kind—he couldn't lift his knees and his head brushed against the roof. Why had he crawled in here?

He turned his head to take in more of his surroundings. In front of him was a torn bag of cat biscuits, its innards splayed across the ground. The little brown stars smelt of false meat and were bunched around a clear plastic mound. He stared at the arrangement for a long moment, unable to make sense of it. When his focus shifted, he saw an unconscious woman beyond them, hanging upside down. He didn't recognise her but knew she was hurt because of her blood-matted hair.

Synjan! He couldn't move around much but he knew she wasn't in the car with him. The plastic mound made sense now; it was a light. The car had landed on its roof. It had been crushed like a paper bag; its sides had buckled and the back seat had fallen free of its anchor, onto his legs. He could move them, no bones were broken... or they *had* been broken and that was why he was thirsty now. It was so hot he couldn't tell whether he'd sweated all his body's water out or used it up with his power.

Daeson dragged himself forward with his elbows, shuffling his legs to and fro to free them from the weight of the back seat. He got close enough to the upside-down woman that he could check for a pulse in her neck. It took some searching before he finally found a beat against his fingertips, filling him with relief. What was her name?

He remembered then, what he and Synjan had done. The woman's name was Peri and she had a man named Dave and a cat called Biscuit. Synjan had forced her to drive them to the Portal. They'd Wandered and then they'd crashed. He hadn't expected the car to come along with them—he'd thought they would disappear out of it instead.

Guilt, shame and fear wracked his body in waves, making him feel nauseous and hollow at the same time—contradictions that he couldn't fix, not if this woman died here.

He forced his upper body through the space between the two front seats.

"Please wake up," he pleaded, placing his hands on Peri's head, over the wound. A puddle of red had absorbed into the sand and he could feel fresh blood on his palms, warm and sticky. This close, he could smell it in the air. They hadn't been unconscious for long. He didn't want her to grow weaker and die. If he let her die, that would be his fault.

He wanted her to be okay—he allowed the desire to flow out of him and into her. He sensed it going into the gash on her head, then it spread deeper into her body. Perhaps she had internal injuries? He continued Healing, not daring to stop in case it wasn't enough to save her.

It felt different to what he'd done for Synjan; Peri wasn't taking as much out of him, but he could still feel himself tiring as he fed his power into her. He had no water to replenish himself with, but he owed her. If she died now, then he'd taken her life as surely as if Synjan had pulled the trigger of her gun.

———————— ·✦· ————————

Persephone Brown had had the most refreshing sleep. In all her twenty years as a primary school teacher, she'd never felt so good, not even when she'd gone on a cruise around the Pacific Islands. Relaxed, yes, but the feeling thrumming through her now went well beyond that. It was like she'd caught up on every second of lost sleep in her life and not gone a moment over. She was *revitalised*.

Her eyes sprang open and then squinted because of the

light. A few rapid blinks reduced the blinding dazzle to an insistent glow and she looked around as best she could. The world was upside down—she was looking up at her steering wheel—and there was a great deal of pressure on her legs and body. She felt bent at odd angles, her chin pressed to her chest. Her belt was a vice, further restricting her movement and making it hard to breathe but she could see clear blue sky beyond her open window. No traffic. Oddly, there was no noise at all. That couldn't be right, she'd definitely been driving... she'd been in an accident! She'd never been in an accident in her life!

Cautiously, she tested her body with little movements and ascertained that she was whole. No injuries, though she must have rolled the car. Still, she was filled with the most reassuring feeling of rightness.

With some difficulty, she grasped the seat-belt and tested it, trying to figure out how to get it over her head. As she squirmed, something in her peripheral vision caught her attention. She swivelled and saw a man laying on the ceiling of her car. He was asleep, his chest rising and falling in a relaxed rhythm that matched her own. There was blood on his hand, which mildly disturbed her, but he looked otherwise peaceful, his long, dark lashes casting shadows across his cheekbones. She didn't remember who he was but his beauty was reassuring. Men that good looking couldn't be all bad.

The longer she stayed, the harder it was to breathe. She had to move. With another determined burst of effort, she scraped the seatbelt a short distance across her torso, wincing as it threatened to slice off her padded stomach and garrotte her breasts. It was no good. Even if she got it over her head, there was still the section at her hips cutting off circulation to her legs. She had to unbuckle properly.

Peri reached up and braced her arm against the roof of her car. It was warm and sprinkled with cat food and... sand? She couldn't remember where it was she'd been driving when the accident happened but there was a lot of sand around. It looked like a beach. When had she ever driven on a beach? Her other hand felt around for the seatbelt clasp. She found the button and, with a deep breath, she pressed it.

Her arm collapsed beneath her excessive weight and she dropped, expelling all her air with an indelicate grunt and painfully scraping her face. That hadn't worked, then.

Peri wriggled and heaved until she was on all fours, marvelling that she hadn't woken her passenger in the process. He looked so serene, his bloody hand stretched towards her like a lover silently begging her not to go. He'd been dusted in a light coating of sand too, she observed. Why was there so much of it in her car? How had it got in? She looked out the windshield, amazed at how clean it looked. It took her a moment to realise that the glass was no longer there. It must have shattered when her car rolled.

Peri spat out as much sand as she was able, brushing it off her face and away from her eyes, while she stared bemusedly out of her non-windscreen. She was unable to dislodge most of the grains upon her lips, regardless of how many arm-wipes she carried out. It kept falling out of her hair or was stuck to her sweaty skin. She gave it up and looked around to determine her best method of exit. She spied her handbag resting below the crumpled dashboard and grabbed it before she half-crawled, half-dragged herself towards freedom, crying out when her hands and knees landed on sharp or bumpy items. How could they be the only pains bothering her, if she'd had such a terrible accident?

Peri laboured to her feet and looked around. There was nothing to see but giant sand-dunes. Deserts made people hallucinate, right? Could she be imagining the desert itself? She took a deep breath, the dry air and dust she inhaled causing her to cough. She scrabbled in the handbag hooked over her arm and pulled out the water bottle she always had with her. Taking a swig, she noted the bottle was mostly full. She'd been grocery shopping, she recalled. The shops were nowhere nearby. She blinked as she looked around, trying to align what she was seeing with what she knew.

She was in a valley between towering golden dunes of sand; the sides of the one in front of her even had wind ripples snaking across it. She'd had a calendar with pictures just like it, once, with scenes from all over the world. This desert didn't look anything like the red heart of Australia but that was a ridiculous thought. Almost as ridiculous as the notion she'd been driving on a beach. What was going on?

Peri reached back to steady herself, touching the car and quickly pulling her hand away. The metal was scorching hot. How long had she been unconscious? Had she been drugged, to forget how she'd got here? None of this made sense, otherwise.

She turned to see where she'd come from and her

stomach lurched when she saw the car's tracks only started halfway up the dune. She'd driven off *that*? And rolled down here? Her gaze followed the haphazard path of chewed up sand. Her heart picked up speed as she imagined what the car would have been like, flipping over and over until coming to its final position at the bottom. Upside down. How the hell was she alive?

A cold tendril slithered down Peri's spine despite the burning heat; there was a body lying at a strange angle some distance behind the car. It was a woman and she looked dead. Maybe not dead, but there was certainly something wrong with her. Tracks in the sand and debris woven around her told the story of how the woman had been flung out of the car partway down.

It came to Peri then, that the woman had caused this situation. She'd forced Peri to drive... drive where? Wherever they were. Some weird place. They couldn't still be in Brisbane, yet it was equally as ludicrous to think she'd blacked out and driven them to an unfamiliar desert. Did it matter, though? Knowing how they'd got here wouldn't make their situation any less perilous. Dismissing the black lake of despair threatening to drown her with revelation, Peri dug into her handbag again, this time searching for her phone. She hoped she'd put it inside. Sometimes she didn't because the bluetooth in her car worked with her phone whether it was in her bag or not. She found her sunglasses first and put them on. Her phone was underneath.

Relief flooded through her again. Now she could call for help. Peri unlocked the phone, thinking that this was her second emergency call for the day, and dialled triple zero.

Nothing happened. Her gaze flicked to the battery icon. It was full. Then she checked the signal. No bars. Instead of her usual carrier, something called AUTHNET was emblazoned at the top of the screen. Okay, so that meant the phone had picked up a signal at some stage, to display that weird business name. She took it as a positive sign, even if the call didn't work.

She'd have to check on the woman. She glanced towards the prone figure and a well of apprehension opened inside her, probably because she wasn't moving. Probably.

Peri shoved her phone back into her bag and settled the strap on her shoulder before wading through the soft sand. Halfway along, something reflected in her eyes and she flinched to a stop, supposing it was a broken car mirror. Through a small gap between her fingers, she saw that it was nothing so benign.

It was a silver gun.

Again, the tide of understanding lapped at her subconscious but she pushed it away. She veered towards the gun and picked it up, popping it into her handbag for safekeeping. A few steps later, she did the same thing for an apple and then for the remainder of a hand of bananas. They poked at the underside of her arm as she continued onward, her hands clasped tightly about the strap of her bag. A sense of dread trickled into her chest with every step and she slowed as she saw the horrible angle the woman's arm was at. The greater issue seemed to be half of a tyre iron sticking out of her side.

It looked like it wasn't real, like one of those joke items people bought to freak out their friends or parents—one of those headbands that had the pointy end of an arrow stuck on one side, and the feathery end on the other. She'd had a student once that had slipped on a fake bandage with a fake nail, for a nail-in-the-finger prank. It had worked on his friends because eight year olds were gullible but he'd made the mistake of showing her at the end of a long day. She hadn't had the energy to pretend she was fooled. The tyre iron sticking out of the woman's side was more realistic than either of those.

A groan escaped the woman as her eyes fluttered open. It became an animalistic scream when she moved. Peri's lips pulled apart in a silent, sympathetic snarl as the woman froze in muted agony, veins and tendons straining in her neck, her knuckles white where her good hand dug into her hip. Blood seeped in a growing arc at her side, gobbling up the white of her shirt with sinful speed. Peri shuffled around until she was in the woman's line of sight (and unable to easily observe that spreading pool of blood).

"Can I help?" she asked, deciding to pull out her phone again. Peri frowned in concentration, taking the time to shift the bananas to her other hand and dig up her lifeline. She knew first aid but wasn't prepared for anything like this. The woman was losing blood and was very sweaty. She needed more help than Peri could give.

"Get... Daeson," the woman said through gritted teeth, then made another sound that Peri associated with terrible pain. She was surprised the woman could talk at all.

"Daeson? Who's that?" Peri asked absently, looking at her phone and checking her signal. Still no bars. She dialled 000 anyway. No luck.

"Daeson! He's... I don't... know where. He was... with me—" the woman growled, attempting to look around and screaming when it was too much.

Peri jumped, staring at the woman as she breathed in short puffs of air. She was hyperventilating; that wasn't good.

"Oh, Daeson is that man's name! Got you. Right. Well, he's sleeping in the car, he's okay, don't worry about him." Peri knelt by the woman. "Is there something I can bring you? I have an umbrella, it'll give you shade."

With snake-like precision, the woman grasped Peri's wrist with an astounding amount of strength. Peri cried out in terror and pulled back to no avail, overbalancing and falling on her butt when she couldn't break the blonde woman's grip.

"N-no! Let me go! Stop it! Let me go!" she warbled, her voice escalating in volume as terror overtook shock and the wave of understanding crashed down on her at last. She remembered now. This woman had hijacked her and her car, forcing her to drive to some portal or something, causing them to crash. She was the reason they were here, it was all her fault! Peri needed to get away from her.

Her frantic movements caused the blonde to release her, the colour washing out of her face dramatically.

"Get, Daeson," she panted, her eyes closing as she fought off the pain.

Peri leapt to her feet, wanting to flee across the desert but compelled to stay because it looked like the woman was about to die. "He's sleeping," she argued weakly.

"He'll wake up... soon. He probably... Healed you, you... hurt?" the blonde grunted.

Peri frowned, the woman's question reviving the manic sense of confusion and unreality she'd been experiencing since she awoke. She fought it off valiantly. "No. I'm fine, no thanks to you," she answered brusquely.

"Then get him... water. He needs it. To Heal me."

"He can... he's a doctor?" Peri queried. He looked a bit young to be a doctor, but lots of twenty-something year olds looked like kids to Peri. Being in her forties had changed her perspective of ageing.

"No."

"Then... why do you want him?"

"Just... go."

"But he's unconscious...?"

"Give... water," Synjan gasped and let out another shriek of agony.

"Okay, okay. I'll do it. Stop talking, save your strength," Peri admonished and rushed towards the car, tucking the bananas and her phone back inside her bag as she went.

As she hobbled along, she was forced to acknowledge that she had no idea what she was doing. It made no sense to be heading away from a critically injured woman towards someone who wasn't a doctor but she wasn't about to argue with someone on the brink of dying. Mainly, she left because she was thrilled to be heading in the opposite direction to the crazy woman that had ruined her day.

3

Hjaaloken

WHEN HAWKE WOKE again he was flat on his back with an oxygen mask on his face. Other than the heavy, churning sensation in his stomach, he didn't think he was bad enough to warrant oxygen so he pulled the mask down and tried to sit up. The female medic nearby made a noise of protest and pushed him back down, hard.

"Ow! The fuck? You're supposed to take care of me, not treat me like we're in a wrestling match."

"You sound like you're getting better," the woman replied. She wrapped a blood pressure cuff around his arm and pressed a button for it to puff up. Hawke rubbed his fingers together and she glanced down at them. "Are you numb? Can you feel them?"

"Yeah, it's just a habit."

"Stop moving your right arm."

No please, no requests, just orders. He used his left hand to pull the oxygen mask up and over his head, the elastic too old to retain much stretch. He supposed the medics must always be busy at a training base. He remembered the many incidents during his live-fire exercises. Surprisingly few deaths, considering how many soldiers ended up getting shot.

When the blood pressure cuff came off, he struggled to sit up. The medic gave him a grim appraisal as she packed the cuff back into its case.

"How long was I out?" he asked. She checked her watch.

"Less than an hour. Can you give me your name and rank?"

"Hunter Hawke Donovan."

The medic took his hand and held it so his palm faced down, her touch light. He could see his fingers trembling like a junkie on withdrawal and he snatched it back.

"I'll be fine. Just give me some adreno-pills and I'll be on my way."

The look she gave him would've made him laugh if he hadn't been worried she might stop him from leaving.

"Are you experiencing any dizziness?"

"No."

"Double-vision?"

"No."

"Do you have a headache?"

"No."

"You're lying."

"I want to get up now."

He outranked her but because she was a medic she had the authority to make him wait. He forced a smile to show how amicable he could be.

"I haven't taken bloods yet," she told him.

"Now is not the time for me to be losing any," he said,

unable to keep the sharpness out of his voice. He was relieved when she nodded but then there came another barrage of questions that he answered in the negative—no, he was experiencing none of those side-effects, just the blacking out.

The recovery room they were in was bigger than Hawke expected for a training base. He supposed trainees could arrive in combinations of numbers up to a full unit of twelve and the room would have to accommodate them. A careful look confirmed that it could've held two full units. The walls were a boring antiseptic green but he was grateful they weren't white.

As he waited for the dizziness he'd denied to fade, the attendant left. She came back carrying a glass of juice and a plastic-wrapped sandwich with a suspicious green filling. His stomach flipped at the idea of eating but he took it with a thanks and set it down on his lap so he could ignore it while he drank.

The attendant left again and returned five minutes later, pulling a trolley behind her that had a machine with a bunch of wires on it. Hawke soured when he saw the older woman helping her. She was dressed in the same Authority medic outfit of a white shirt over dark blue pants but had two stripes on her sleeves. The older woman held the rank of Officer and was unlikely to be influenced by any protests he made. Hawke forced as pleasant a smile as he was able, not wanting to appear ill or weak. The first attendant gave a small smile back while the officer looked him over without expression.

"You've been reckless, Hunter Donovan," she announced primly and began fussing with the machine. Hawke sighed, recognising it as a dynamap—it would only show them his vitals, nothing too intrusive. He wouldn't make a fuss.

"The mission comes first," he replied.

The officer scoffed and shook her head at him. "I think the cost of training another *you* is worth more to the Authorities than your mission."

Hawke thought it was wise of her to say so, but also presumptuous. If she knew he was after a Healer Wanderer, she'd agree the Authorities would sacrifice thousands of him in order to get one of those back alive.

The medics needed to put sensors on his chest so he removed his shirt and felt a chill. The air-conditiong was a constant whirr over the bleeps of the dynamap and he thought about the effort and cost of making the base so cold in the middle of a desert. Surely it would make acclimatising more difficult for the trainees based here. Maybe that was the point. Soldiers sent to a desert world might be portalling in from an icy one.

The more minutes that passed, the more anxious he became. Synjan had already landed and she was probably on the move. If she wasn't near Hjaaloken, he had to find out where she was and send instructions that she was not to be actioned. He'd need to figure out whatever base was closest, or if she was even near a base. This world was huge and most of it untouched. Hopefully the portal wouldn't be close to her again. She'd been ridiculously lucky with that thing.

"Have you seen enough yet?" Hawke asked, frowning at the monitor transfixing both women.

"I'm not liking the look of the spikes you're getting now," the superior said.

"They're only there because I want to get going. I risked myself to make good time and you can see I'm healthy enough." He had no idea what they were seeing but he felt good, if queasy.

"Eat first, then you can go."

He stared blankly at the officer and then looked with disgust at the sandwich on his knee. He met her gaze again.

"If I eat that, I'll probably throw up again. And it wouldn't look much different."

"You won't, because it's made from the right proteins and nutrients. Its taste is tolerable."

"Tolerable? Don't get into the sandwich selling business, lady."

"Officer Carey," she corrected but he thought he saw a ghost of a smile behind her serious facade.

"Can I eat it on the go?"

"There are too many bins between here and the central office," Carey replied, her eyebrow quirking.

Hawke dutifully unwrapped the sandwich and held it to his nose. It had no smell, not even the bread. He looked up at the two medics staring expectantly at him, then ate the sandwich as quickly as possible. The taste was unpleasant but subtle and it had a bitter quality to it, like there was mashed up medicine inside. It struck him, as he finished the last bite, that it was like eating mouldy peanut-butter. His stomach flipped again and he stared at the ceiling to focus on keeping his food down.

The attendant had left the room while he'd been shoving the sandwich into his face and returned with another bottle of water for him to drink. He took it and murmured thanks before downing it. After the initial sensation of disgust had passed, he did feel better and told the medics so.

"I've never seen someone recover so quickly," Carey said dubiously.

"It's always been the case with me," Hawke said, wondering if he was bragging. It sounded like it, though he'd just stated a fact.

"You haven't ever portalled within twelve hours before. I checked. You almost died. Nobody comes back from that."

"From *almost* dying? Sure they do," Hawke grinned, plucking wirepads off his chest. The junior medic helped him, moreso because she was taking better care of the equipment than he was.

"You've been put on the no-portalling list temporarily."

Hawke stared at Carey, panic pounding in his chest. The queasy feeling in the back of his throat returned.

"For how long?"

"Seven days."

Fuck! Hawke pressed his lips together and grunted his dissatisfaction. If Synjan wasn't close to this base or its training zones, there was a good chance he'd lost her.

He hastily threw on his shirt and buttoned it up. He'd spied his bag on a nearby chair and grabbed it before leaving the recovery room, putting all his effort into as brisk a walk as possible.

Once he was out of sight of the medical lab, he collapsed against the wall and caught his breath, wiping his lips with the back of his hand and taking in big lungfuls of air. A few soldiers passed by, giving him curious stares. None of them asked who he was or what he was doing, even though he wore plain clothes. Word must have spread about his arrival. He would take advantage of their mute curiosity and recover while he could.

When next a soldier's gaze lingered on him, he called them over and requested they take him to central office. The signs posted around the base were likely helpful but his vision was too blurry for him to read them.

Hawke arrived at central office shortly after, attracting stares as he picked his way through the room towards the swarthy man dressed in the uniform with the highest rank. There was no Division General or Division Overseer to check in with, not at a far-flung training base like this, so the Major was it. He took cautious steps as the other man stepped forward to meet him and saluted him, even though there was no requirement to—neither of them outranked the other. Hawke saluted back to acknowledge the gesture. It would only help his case if he was liked.

"Hunter Donovan, you've recovered quickly. I'm Major Perrecott, in charge of Hjaaloken for the time being. We were about to send some lookout drones for your targets as soon as we were notified of your impending arrival but we've caught a lucky break and no longer need them."

Perrecott's chatty and friendly nature was a welcome change from the medics but it took Hawke a moment to filter.

"How's that?"

Perrecott strutted back to his computer at a pace Hawke couldn't match, so he took his time, touching the backs of chairs and taking smaller steps so as not to overexert himself. His balance was still off.

"We've received an emergency signal. Though it's a weak one, it's enough to pinpoint a location. Someone's used the open Authnet channel and dialled a triple digit."

Hawke nodded, understanding that triple digits were standard Authority world emergency beacons— associated with cries for help. His eyesight sharpened and his heartrate picked up in fear. Why would Synjan ask for help from Authorities unless she was hurt and her Healer was dead?

"What's the location?" he asked. His gaze was directed to a large map that filled the far wall, one that showed the base and the surrounding area. Most of it was desert, though the topography showed some rises and hollows, and he identified the snaking line of a dry riverbed. Perrecott produced a laser-pointer from somewhere and was now aiming a red dot at Hjaaloken Base.

"So, we're here. The emergency signal came from here." The red dot whizzed to the right and bounced around in Perrecott's imperfect hold. "And now the signal is moving—directly towards one of our training zones, here." The red dot moved slowly left until it arrived at a cluster of squares and rectangles on the map, then circled them.

The distance between where the red dot had first been positioned and the cluster of buildings was quite short. Synjan must be alive if she was walking and it seemed she was walking straight towards the base. She might hole up in the training zone for a while and Hawke could collect her from there without fuss.

"We have a unit already there led by Sergeant Mallory, which will make your job easier. They'll have the opportunity—"

"They'll have no such thing!" Hawke interrupted. "This is a special mission. Nobody is allowed to run interference. Can you radio them right now?"

"They're… they're out of range," Perrecott said, his eyes wide. The laser-pointer disappeared into his shirt pocket. "They have a Trundler, we can fax them through that."

"Do it right now. How long will it take the target to reach the town? What's the rate of travel?" Hawke barked, looking back at some of the technicians who were staring at them. Fingers flew over keyboards and one of them answered quickly.

"At their current rate, about an hour, sir. Give or take five minutes."

"They might slow. Progress is difficult where they are, it's all dunes," said another technician, showing Hawke a foldout map. He took it from her, even though he didn't think she was giving it to him. It would come in handy.

"What's the drive from here to the training zone?" Hawke asked.

"Eighty minutes," two of them replied at once, though only one continued. "You could knock off ten if you go full throttle the whole way."

Perrecott frowned deeply. "I wouldn't advise it, Hunter Donovan. There's a lot of unsteady ground in between."

"You have dirt-bikes?"

Perrecott shook his head. "Trikes and quads. I'll give you the latter, they're faster and steadier. Gimble, can you take Hunter Donovan to the garage? I'll call ahead and have one

27

fuelled and waiting."

Hawke took a moment to thank the major before rushing alongside Gimble, wanting to take advantage of the wave of adrenaline as long as possible.

4

Unorthodox Approach

YIELDING SAND MADE walking difficult and relentless sunlight enveloped them in a bubble of heat. Synjan squinted against the glare, feeling hemmed in by the walls of sand rising either side of them. She wanted to suggest they climb out of the baking valley but she wasn't sure she dared. Daeson wasn't interested in conversing with her and Peri was sticking so close to him, she was practically in his pocket.

Their uninvited companion squawked as her skimpy footwear got caught and she stumbled. Daeson instinctively grabbed the older woman's elbow, steadying her.

"You okay?" he asked.

"Yeah. Stupid shoes. Thanks," Peri wheezed, swiping at a lock of hair plastered to her red, sweat-streaked face. She withdrew her arm from his grasp once her balance was restored, not looking Synjan's way.

The scratch of footwear finding purchase on sand and the rhythm of ragged breathing rose around them once more. It warped the heat bubble with undulations of sound that further distorted Synjan's perception. From the moment she'd awoken to searing agony instead of the usual Wandering bliss, she'd been a beat behind everything in this world. She felt desynchronised.

After Daeson had saved her life (again) and passed out from dehydration (again), Peri had asked one tentative question. Sitting with Daeson's head cradled in her lap, pouring sips of water down his throat, Peri had warbled, "Where are we?"

Taking a deep breath, Synjan had answered as gently as she was able. Peri's initial response to being told they were in a new world was to widen her eyes and simply say, "Sure." Her tone was disbelieving. Further details about their Wanderer talents had been met by Peri repeating the last word Synjan said and finishing with varied affirmations, none of which were convincing. The way Peri looked at her deterred her from insisting it was the truth. Synjan was sure she'd come to believe it in her own time.

Once Daeson was on his feet again, Peri had stuck to his side. While the three of them collected everything useful from Peri's vehicle and their surrounds—none of which was a decent pair of shoes—Synjan had felt the weight of the other woman's stare. She admired Peri's ability to act, even though she couldn't comprehend the scope of the situation. Daeson had mostly glared and avoided speaking to her about anything unrelated to gear. Synjan felt at once like throwing her hands up and screaming at the sky in frustration and falling down, crying until all the water was gone from her body.

Now, there was nothing left to do but walk. She'd used

precious water and mapped the Portal before they left the vehicle wreckage, confirming it was too far across this brutal wasteland to be a realistic target. It would take months to get there—if they lasted that long. Their immediate goal was more practical; a group of nine people gathered at a place within walking distance. They should have ideas about surviving in this world. She'd only ever read about deserts in books but knew they'd need a lot of water.

Synjan realised she'd been lost in her thoughts and had begun to stride ahead of her companions. She stopped and turned to watch them, silently assessing. If the Gods were smiling, their destination would have some sort of transport. The Earth woman was not built for walking and the Portal was a ridiculous distance away. Her excessive bulk already hampered her progress. She gasped for air with every incoming breath and whimpered with pain on most outgoing ones. Her feet weren't adequately covered so they were burning and blistering. Every visible bit of her skin was pink and slick with sweat. Her clothes clung to her. She looked like a victim of torture.

Likely feeling the weight of Synjan's stare, Peri met her gaze. Despite the challenges, there was nothing but grim determination in her dark eyes and her jaw was set. Synjan's estimation of the woman rose and pride swelled on the other woman's behalf. Peri was a fighter, unwilling to let catastrophe knock her down. She also looked like she had something to ask but was either too polite or too afraid to speak, lest Synjan overwhelm her with more crazy information.

As they caught up, she fell into step beside Peri and tried

a different tactic.

"I am sorry about bringing you to this world, you know," she began, meaning to say more when Daeson interrupted.

"You've said that."

Synjan frowned at him over Peri's head then Peri looked away and the moment was lost. Synjan closed her mouth and concentrated on walking instead.

Was Daeson so disgusted by her that he'd never forgive her? Did he hate her? Everything she'd been imagining for them in the shopping centre on the last world now seemed unattainable. Worse, it seemed silly. Synjan felt hollow. She understood how completely inadequate 'sorry' was in the face of such overwhelming miscalculations—there was too much to apologise for—but what else could she say?

When she'd decided to continue Wandering, she couldn't have predicted the magnitude of trouble her choices would get them into. Who knew entire *vehicles* could Wander?! She was certainly to blame for the stolen goods, the choice to force Peri into helping them, the mad dash to the Portal. But beyond that? She'd been just as overwhelmed as Daeson to find Peri and her vehicle here. *That* hadn't been her fault, it had been an unforeseen accident. Her companions mightn't want to hear her repeated apology but Synjan needed to say it to believe it. To accept the enormity of their situation. To own it.

Let your time upon the worlds not be tainted by your misdeeds; a cosmic balance will ensure you pay the cost. Trust in that. Fear it only when you have the time.

Freddie's words were a condemnation, yet she found them reassuring. She was already paying the cost in guilt and in the burden that was Peri but she anticipated even higher costs... the notion that one could be Daeson's friendship closed her throat and constricted her chest. It didn't bear thinking on now.

Swallowing yet another layer of grit in order to speak, she stopped and turned to face her companions. They stopped also, looking at her like baby animals awaiting instruction from their mother. Angry baby animals.

"We need to climb up there." She pointed to the top of the dune on their right. "I believe we're going in the correct direction but I need to see it because I can't map."

Daeson looked where she pointed and shook his head. "We should walk along the bottom. There's more cover from the sun."

Synjan frowned at him, suspecting he was being purposefully contrary. The sun was at its midpoint. "There's not enough shade to warrant staying down here. I know it'll be difficult to walk up there but it's the best vantage point and we might be able to figure out a more direct route."

"Let's just do what you want, then."

Synjan blinked, his words pushing the breath out of her. His face was shuttered with resentment and she couldn't think past her shock to reply to him. She looked apologetically at Peri instead. "I'm sorry about this. Do you need some help?" she queried, taking a step towards the older woman, extending her hand.

Peri drew closer to Daeson as if expecting an attack. "You can't be serious?"

"Um, I am," Synjan confirmed, beginning to feel a sensation very much like one she'd had as a child when she'd ridden on a wooden circle swing in a park. They were going round in circles. "We need to see where we're going."

"Where *are* we going?" Peri demanded bravely.

"To the people I mapped earlier."

"Mapped?"

Daeson leant towards Peri. "With her Wanderer talent," he said gently.

Peri carefully turned from looking at him to blink at Synjan before gazing back up at him again. "Okay."

Frustration welled in Synjan as the familiar word and tone resurfaced. She swallowed it because Peri next turned her attention to assessing the dune and her skimpily clad feet.

"Okay," Peri repeated and powered forward, clambering up the dune herself.

Synjan and Daeson looked at each other.

"You know she's not really okay," he informed.

"I know," Synjan replied quietly. "She's in shock. It'll take a while to sink in. Are you okay?"

"I'm really not. You made a decision for both of us. Being sorry isn't good enough."

He might as well have slapped her. Again, Synjan swallowed but this time she was trying to eradicate the lump of emotion that suddenly clogged her throat. "I know," she whispered. "But it's all I've got." He looked at her as if he was thinking of more awful things to berate her with so she rushed to fill the silence. "Can you forgive me?"

Daeson considered only momentarily. "Not right now."

Synjan took a shaky breath, her attention drawn towards Peri as a squawk of pain came from up the dune.

"Do you think she will forgive me?"

Daeson shrugged and walked away.

The dunes ended abruptly as they drew nearer to their destination. It seemed strange to Synjan; she'd expected the dunes to flatten out gradually rather than just... stop. At least Peri had less trouble walking. Synjan shifted focus off her companions and forward to the odd collection of buildings that appeared to be wavering in their path. An island of civilisation in a sea of sand.

It was a town but, even from a distance too great to make out all the details, there was something not right about it. It wasn't just that it was very small, the proportions of the buildings were off. Some seemed complete, yet many didn't have. She supposed the town must be under construction but that didn't satisfy the notion of wrongness or stop her from squinting at it.

It only got stranger the closer they got. There were indistinguishable lumps on the outskirts of the town, spread randomly across the space between them and where they were headed. As they closed the distance, she could tell they were barriers of uncertain purpose. They were different sizes, constructed from a variety of materials and they gave Synjan a feeling of unease she couldn't explain. Her steps slowed. They would be within the limits of the town in minutes, yet she began to think that wouldn't be the best idea. Her instinct to map warred with her desire to preserve water.

"I'm not sure about this—" she began but was distracted

by a small puff of sand erupting a few metres ahead of them. She stopped walking, her head cocked, but only heard Peri and Daeson coming to a stop beside her. She looked around, frowning, entertaining the notion that she was missing something she ought to *know* but failing to deduce what it was. Not far ahead was a long grey brick wall, constructed from cinder blocks. It was only a half wall, no taller than her chest, connected to nothing, going nowhere. As she stared at it, another spray of sand exploded at its end and was carried away on the hot desert breeze.

Everything connected with such violence that her heart lurched.

"WE'RE BEING SHOT AT! RUN!" she screamed. Instinctively, she looped her arm through Peri's and began dragging her towards the cinder block wall. Daeson reacted almost as quickly, hooking Peri's other arm in his own and striding forwards so rapidly that he was almost dragging both of them. Peri wailed questions that no-one had time to answer and thereafter made terrified shrieks as more sand fountains appeared in their path.

Synjan tried to push and pull her cargo, aware that they were running directly into the range of the bullets that had thus far avoided them but Daeson was having no part in her attempt at evasive manoeuvres. All she ended up doing was repeatedly body slamming Peri until she gave up and just sprinted.

"The wall! Get to that wall!" she shouted, pointing. Daeson was already headed for the barrier in front of them but there were other offerings to the side that he might be tempted by. Everything else was made of wood or bullet-riddled, rusty tin.

They reached their target without incident but, as they slid down behind its concrete safety, Daeson let out a noise of anguish. Synjan saw he'd taken a fraction too long ensuring Peri was safe and been shot in the ear as he dropped down beside her. Blood poured out of the wound and Synjan scrambled frantically towards him, yanking his hand away to examine the severity of it. Breath started coming back into her body only once she'd ascertained it wasn't fatal, though most of his earlobe was gone.

"It's messy but you'll be fine," she told him, having to raise her voice as the other side of their wall exploded with gunfire.

Peri flattened herself as close to the wall as she could and Synjan wormed her way past, pulling her arms free of her backpack. She upended its contents on the sand, watching for the glint of her two big guns. She'd lost her small one in the crash and the other two had been secreted at the bottom of her pack since they'd been given back to her on Femme. Her ammo and spare magazines came tumbling out with them and relief rushed through her. She tucked two mags into her pants pockets and thumbed the safeties off both guns as she threw her back against the wall. Glancing over, she saw both her companions looking at her with wide eyes.

"Cover your ears. This will get loud. And I'll need to map," she warned.

Obediently, they tucked their heads down between their hands. They were pressed against the wall, for which she was thankful. She could move easily to either end as necessary. Taking a swig of water from her canteen, she closed her eyes.

Even though adrenaline hammered through her system, the sight of her inner world was so familiar that it calmed her. There were nine patterns spread throughout the town. Nine scrambling, excited patterns moving with tactical purpose to find the best positions to kill her and her companions. From their movements, she assumed them to be Authorities.

5

In His Sights

THE QUAD-BIKE ROARED across the encrusted plains, kicking up plumes of dust and sand. With the throttle all the way open there was no asking for more speed but Hawke leant forward over the handlebars all the same, willing the bike to get him to the training zone before Synjan. He didn't want to field questions from recruits or their Sergeant, or have them witness him ushering the Wanderers away.

Pain radiated from the top of his head, throbbing in a sadistic rhythm that forced him to squint. It was like a dehydration headache, though he'd had a lot of water at the base. It had been a long time since he'd travelled through a desert.

Tension and unease mingled with the headache. Who had dialled the emergency number and why? After his time alone on the long ride over, he'd decided Synjan or her Healer friend wouldn't have alerted the Authorities but the reports of a stolen car hadn't identified anyone else. Perhaps they'd picked up another Wanderer on the way? Maybe... a hostage?

His stomach turned and he swallowed hard, pressing his lips together. He wanted to blame the lingering effects of too much portal travel for the sick feeling but he was too self-aware for that. He shunted the idea of a hostage aside. No point analysing what might be when there were too many actuals to deal with.

Hawke saw impressions of buildings, hazy in the distance. As he drew nearer, the shapes were unmistakable.

The closer he got, the lighter he felt. Now he could see individuals from the training unit gathered together in the middle of the makeshift street. Their Sergeant must have received the order issued from the base and called the team in... Hawke's relief was shortlived as the group scattered in multiple directions. He made a noise of dismay because they were getting into position for an ambush; if they'd been angling for an arrest, their behaviour would've been different.

Hawke parked the quad-bike in the shadow of the Trundler—a squat, all-terrain bus that rolled on tracks. He didn't have time to check the fax machine but he leapt off the bike and tried the door anyway. With orders in hand, he would be able to take control more easily. Even though Hunters had rank over all officers, it wasn't always recognised or respected—even less so when fresh recruits were involved, as they weren't familiar with exceptions in the chain of command; the Hunter Division, the Spy Division and Interworld Tactical Response answered only to Generals.

The Trundler door was locked. Hawke slammed it with

the side of his fist and moved away, passing a building of sun-bleached slats. He rounded the corner and recognised the Sergeant standing in the shadow of the wooden building opposite. A quick glance down the short 'street' showed Hawke several places for soldiers to hunker down and hide. Not all the buildings were real—some of them were merely facades, props to create the illusion of a small town centre. Looking at various windows and rooftops, Hawke identified three trainees moving around, getting into position. They weren't discreet about it.

He jogged across the street.

Sergeant Mallory was a broad-shouldered giant of a man, rivalling the likes of Kegan Frederickson. In the man's meaty fist was a large black rectangular object—a walkie-talkie. Mallory raised it to his mouth and spoke into it as Hawke got closer but he didn't catch what had been said.

"Sergeant Mallory," Hawke said as he got within earshot. "I'm Hunter Hawke Donovan. Some people of interest are—"

"We seen 'em," Mallory said in a gravelly voice, then bared his teeth in a smile that didn't reach his eyes. "I got my newbs on 'em."

Hawke was incensed at the interruption and further aggravated by the interference of his task.

"Then get your 'newbs' off them," Hawke replied.

The bared-teeth smile disappeared. "This is good training, Hunter. Just sit back and we'll squash the Wanderer maggots for you," Mallory said. One side of his mouth twisted into a smile, showing his contempt.

"This mission isn't stan—"

Standard, Hawke intended to say, but the walkie-talkie

erupted into life with a screech from an excited trainee soldier.

"They're in range! Three of them!"

Mallory raised the walkie to his lips.

"Don't you fucking dare," Hawke said.

There was the tiniest pause before Mallory gave his order. "Fire at will."

"Recall that command!"

"Don't you get upset 'bout—" Mallory started to reply, but Hawke wasn't about to argue the finer points. He drew his pistol and aimed it at Mallory's head, much to the sergeant's surprise. Hawke hoped he wouldn't notice the slight waver of the barrel, another unwelcome repercussion from his excessive portalling.

"Recall that command, Sergeant. That's an order."

"Get that gun outta' my face!" Mallory returned, his cheeks reddening with rage or fear. When his hand moved to the butt of the gun in his holster, Hawke flicked the safety off his pistol and moved his finger to the trigger.

"Recall that command before they start shooting!" Hawke yelled back.

It was too late. Before he finished speaking, the first shot rang out. Both Hawke and Mallory glared at each other. "Recall that last command, NOW!"

More shots rang out and Hawke knew he was too late. Synjan was in trouble and he had to help her fast. His skin prickled and the hairs on his body stood up.

The Sergeant moved things along by drawing his pistol. Hawke pulled the trigger, meaning to get Mallory's shoulder but the bullet tore into his neck instead. Hawke's stomach hollowed out as Mallory crumpled to the ground, blood spurting onto the walkie as it fell to the sand. Hawke grabbed it, repulsed by the warm stickiness on his hands and the smell of death in the air.

"Disregard that last command! Hold your fire! I repeat, hold your fire!"

There was a brief pause in the shooting. Hawke had enough time to hope that he'd averted catastrophe, that he would be asked to identify himself and that his rank would help calm things down.

Then Synjan started shooting back. And one of the trainees noticed what had happened.

"He shot Sarge! Holy shit, Sarge is down! He's down, he's down!"

Hawke swore and dove for cover when bullets started chipping away at the wooden posts beside him. He ran into the building and found it was being used as a temporary supply room, miscellaneous gear shoved in the corner beside stacks of water and fuel cubes. A staircase led upstairs. He hadn't seen anyone moving around through the upstairs window when he'd approached but that didn't mean a trainee wasn't up there. It was impossible to hear anything subtle like footsteps over the sound of gunshots. He had to do something before Synjan was overwhelmed and killed.

If she wasn't bleeding out on the sand already.

No time to think that way. He had to act.

Hawke moved quickly up the stairs, carrying his pistol close and at the ready. Dust motes were visible in the rays from the row of windows. This floor was also bare of furniture and people. He wasn't going to risk looking out the front so he checked the single window set in the back wall. A convenient narrow platform had been built on the sill, perfect for him to shuffle across and reach the next building.

It was typical to find such a thing in a purpose-built training area. He checked every angle before climbing out, disliking the vulnerability of the ledge but unable to make an escape any other way. A drainage pole—more township cosmetics because it wasn't attached to anything—gave him the option of going up onto the roof. He could also continue past it to the edge of the building.

He went up.

A soldier lay prone on the roof, looking down the scope of a rifle towards dunes in the east—presumably the direction Synjan had come from. Had this soldier not heard about their sergeant getting shot? Hawke crawled onto the roof and got to his feet, about to identify himself and issue a command when he attracted more fire from an adjacent building. He dropped to his stomach just as the trainee sniper looked over her shoulder. She was a girl rather than a woman, but to be involved in live-fire training, she had to be at least sixteen.

Hawke didn't miss the way her eyes widened, nor the fact she was bringing her rifle around. He had no time to speak. Hawke shot her, pulling the trigger three times before the youth stopped trying to shoot him back. Hawke's chest tightened with guilt. He forced it down. Screw it. This fuck-up wasn't his fault. Sergeant Mallory had risked the lives of his trainees with his stubbornness and insubordination, now Hawke had a mutiny on his hands. There was no coming back at this point, it could only end one way.

He crawled over to the dead sniper and grabbed her rifle, using the scope to identify where the other trainees were. There were only eight in this unit, so there were seven targets left. He had no idea if Synjan had managed to take any out so he would have to operate on the assumption that the remaining seven were still alive.

He spotted two in a building opposite. One had a set of binoculars and was sweeping the street, likely looking for him. In the corner and in a vulnerable position was another soldier, aiming at something at the eastern end of the street. At some*one.*

Synjan.

Hawke took him out first, seeing the large splatter of blood on the wall as the soldier disappeared from view. He shifted the barrel of the rifle to the one with binoculars, who hadn't the common sense to take cover. Instead, he looked for where Hawke had shot from, holding a walkie-talkie to his mouth, reporting everything he saw. He went down next.

Hawke shuffled back and left his position. He'd fired two shots, he had to reload and move. So far he'd taken out three hostiles and their leader, which improved the odds for Synjan. He hoped she was doing her part.

6

Cease Fire

NO TWO GUNFIGHTS were ever the same yet, in essence, they were. The landscape varied, the obstructions were different and nothing could be accurately predicted except for adrenaline, blood and risk.

Synjan was as grateful as she was dismayed by the ease with which she surrendered to the throng of battle. Her breath echoing in her ears, blood thumping through her veins, the feeling that her mind and heart and feet were one with the world—like she was a tree with roots that extended everywhere. She moved with precision; the dimensions of the barrier wall were the limit of her world, her companions a tether of awareness she couldn't sever. The sun, the wind, the sand; none of these registered. Her immediate surroundings and the patterns she had yet to conquer were everything.

They must be Authorities and figured she and her companions were Wanderers. Frankly, who else were they likely to encounter out here? Of course, they could just be highly-militant locals that had a thing about defending their home from foreigners but she doubted it.

When two patterns began wending their way through the buildings, moving towards better vantage points, Synjan decided it was time for a better look. She scrambled past Peri and Daeson to the wall's other end. Her movement attracted a flurry of shots. Synjan remained low until there was a lull and then peered around the edge of the wall.

She'd been right in her suspicions about this town. It consisted of two lines of incomplete buildings, facing each other across a central, sandy street. Their cinder-block wall stood about twenty metres from its end. Her glimpse told her that this town wasn't anyone's home, despite some establishments having porches, verandahs and window openings.

As she watched, two young men in Authority uniforms reached the building ahead of her. They were attempting to strafe along the porch but were more interested in getting to fire their weapons than staying behind cover. She pulled her head out of view, leaving only her gun visible at the wall's edge. Taking a steadying breath, she returned to mapping, watching as they hung back to argue. They jostled with one another, before one went high and the other stayed low.

Synjan shot the man duck-walking in front of his team-mate, her bullet entering his left eye and throwing him backwards into a messy sprawl. His pattern blinked out as his companion instinctively tried to catch him, exposing himself. She got him just below his ear, an arterial spray of blood grimly confirming she'd successfully executed the shot that had failed to kill Daeson earlier. The soldier fell on the porch, also fading from her mind map as he died.

Regaining her cover, Synjan mapped again, knowing there were seven patterns to eliminate before Daeson was safe... no, six. There were six patterns left? Hadn't there been nine to begin with? It didn't matter, she had no idea if she had time or enough cover to move into the town to find a better position but she knew she needed to if she was going to get them all. Of course, that would also leave her companions exposed—

Something wasn't right. There weren't six patterns left in the town any more, there were only *five*. Friendly fire? Even as she contemplated what a ridiculous notion that was, something even weirder happened; two more patterns blinked out at the far end of the town, one after another. Someone else was killing her targets, yet there was no pattern in a position to do so.

Who in all the worlds could be helping her?

So there were three left. Two were in buildings on the left side of the street, one on the right. They all stopped shooting at the same time and a deafening silence rushed to fill the void.

Synjan stopped too, and watched.

The patterns began talking into communication devices, heads tilted and arms waving with a meaning only they understood, all concealed behind walls and out of one another's line of sight. That was to her advantage. The two on the left were separated from each other by a couple of buildings and the single guy on the right was the closest to her position. Synjan supposed she should head for him, run him down, but the thought of leaving Daeson and Peri undefended held her in place. She couldn't go after one with the other two on the loose, nor was it wise to head for them.

The closer male on the left headed towards Synjan's end of town, apparently sick of talking and planning with his colleagues. He moved stealthily, with a speed she hadn't expected, weaving in and out of the buildings inexorably. The way he held his arms told her he had a rifle. The distance he could shoot significantly outstripped what she could achieve with her pistols and he appeared to be heading for the last building. Very soon, *he'd* have all the advantages.

Nerves tingled down her arms and she released her guns to her lap, making fists and shaking out her fingers. She couldn't just sit here and let it play out. She had to *focus*. She picked up her guns again. Shuffling around Daeson and Peri, Synjan hastened to the other end of the wall. Easing her head around the edge, she risked a look with her eyes.

All of the buildings were two storeys, though some were facades. Flicking to her mind map, she noted that the rifleman was climbing upwards; fuck. There was a verandah around the top storey of the final building, with wooden signs spaced along the balustrade. There was also some floor to ceiling lattice with material flapping around it for extra cover. The roof was even worse. It had built-up sides of brick in a battlement pattern and there were extra walls or structures up there that she couldn't properly make out. If the soldier got onto the roof, he'd likely have the angle to pick the three of them off and the cover to avoid her retaliatory shots. She had no idea how to stop him.

The other two soldiers started to move as well and Synjan's heart sank. Tamsin was smiling upon her, however, because the guy at the far left end of town decided he had to catch up quickly and he couldn't be bothered with stealth, or he was overconfident because Synjan hadn't kept shooting. He sprinted out of where he'd been hiding, affecting a strange gait because he seemed to be trying to keep his back angled to the buildings he was passing. It didn't work in his favour; Synjan was able to aim while he raced into range and shot him twice in the body and a third time in his shoulder as his wounds overcame him and he pitched forward. Momentum carried his body in a noisy slide along uneven porch floorboards and by the time he came to a stop, he was dead.

Encouraged by this tiny victory, Synjan believed she had a decent chance of getting out of her predicament. She reverted to her mind map. The ostentatious death of their friend had registered with both of the remaining two soldiers but they both broke out of their momentary pause and kept moving soon after. She was dismayed to note that the guy on the left was definitely climbing towards the roof when her attention was grabbed by an agonised scream. The sound of flesh striking flesh travelled to her on the wind.

The soldier on the right was *fighting* someone. A completely invisible but absolutely real someone that was knocking him around. The Authority's pattern flared and strobed as fists and feet pummelled him, pulsing when he was thrown onto the ground. The dark shadow of a knife pressed him down and his pattern seeped and faded as the blade opened his throat.

Synjan peered around the wall, hoping to confirm her suspicion that a Wanderer Shielder was her anonymous assistant. She was desperate to catch a glimpse of them but she couldn't see beyond the building fronts. As she shifted lower, a bullet struck the wall where her head had just been.

"Shit!" she yelled, panic infiltrating the shot of adrenaline her brain dumped in her system. She fired two wild shots, ducked and rolled back, mapping. She'd been so enthralled by the eighth soldier's ending that she'd forgotten the ninth! The asshole had gained the roof while she'd been distracted and had taken a shot when he'd seen her head. As she pressed hard against the wall, he lifted his rifle and moved again; perhaps he hadn't found his optimal shooting position after all. There was still time and she had an unexpected ally.

She tipped her head back and screamed a message to the sky, hoping the wind would carry her voice where it needed to go. "There's only one left! End building, the roof!"

"What?" Peri asked hoarsely, peering up at her from beneath her folded arms. She had sand all over her face. Synjan's spirit was unreasonably buoyed by the sight.

"Nearly there," she told the other woman, leaning across to squeeze her elbow before she returned her attention to the fray.

A cacophony of noise erupted from the buildings to the right; the soldier on the roof swung his rifle in its direction and Synjan chanced a peek. The Shielder was a blur moving past the numerous window openings on the unfinished second storey, banging on the wall as he went.

The rooftop sniper took the bait and started firing, unleashing a spray of bullets that made up in brute force what they lacked in finesse.

Two things happened simultaneously. The Shielder's course was changed dramatically by a bullet hitting him and Synjan realised the Authority had left himself exposed. The Shielder dropped out of physical sight but she barely noticed as she aimed her gun at the head and shoulders she could see on the roof of the building. She had a shot and she took it. The soldier dropped the rifle with a clatter as he fell and then all was silent (except for the sound of her heart pounding in her chest and the distant murmur of what she thought was a groan). To be sure it was safe, Synjan mapped again.

It had been a long time since she'd been surprised by what she witnessed with her mind but her breath caught when she saw that the Shielder wasn't invisible any more. He was definitely male and his was the only pattern visible in the town.

It was the purest, starkest shade of white she'd ever seen. She felt the muscles around her closed eyes squint as she did her best to make out a design within the overall whiteness of his beautiful pattern. It took a few breaths before wavy lines that were complete *absences* of light revealed themselves to her. They were hard to keep track of. Was this the kind of brilliance Daeson saw when he looked at the Portal?

"Whoa," she breathed.

"What is it?" Peri asked querulously.

Synjan shook herself out of her pattern fascination—flaring obviously around his shoulder, where he'd been shot—and turned to smile at her companions. "Nothing. Everything's fine," she reassured them.

"It doesn't feel like nothing," Daeson pointed out and she blushed.

"Oh. Well, yeah, I was looking at the pattern of the man that helped us but it's nothing to *worry* about. You're safe. You can get up now." Synjan got to her feet.

She wasn't very tall but she felt oddly vulnerable when her head was exposed over the top of the wall. Still, Synjan hoped her smile was convincing as she beckoned them to follow.

Both of her charges gazed up at her and again she felt like the mother of mistrusting, angry babies. She sighed and when her head dropped, everyone's gaze became directed towards the guns she still held.

Curse the favour-giving soldiers and give me strength, she silently appealed to the Gods as she spun around and hastily repacked her backpack, tucking the hot pistols in at the top. The urge to keep them out was strong but, rationally, she knew it was unnecessary and would only serve to discomfort her companions. She was fairly certain she hadn't packed a cleaning kit. Guilt trickled through her as she contemplated what she'd be able to find in the dead soldiers' gear but she quelled it. Practicality was key when Wandering and she'd take what she needed to maintain her weapons as necessary. If Daeson had a problem with it, she'd throw his hero Roman at him. That fucker was bound to agree and Daeson was unlikely to argue with Roman reasoning.

Synjan pulled on her backpack and turned to face Peri and Daeson. They'd sat up but hadn't moved beyond that.

It might be a very slow process to get them to enter the town but she had to persevere. Her teeth pressed together in determination as she widened her smile.

"C'mon guys. Everything's fine. Please get up! We have somebody we need to go and thank."

7

Integration

HAWKE'S UPPER ARM burnt and throbbed with an intensity he'd only encountered once before. He knew a bullet was the cause of it, even though it had been years since he'd weathered this kind of pain. It wasn't the stinging radiance of being slashed with a knife. There was a heat that came with bullets, the kind of burn that even the desert sun couldn't compete with.

This time he'd been hit in his right shoulder. Not great, since that led to his dominant hand. Falling from the second floor might also have broken bones or punctured something internally. He felt like he'd been pummelled but nothing matched the searing pain of the bullet-wound.

He could feel the gritty sand beneath his back. He tested his fingers and toes, then progressed up the joints. Everything moved, though shifting his right arm pulled the muscles of his shoulder in a ghastly way. He groaned through his teeth and squinted, unable to see anything beyond the brightness of the sun. It blazed heat like a flamethrower, making his skin feel like it was tightening and cracking. He had to get to shelter and assess his wound before he bled out. Water would be great, too.

Shadows fell across his face and he opened his eyes more fully, seeing dancing sunspots and dark outlines of people before he could resolve details.

A tall, muscular figure. Daeson.

A short, athletic young woman. Synjan.

A plump figure of medium height and indeterminate gender. He remembered the emergency signal and recoiled, his shoulder reminding him with a flare of pain that sudden movement should be avoided. His gut wrenched and twisted, hollowed out and remained empty.

They'd stolen a person. They'd stolen them out of their world... and because they were from Earth, they couldn't go back.

He could feel intense hatred twisting his lips and burning through his gaze. He didn't want to look at Synjan with that heat so he turned it onto Daeson, who flinched from it.

"Are you a Wanderer?" Synjan asked, the question tumbling out of her mouth with the kind of casual nonchalance that didn't suit the situation. He looked at her, the burn in his gaze dissipating.

"I have the blood. See?" He pointed at the red bloom on his shirt. Somebody had written a poem about someone's heart blooming. Or had it been when somebody was dying?

"Shielder."

"Guilty." Hawke struggled to get into a sitting position as he weathered Synjan's curiosity. He stumbled onto one foot but couldn't get the other one beneath himself to finish standing up. The world spun around him.

"Easy," came a female voice. Synjan's face was very near his as she crouched beside him, a hand around his waist. Her other hand began working on the buttons on his shirt.

He wanted to say something light and funny—probably about what a fast-moving woman she was, but when she shifted the shirt and peered at his arm, pain flared so brightly that he fought to remain conscious. He gritted his teeth, wondering if he'd be so adversely affected if he hadn't punished his body with too many portal trips. He'd already crashed this morning and now he was throwing himself out of buildings. Had Synjan asked him about undressing?

"I wouldn't normally," he told her, earning himself a confused glance before she turned away to talk to someone else.

"The bullet's still in there," she said. The other person didn't reply. "Let's get him out of the sun."

"First building, this side. There are cubes." Hawke hadn't seen a medi-kit while he'd been racing through the buildings before his shooting spree but he'd noticed the trainees had put their supplies together.

"Cubes?"

Hawke heard the confusion in her voice. Of course she wouldn't know the Authority nicknames for the rectangular containers.

"Water and fuel."

"Excellent." She picked up the pace and he found it easier leaning on her for support.

"You're the perfect height for a crutch."

"Not the first time I've heard that... sadly."

Hawke laughed his surprise but it hurt his stomach and

chest too much for it to last. He heard footsteps behind him as Daeson and the Earther followed. Other than the noise made by their peculiar little group, it was silent.

<hr />

So many bodies.

Daeson's gaze flicked from one soldier lying on the verandah to one half out of a doorframe. His eyes kept finding isolated splashes of blood before he forced his gaze away. He thought he would be horrified to see so much death but all he felt was relief. Relief that he hadn't been shot. Relief that he hadn't had to pull a trigger.

His hand moved to his left ear. It felt... diminished. A bullet had stung him, ripping through his earlobe and taking a chunk away. His body had healed itself around the absent flesh, leaving an indent that felt the size of a horseshoe to his worrying fingers. It was the first imperfection he'd ever had.

The first time he'd Wandered, he'd been stopped by Authorities intent on questioning him. They hadn't shot at him, they'd simply approached and talked to him. They probably would have arrested him for being out after curfew except Nick ambushed them. Daeson had been caught in his first gunfight. He'd thought it would be his last.

He pulled at his ear again. His absent lobe would serve as a permanent reminder that without Synjan, he would have died. He disliked the sight of her guns but he wasn't foolish enough to believe they weren't necessary. He hated them but she needed them. And he needed her.

He glanced at Peri, cowering beside him as they followed Synjan through the graveyard she'd created. The Authorities had shot at all of them. They weren't criminals because of their crimes but because of how they'd travelled. Wandering was illegal—Omerri hadn't lied to him about that. So either the Authorities hadn't known about Peri or they didn't care that she'd Wandered without consent. How could he help a woman who was condemned for an act she hadn't wanted to commit? There was nobody to reason with; everyone was dead. They hadn't wanted to talk when they were alive, either. His stomach tightened.

Daeson looked away from Peri and found himself staring at Synjan's back as she hobbled alongside the blonde man who'd saved them for no reason. He resented the stranger's presence, even though Synjan wanted to thank him. That *look* he'd given when they'd first laid eyes on each other... it had disappeared suddenly, and Daeson trusted that even less than if it had stayed.

A Wanderer Shielder, by his own declaration. Synjan had guessed his talent, probably because she was a Navigator. What did a Shielder do? He obviously couldn't stop bullets.

"Oh my God," Peri collapsed against Daeson, clutching his arm to stay on her feet. He looked at her downturned mouth and shiny face and then at what she was staring at. A big man lay in the sand with a large puddle of blood pooled around his head. His body lay in front of the building that Synjan disappeared into.

Peri released Daeson to stagger away from him, a hand covering her mouth. She managed to hook her arm around a post before she threw up. Daeson frowned and looked away. He thought back to Synjan's actions after the gunfight. She'd stared down at them and he'd got the sense she was disappointed—that they'd cowered while she'd had to take care of them. Then she'd hastily packed up her things, taking no care about what went where except for the weapons at the top. He'd almost requested that she leave them out, just in case someone wasn't quite dead and would fire on them again, even though he knew that Synjan could see everyone was dead.

He didn't envy her, though he was concerned by her strange behaviour afterwards. They'd been so tired after their journey through the dunes but Synjan became energised, like the gunfight had perked her up. What was a normal reaction, anyway? Laughing out of relief? Throwing up out of shock? Thinking about the person who'd saved them? Depending on who talked about Synjan's actions here today, she was either a murderer or a hero. She'd saved his life and Peri's. And while he wasn't innocent of committing crimes, Peri was. Synjan had saved someone who didn't deserve to be killed, and killed those who didn't care about innocence or guilt.

So who was better? Was anyone better? Or were they all the same, just positioned in different starting points in life with multiple choices for endings.

Synjan reappeared in the doorway, glancing at Peri before looking at him in concern.

"What happened?"

"She saw him," Daeson said, pointing at the corpse on the ground. His voice sounded like it was coming from somewhere far away. Synjan approached him.

"Are you okay?" she asked quietly. The way she spoke, he

sensed it carried weight. Was he okay? He couldn't properly answer.

"I'm not hurt."

She almost reached to hug him but he saw her pull back and her fingers fidget instead. It hurt his heart, that she second-guessed comfort with him. He'd damaged their relationship with his resentment.

"Is there anything I can do?" she asked.

It was another question he struggled to answer. He reached for her and pulled her into a hug, wanting them to trust one another again. He'd given her a hard time and that had to stop. "You saved us," he breathed into her ear. "That's enough."

Synjan clung to him, trembling like she was drowning and he was her lifeline. She made killing look easy because she hadn't hesitated to pull her guns and start shooting back. With her pressed against him, he could feel her heart hammering in her chest, the weakness and tremor in her hold. Standing before him, he hadn't guessed she was like this inside. She presented herself bravely, detaching herself from the violence that he now knew affected her— it reassured him that he hadn't been wrong about her.

The sound of Peri sobbing made him feel awkward and inappropriate. She was the constant reminder of Synjan's mistake. Her presence alone would pile on the guilt. He pulled back from Synjan and looked at his hands on her shoulders. "I'll walk with Peri into the building," he offered, knowing that both women would prefer it.

Synjan lingered. "Do you want to Heal him?"

'Sure' danced at the tip of his tongue but he didn't want to commit to it.

"We don't know him."

"That's why I asked," Synjan replied, nodding.

Daeson was aware of Peri turning away from her vomit. He let go of Synjan and moved to help her, leaving the question unanswered.

"Just a few more steps," he encouraged as Peri walked unsteadily towards the building.

When they entered, Daeson saw a stack of rectangular containers in the corner—some white, some red—and a pile of clothing and equipment. The blonde man sat on a white container pouring the contents of a small bottle on his bullet wound. He had his belt clenched between his teeth. Daeson looked him over. His blonde hair was a great deal lighter than Synjan's. His skin was tan and rough-looking. Wrinkles around his eyes and mouth had him around the same age as Peri, who'd said she was forty something. He hadn't been as tall as Daeson, though he wasn't short, either. He looked fit, healthy, capable and ruthless. Daeson didn't like him already.

While he stared, Peri headed for the staircase in the corner and lowered herself onto the third step, extending her legs.

"Kweezersh," the stranger requested around the belt. Daeson watched Synjan pull tweezers out of a large white box with a red cross on the lid. She handed them over and the blonde man took a breath then pushed the tweezers into the hole in his arm.

A surge of admiration and disgust enveloped Daeson as the man sweated through his own surgery. What kind of person pulled a bullet out of themselves? It didn't feel right to have this unknown man suffer after he helped save their lives and took a bullet for them. But how had he known to help them?

"What were you doing out here?" Daeson asked him.

The blonde man glanced over but returned to his task. Daeson thought he wasn't going to say anything since he had a belt in his mouth, but an answer came—though it wasn't much of one.

"Coo ashk ga shame abow oo."

Could ask the same about you.

Peri opened up her handbag and shuffled around in it. She pulled out a water bottle and extended it towards Daeson. "For when you do your Healing thing," she said. Daeson looked back at her with an expression that he hoped would convey his wish for silence but she didn't seem to understand. "Aren't you going to fix him too?" Peri's gaze slid off Daeson and then past him to where Synjan and the stranger sat.

Daeson heard the belt and buckle hit the floor and turned to face the wounded man. He looked more amused than upset to learn this new information. Shouldn't he be angry that he hadn't been Healed straight away?

"Secret's out. You might as well." He pointed at his wounded arm.

The demand irked him. He didn't know this man and didn't want to help him. It was petty, he knew, especially since he'd helped to save their lives, but Daeson didn't care. It might not have annoyed him as much if it had been voiced as a request, with a please attached to it. With Synjan watching, he thought it best not to make a fuss so he nodded and stepped forward. "What's your name?"

There was a pause. "Aron."

Just before his hands made contact with the man's arm, he lowered them.

"That's not your name," he said, but Daeson had felt a discomfort that didn't come with the full force of a lie.

"It's one I was born with," Aron snapped. "Do you use your real name on every world you travel through?"

Synjan and Daeson exchanged a glance.

"Can I be Healed now?" Aron prompted.

Daeson didn't particularly like Aron, even though he reminded him a little of Roman, and he now understood Synjan's initial dislike. Grudgingly, he placed his hands on Aron's shoulder and arm and felt the warmth of the Heal take over.

Synjan caught the bullet when it popped out of his arm. "Souvenir?" she offered. Daeson thought it was repulsive but Aron took the bullet and pocketed it. Aron's eyes glazed over and he had a peculiar smile on his face. Maybe under the Heal's influence, he would be more open to answering questions.

"So what were you doing here?" Daeson repeated.

Aron moved off his makeshift chair, rubbing and pressing his right shoulder where the wound had been.

"I turned up here not long before you did. Almost the same time. I had a gun on the big guy out there. I thought I could talk my way out of a firefight but then you lot started shooting. You know the rest."

"They shot at us first," Synjan pointed out.

"I'm sure they did. They were set up for an ambush. Good thing I came along," he grinned at her.

They were set up for an ambush. Daeson swallowed the spit that flooded his mouth and his hand found his left ear again to worry the tiny part of lobe he had left. He opened his mouth to say thanks but Synjan got in first.

"It is a good thing, actually. Without you, we wouldn't be here. I'm grateful."

Daeson's stomach dropped at her words and he looked Synjan's way. She'd often said such things to him, looking at him with admiration and appreciation. Seeing it directed at someone else made him feel hollow and angry inside. Aron didn't deserve that look. He had the sort of arrogant bravado less like Roman and more like Nick. He was untrustworthy and if he came along there would only be tension and unhappiness. He didn't want Aron around but judging by the way Synjan was looking at him, Daeson didn't think he had much of a choice.

8

Cayden And Nick

DIVISION GENERAL IRIAN Cayden brought the cigarette to his lips and pulled on it before harshly coughing the smoke out. He could imagine the comment his wife Mary would make if she were here. He grunted acknowledgement of his mental reprimand and dropped the cigarette onto the ground, stamping it out with a booted heel.

Cayden looked across the road at the front doors of Hill End Medical, where he'd seen Division Lieutenant Kegan Frederickson—Kegsy—walk in holding a small box. He assumed it was a gift for someone who was unwell but he knew it wasn't for Kegsy's longtime girlfriend, Tiln—he knew this because he'd gone to Kegsy's house first.

He'd intended on surprising his friend, to catch him off-guard and unprepared so Cayden's questions were more likely to get truthful answers. Before he'd crossed the road, the front door opened and Kegsy stepped out with Tiln just behind him. She'd given him a peck goodbye and disappeared behind the closed front door. Cayden might have approached if it hadn't been for the small giftbox in Kegsy's hand. It was wrapped with a silver ribbon and looked like the kind of box a man might give a romantic interest, except he hadn't kept it hidden from his live-in woman. His instincts told him that he'd learn more by observing from a distance.

It had been a very long time since Cayden had tailed anyone. He felt obvious following a man he'd known for over two decades, dressed as he was in full uniform—except there were a lot of Authorities patrolling the streets of Gredann lately. Not only had the bombing at Oceangate put the city on high alert but ID cards were rolling out, so temporary processing tents took up the footpaths. With so many varieties of Authority uniforms milling about, he didn't look out of place.

Barely ten minutes passed before Kegan left the hospital. A quick visit, then. Just enough time to drop off the giftbox. Perhaps the patient wasn't a close friend? It wouldn't be someone from his unit as they would have gone to the infirmary at Blackmoor Base on the world of Xavier.

After Kegsy had walked far enough down the street that he definitely wasn't coming back, Cayden crossed the road. He walked through the hospital's wide glass doors into a foyer that was crisp and modern, smelling of lavender rather than eye-watering disinfectant. The nurses and doctors didn't have the haggard look of the over-worked and under-staffed. Hill End Medical could afford what it needed and got what it wanted.

He approached the front counter, aiming for a sensible-looking woman with a long white coat over plain clothing; a doctor or an administrator. She turned away from the nurse nearby to greet him with a pinched smile, giving his uniform a quick appraisal.

"How can I help, General?"

He liked that she knew his rank, that she was aware of his importance. He didn't think she would simply hand over the information he was after but he would certainly try.

"The gentleman who left a moment ago… I was wondering who he was here to see?"

The woman stared at him, likely assessing the most diplomatic way to deter him. The young nurse behind her looked up from her task so she could roll her eyes.

"Another one for Omerri Backhouse. That woman."

Cayden glanced from her to the serious-looking one, unsurprised when her smile tightened into something grotesque. She gave him a perfunctory nod.

"Room two-five-eight. Up one floor and at the end of the corridor on the left." She indicated the lifts.

"Thank you," Cayden said, moving to the stairs instead. He took them two at a time and then gathered himself at the landing before heading down the corridor. Now the smell of disinfectant was in the air and the hospital lost its modern edge, turning into every hospital on every world that Cayden had ever visited. What was it about pastel green?

As he walked, some doors were open and he looked in. At the start, rooms had four beds in them. Then it became two. By the time he reached Omerri Backhouse, the number of beds per room had whittled down to one.

Standing at the doorway, he was assaulted by a colourful parody of cheer. A variety of flowers covered every surface. Their aroma overpowered any disinfectant smell that remained. His throat clogged, his nose tickled and his eyes began to water. He'd seen the cause already—a ridiculously large bunch of chrysanthemums were in a bright red vase on a table by his elbow. He entered deeper into the room to escape, which earned a glare from the man sitting at the bedside.

Sporting unwashed black hair and red-rimmed eyes, he looked a mess... but not as much as she did.

She wore a long white nightgown with no sheet to hide her body or her multiple casts. Every limb had one, and there was a serious bandage around her middle where one or more of her ribs had been broken. The casts and bandages didn't hold his attention long because the frame and pins along her lower jaw mesmerised him. It was held shut by a stretchy blue material that encircled her face, rivalling the impact of stitches and a taped nose beyond it.

Through watering eyes, Cayden looked at the apparatus fixed to her bed. It supported a sling that currently lay slack beneath her. When suspended, he could tell she would be supported from the small of her back to the tops of her thighs. It looked absurdly medieval amongst the high tech machines that bleeped softly beside her. Computers weren't publicly available on this world, nor were cameras and other monitors, but the rules didn't apply to the rich. Omerri Backhouse was obviously a woman of means.

Since when did Kegan Frederickson rub shoulders with the wealthy and influential? And what kind of devastation had happened to this woman? There were no bruises on her face or any part of her skin that he could see, he assumed they'd faded by now. She'd been here a few weeks, at least. He coughed. Damn, it was hard to breathe in here.

The man at her bedside stood, his hands resting on the woman's mattress as he leant protectively over her. He looked sharp beneath his despair.

"Can't you fuckers leave her alone for one minute? She's asleep," he hissed.

"I'm Division General Irian—"

"I don't give a fuck about that. I didn't enlist. If you care about her, come back tomorrow." He sank into his chair and went back to staring at the woman. Apparently he believed Cayden cared about her. A picture was forming about the kind of influence she had.

Cayden reached into his pocket and took out a handkerchief to first wipe his eyes before he held it over his nose and mouth. He mentally cursed the presence of chrysanthemums but was lucky there was only one bunch of them. Tulips appeared to be a popular choice and he figured they were her favourite.

He spied the box with the silver ribbon on a credenza against the wall. It was the only surface that had some available space. He went to it, expecting the man to confront him but he said nothing. Maybe he'd zoned out. Cayden didn't waste time checking.

He set his kerchief aside and tugged the silver ribbon loose, moving it off the lid. The giftbox itself was glossy black. When Cayden lifted the lid, he found a diamond-encrusted bracelet inside worth thousands of dollars, if the diamonds were real. He thought they were. There was no note with it, no way for her to know who it was from.

He closed the lid, doing a poor job of re-tying the ribbon.

"Thanks for the gift, now get out," the man said quietly. He must've thought Cayden was dropping something off rather than investigating what Kegsy had left behind.

Cayden turned and gave the man a brief nod before leaving the room, pressing his handkerchief over his nose and mouth as he passed the flowers near the door. His eyes stung and watered so much that he had to stop a few doors down and wipe them again, lest he plough into someone because of his blurred vision.

Now that he was out of her room, he allowed the sneezes to come. There were only two; he'd escaped his allergies with a light smack on the wrist.

Instead of using the stairs again, Cayden waited at the elevator. He was fairly sure there would be a carpark beneath Hill End Medical because those who lived in this section of the city could afford cars. When he stepped into the lift, he saw a button marked CP and pressed it. He hoped there would only be one level of parking. Now all he had to do was wait.

Irian Cayden was a patient man. Through the years he'd set numerous plans in motion, quietly monitoring their progress as he worked his way up the Authorities' ranks, making good impressions, collecting favours and securing loyalty. Some ventures had succeeded while others dissipated. A lesser man might be disheartened by the failures but he understood the odds. The best opportunities were the ones that had fallen into his lap—

lightning strikes he couldn't have planned for. They were the people he'd gambled on, the ones who'd ended up catapulting his career well beyond expectations.

Kegan Frederickson was one such person. Their friendship had begun by Cayden's design, though the rest of the worlds—and Kegan himself—would believe it had come about by chance. Kegsy had made a huge name for himself at the beginning of his career; he'd enlisted in his early twenties and demonstrated an extraordinary breadth of skill and knowledge of multiple disciplines and close combat techniques. His superior fighting abilities had vaulted him to fame within the organisation, following him as he moved out of the ranks of the general forces and into the elite extraction division at twenty-five.

The ripples of Frederickson's fame had lapped against Cayden's shores early on and he'd manoeuvred circumstances so that they worked together numerous times. Kegan was easy to like so their relationship had continued organically after Cayden's early manipulations, though Kegsy's lack of ambition had always grated. It was baffling that Frederickson had been Unit Commander of the ITR most of his life, resisting moving up to Division Lieutenant until he was *fifty*. Cayden had been a DL at twenty-six! Still, it was the only flaw he'd managed to discover in all the years he'd known Kegsy.

Cayden was not just patient, he was canny. He decided to use his waiting time wisely when he spied a payphone bolted to the wall by the lifts; he called Oceangate and asked for the Local Enforcement division.

He received a lot of information on Omerri Backhouse. She was the madame of a successful brothel, Queen of

Hearts, which also ran an illegal gambling club and nightclub that served alcohol during prohibition. Most of her clientele were Authorities so it was seldom raided. A woman like that would have a lot of secrets and a lot of enemies posing as friends. He doubted Kegsy would be so duplicitous—he was too much of a lamb. They had to have some form of genuine connection.

The second-in-command, the club manager, fit the description of the man in Omerri's hospital room—Nick Logan, suspected terrorist. Cayden questioned the seriousness of the suspicion but it turned out to be a matter of procedural record only. Every crook in Gredann had been put on the suspect list since the bombing of Oceangate. Nick Logan had been brought in for questioning and released the same day because he'd had no ties with GOAL. Lucky for him.

By the time his phone call finished, the last of the sun's rays mingled with the constant lights overhead, battling for dominance. Visiting hours were almost over.

The elevator doors opened and Cayden peered around the pillar he stood behind. A well-dressed woman stepped out and headed towards a glossy red sedan, the sound of her heels echoing through the concrete carpark. There were more empty parking spaces than cars. Most of them were compact, designed to navigate the narrow streets of Gredann City. Cayden figured those belonged to the staff who couldn't quite afford to live in Hill End, or those who viewed practicality over luxury. In every case except for one, the cars were well-kept. A small white car, nondescript except for the dents and minor spots of rust upon it, was parked by itself near the wall opposite the lifts.

Nick's car. If his assumption didn't pan out, he'd wasted only a few hours of his life.

A nearby pillar gave Cayden the cover he needed as he waited. He shouldered it, an eye on the numbers above the elevator doors. Every time they showed movement, he tensed and focussed on his breathing. It had been a long time since he'd worked the field and one wrong word could screw his opportunity. He couldn't rush querying Kegsy's name, he had to push Nick Logan first, to get a read on him.

The elevator numbers moved up, then down. Somebody was coming to the carpark. Cayden held his breath, then released it when the doors opened. Nick Logan stepped out, hands in pockets, shoulders slumped.

Cayden pressed his back to the pillar and listened as footfalls drew closer. He kept his breathing shallow to not give himself away, debating whether he should grab the thug before he got into his car. He decided against it. Small-time crims knew how to fight and, as defeated as Logan looked, Cayden had no doubt that the bastard had bite when attacked. He'd have to outmanoeuvre him verbally, not physically.

Cayden heard the jangle of keys. The jangling muffled almost immediately; he could picture Logan palming them, separating the key that would unlock the car.

As soon as the other man came into view, Cayden cleared his throat and shifted away, not wanting to get too close. His instincts proved him right—Logan spun and drew back a fist, ready to strike. He'd flicked his keys around so one of them poked out to do extra damage with a punch.

"I'm here to help," Cayden declared, spreading his hands apart. Logan glanced at them, then back at his face. "We're on the same side."

"Fuck you, we're not," Logan seethed. He glared with red-rimmed eyes that had nothing to do with allergies. Cayden needed to use that emotion, to squeeze him at his weakest point.

"If you tell me who did it, I can find them." He watched as Logan's expression shifted into something less angry and more suspicious. "I can do it unofficially. Wouldn't you like to give it back to them?"

Nick lowered his stance and fell back against the car, shaking his head and laughing without mirth.

"You don't have a fucking clue. I can't do shit. *You* can't do shit."

Cayden studied him. Now that he had the words to go with it, he saw the fear. What he'd mistaken for anger was a cover for being scared. He didn't know much about Nick Logan but he wasn't going to underestimate a criminal who'd held an esteemed position in a successful business for a long time, without ever being arrested. Perhaps Omerri Backhouse's injuries were a consequence of his misdeeds? But who would lay a hand on someone with so many Authority ties?

"Look at my rank, Logan. I'm a Division General. I can help you."

They stared at one another. He could feel Logan wanting to make the leap but years of conditioning as a criminal would work against them both. Snitches didn't last long in any world—they were treated poorly on both sides. The ones who could traverse worlds under Authority protection were the only ones who could survive. Maybe Logan would angle for that. It had to come from him, for it to have any potency. If it was offered, it might be declined. He had to ask. Logan's focus moved away as he studied the keys in his hand.

"You care about her, right? Who did that to her?" Cayden prompted, wanting to keep Logan on track.

It was the wrong thing to say. Logan made his mirthless laugh again and then wiped his face with his free hand. He pressed so strongly that it contorted his features on one side and the laugh choked off. "Aw, General Whatever-the-fuck. If only you knew. If only you fucking knew."

"I'm trying to know," Cayden hissed, stepping closer. "You're telling me I can't do shit but that's on you! You have to trust somebody at some point to get out of whatever mess you're in. Might as well be me because I can pull a lot of different strings on a lot of different worlds, right?" He smacked himself on the chest, wanting Logan to look there, to look at his rank, so he would believe him.

Logan's gaze followed obediently, roving over Cayden's shirt and pausing at the insignia that only Generals wore. Cayden watched as Logan's expression shifted yet again. He held his silence, giving the criminal time to think it over. He didn't want to interrupt justification. He needed Logan to make the connection.

"You're not based on this world?" he asked. Cayden's heart hammered in his chest as victory came into his sights. Logan was going where he needed him to.

"Trent is a shithole, Logan. Why would I be stationed here?"

"Gredann isn't the only city on this world," Logan replied slowly.

"You've been sightseeing, have you?" Cayden asked, sliding his hands into his pockets.

Nick Logan swore and folded his arms atop his head, looking agitatedly around the car park. "It doesn't matter where I go, he can find me."

He. One man.

"You underestimate me," Cayden began.

Logan met his gaze, scorn evident in his eyes. "You underestimate *him*. He's gone now but he'll come back! He *can* fucking come back."

"He's a simple bully, can't you see that? A man who beats up a woman and takes off is nothing but a coward."

"For all the Gods, I could park a fucking limo in the space of the shit you don't know," Nick half-laughed, half-moaned.

"Then who did that to her, if it wasn't him?"

"ME!" Logan's scream bounced along the concrete walls and returned to them, echoing in a combination of madness and agony. "He made me do it! And it wasn't an order, I would never do that to her willingly, he fucking *made* me. He used me, my hands, and fucking made me," Logan sobbed. Keys fell to the carpark floor as he held his face in his hands and sobbed like a broken man.

Cayden had a rush of clarity. He'd never personally met the kind of Wanderer Nick was talking about but he understood the devastation they could cause and why Logan was bawling in front of him, feeling like there was no escape. Every now and then one of them would go on a spree and everyone would work together to take them down. They were the bogeyman to every Authority and Nick had experience with one.

A Wanderer Controller.

"I need his name." He thought of Kegsy and dismissed the thought... but it wouldn't go entirely. Kegan Frederickson led a very private life and he had a home here, in a city on a world that he wasn't stationed in. Men of his rank moved their partners out of shitholes like this and set them up somewhere nice. Cayden had never understood why Kegsy would keep a home here. There was no logic to it. He'd always been suspicious of illogical moves. The comraderie and connection he had with Hawke was also difficult to justify. But no, Kegsy's blood was tested every time he was sent through the portal, when he was asleep. Could a Controller somehow manipulate people's actions throughout a specific task?

Logan mumbled something.

"Give me his name and you can go to any world you want, along with a healthy bank account with many, many zeroes."

Logan looked up at him, dubious but hopeful. Yes, Cayden was a patient man but if Kegan Frederickson was a fucking Controller—

"Ellis. Howard Ellis. He's... he's gone off world. He's looking for her."

He's looking for her. Cayden's gut clenched. Kegsy was involved in all of this somehow, because Hawke was doing a favour for him, trying to find someone for him. Someone who had a fucking Controller on their tail.

"What about Kegan Frederickson. How's he fit into this?"

"I'm not saying shit until you make good on your

promise."

Nick Logan would talk because he'd already started but Cayden nodded in appeasement. He could wait a little. There were still questions unanswered but he had clues to work on. He organised a discreet place for his newest songbird to meet him at Oceangate later that evening and they went their separate ways.

When Cayden got back to the base, the first thing he did was find a terminal that gave him access to the Authority register of identified Wanderers. It took him very little time to figure out that Howard Ellis was an unregistered Controller. Rocking back in his chair, Cayden gazed sightlessly at the uniforms moving about him.

He wanted to be able to tell Nick Logan that he had the power to place a kill order on his bogeyman—which he did—but he couldn't be certain it was the right play. Kegan Frederickson was an unknown quantity. Cayden still needed to understand Kegsy's relationship with Omerri Backhouse. If Howard Ellis had used Nick Logan to beat her, was he known to Kegsy as well? Cayden didn't want to contemplate the possibilities without asking further questions. He'd have to ask them in person.

Cayden's social calendar was beginning to look very full.

9

Scavengers

HAWKE DIDN'T TELL Synjan about the soldier on the roof. She wanted to find boots to replace Peri's sandals but he didn't want her up there watching as he made his way to the Trundler, so he said nothing.

He knew the large Authority vehicle was locked and he suspected the key was in Sergeant Moron's pocket. A mixture of regret and resentment burned in his chest as he crouched by the body and rummaged through its pockets. He found a bunch of keys attached to a carabiner by their rings and palmed them. When he jogged across the street, he could feel his skin tightening as his defensiveness triggered his power. The hairs on his nape prickled as he tried the first key with no success and he resisted the urge to check over his shoulder. The second key slid home. He opened the narrow door, stepped up into the vehicle and closed it firmly behind him. He took a moment to get his bearings; driver's seat a step down on his left, the rest of the Trundler on his right. There were double-seats on one side of the vehicle and a small computer bank on the other.

A white piece of paper sat on the holding tray and he strode to it, yanking it out with more force than necessary. A chunk of paper ripped and remained in the printer. He looked at the piece in his hands. A report summarising his movements at Hjaaloken, indicating that Hunter Hawke Donovan would be requiring cooperation on arrival at the training area. He ripped the evidence into small pieces and pulled the remaining chunk out of the printer so he could rip that up, too. In the back of the vehicle was a stack of live-fire helmets, a section of track for repairs and a prybar. Hawke took the prybar and hefted it, testing its weight in his hand.

The printer was his first target. He unplugged it and struck it a few times, satisfied by the sound of crunching plastic and pings as small metal parts flew off. Next, he took aim at the monitor for the navigation system. One solid swing crunched the glass into a spiderweb. He opened the cupboard doors beneath it and looked at the mess of cables and wires. Hawke shoved the curved end of the prybar into it and hooked as many of the colourful strands as he could before yanking it back. He was dismayed that he needed a few goes to pull them out; maybe he shouldn't have hooked so many at once.

The radio was the last thing he needed to demolish. It sat near the driver's seat with a hand-held mouthpiece attached by spiral cord. Electronic parts and black plastic flew before he thrusted the prybar deep into the guts of the equipment. He knew they were out of range, but on the off-chance one of the Wanderers came in here and tried to use it, nobody would be able to pick up a transmission with it.

This was it, there was no going back now.

He intended on travelling with the trio and taking Daeson and Synjan back to Kegan. The only thing now was to leave a recorded message for Cayden... but not here, where his transmission would be lost among the mess of plastic and metal pieces scattered across the floor. He had to leave it where it would be found and quickly, before his actions were deemed treasonous and drones were deployed.

Hawke left the Trundler and locked the door again. He separated its key from the ring before throwing it a great distance into the desert. Not much time had passed; it didn't take long to trash a few pieces of equipment. He doubted the others would have heard his handiwork— though if questioned, he could always tell them the truth. That he'd trashed the Authority vehicle to stop it from being used against them.

He looked at the other three keys in his hand. They all looked like his quad-bike key. Around the opposite side of the Trundler he found three parked trikes with trailers attached. His stomach churned unpleasantly as a memory of riding in a trailer surfaced.

He hurried away to perform the task he'd volunteered for; collecting gear off bodies.

If he kept moving and acting, he wouldn't have to stop and think. A voice in his head told him he was insane, risking his entire livelihood to bring back some Wanderer bitch and her piece of action. And they were kidnappers, fucking *kidnappers!* Just like Eddie and his ignorant gang. Why was he doing this?

The building he entered had limited natural light. Only small streams trickled in through the badly-positioned planks that made up the walls, purposely designed to blind any trainees leading an assault on the building during daylight. It would've been a tactical mistake. He stood in place and let his eyes adjust before moving around tables and chairs positioned as obstacles.

Upstairs, he found the sniper and his spotter. Looking at the remains of their faces, they weren't much over sixteen. This had been a whole unit of fresh soldiers, who were probably on their first live-fire training exercise. It explained why he and Synjan had been able to take them out without much difficulty. Sergeant Moron had made a monumentally bad call. Rage, shame and guilt built up in Hawke, refusing to be squashed down.

"Fuck!" He dropped to his knees by the bodies and took a moment to collect himself before inspecting their equipment. They each had personal medi-kits attached to their belts by carabiners. He unclipped both and checked one. The usual desert supplies were held within; a small tube of sunscreen, collapsible sunglasses, a thermal blanket folded into a pocket-sized square, a multi-tool, a piece of rubber hose, waterproof matches, a dust-mask, a plastic beaker and a compass and map. The map was useless, it detailed a smaller area than the one he already had. There was also a bullet-sized gadget that he recognised—an electronic device for making reports. This one hadn't been used, nothing was lit up on it. The other soldier also had a blank one. Hawke made a mental note to check all of the other kits before they left. It wouldn't be good for him if there were conflicting reports about what had happened.

Hawke moved away from the windows and took out his own reporting device. He twisted it and checked the green light had come on before speaking.

"This is Hunter Hawke Donovan, identity Redrock Two Zero Zero Echo Bravo. This message is intended for Division General Cayden. While on mission, Sergeant Mor... uh... Mallory, refused my order to stand down. We both drew and I fired, thereby turning his unit against me. To protect the mission and myself I, uh, I fired on blue." He frowned, glancing over at the bodies as they lay accusingly on the floor. "They were following an illegal command. I tried to stop it before it got away from me. I grabbed the walkie, tried to explain, but they fired on me. It was out of my control the instant Mallory issued the order. I... I didn't want to kill those kids. I don't... want that blood on my hands." But the blood was there and he couldn't undo it. Here was not the place to defend himself. Hawke closed his eyes and continued. "I acknowledge that I will face an investigation and request that it hold until completion of my current mission. I further request that all flares on this world and subsequent flare-streams be reserved until mission exit. End report."

Hawke snapped the device closed and stared at its blinking red light before shuffling to the closest body. He took the boy's hand, already cooling even in the room's surrounding heat. He pressed the report into his palm, folding the fingers and thumb around it into a fist.

He wanted to say sorry, but it wouldn't change anything. He said nothing.

Hawke spied four clips of ammunition on a table nearby.

Two of them were black, the other two were blue, indicating rubber bullets. They'd swapped out the blue clips for black ones in their weapons. Incensed by their choice, he took a pistol and the black clips with him and headed for the soldier on the roof that had shot him. From that body, Hawke looted another medi-kit, a rifle and as much ammunition as he could find to suit it.

If Cayden heard the report and delayed proceedings as per Hawke's request, it would add to his debt. He was already in beyond his means, he could never repay that man. Was doing all this going against him? His loyalty to Cayden should be greater than his connection with Kegsy. Divided loyalty would break him and he hoped neither of them would demand he choose. He grunted; too much thinking, not enough action. Keep moving.

Hawke jogged back across the street and into the supply room where Synjan was already waiting. An impressive pile of equipment lay at her feet but she didn't look happy.

"I can't find any boots for Peri," she said as her gaze dropped to his armload of things.

Hawke dumped them onto her pile and pointed upward. "Did you check the soldier on the roof? Was she—" He stopped talking when Synjan hurried up the stairs.

Daeson and Peri both stared at him when he looked their way. Not wanting to start up a conversation with either, Hawke crouched and went through all the medi-kits. Nobody had left a report.

"What are those things you're taking out?" Daeson asked.

"Electronic gadgets."

"What are they for?"

Hawke glanced at him, irritated by the questions. They

had to get moving before the Authorities decided to send a team. The sergeant would have check-in protocols to follow and if they didn't radio in, then a small, heavily armed troop would be sent to investigate. Hjaaloken was a small base, but it would have a lot of the latest gear and weaponry.

"I don't know but they shouldn't come with us." He stared Daeson down. Before the Healer looked away, there was a strange look on his face, like he'd smelt something bad. Hawke dismissed it and kept looking. Once satisfied, he moved over to the pile of jackets. He tried a couple on before he found one that fit snugly.

"Have you both got jackets?" he asked the pair still sitting on the cubes, like it was leisure day and they were waiting for someone to bring them a beer.

"I've got one in my pack," Daeson replied.

"An insulated jacket?" Hawke checked. "These are sturdier than normal jackets. Deserts freeze at night."

Daeson made the same bad-smell face as he had earlier. "They don't *freeze*," he argued.

"Alright," Hawke said, not caring enough to push it. Perhaps Healers didn't feel the cold. He sorted through the rest and found a 4XL that would fit the Earther. A Sergeant rank had been stitched onto the shoulder and collar.

When helping Peri into the jacket and then out of it, he discovered how the emergency signal had been sent. The Earth woman had set down her phone before trying on the clothing. Hawke resisted the urge to grab it right away and frustration welled in him when she picked it up again, toying with it until Synjan came back downstairs, holding a pair of boots in one hand and socks in the other.

Hawke watched as Peri sat motionlessly, allowing Synjan to measure the boots against her feet. He wondered how long it would take for the woman to get her hackles up, or if she was so soft that they would never show. He would respect the former but preferred the latter. Would he be able to bully the phone from her?

"I'm glad you got jackets but Peri needs clothes," Synjan told him while wiping the knees of her jeans.

"The only clothes are the uniforms they're wearing."

He watched Synjan grimace before she corrected her posture. He supposed she was psyching herself up for the grisly task of undressing bodies. The pants would have to come from the sergeant. Nobody else had the girth. They might have to take his blood-stained shirt as well. It would be a difficult job even without looking death in the face.

"Want help?" he offered.

"Please," she said, and he found himself smiling at her, even though it wasn't that kind of task. Incredibly, she smiled back.

Hawke had scored when they'd handed Peri the Authority uniform she was supposed to change into. She'd set down her phone in order to better accept the clothing, then tromped upstairs, pausing only to collect her handbag. Hawke pocketed the phone, expecting to be questioned about it, but neither Synjan nor Daeson had noticed, too busy chatting quietly with one another.

Time stretched.

Hawke listened to Peri sobbing upstairs. She was

supposed to be changing but he couldn't hear movement. He'd have to go up and yell at her to hurry her along. The longer they waited, the more anxious he got.

They stood in a loose huddle in the middle of the room. All three trikes and their trailers were parked outside so they could take some of the cubes. They had loaded all the fuel and water that was left, only two cubes of each, the others were empty. The second trailer held Synjan's and Daeson's pack, but Hawke had opted to keep his messenger bag with him. The trailer of the third trike had all the medi-kits and extra equipment they'd salvaged, so they wouldn't have to waste time repacking them into the bags.

"Maybe we should leave Peri here," Daeson suggested.

"That's not a bad idea," Synjan mused.

Hawke frowned at the pair of them. "So both of you *want* the Authorities to know everything about you when they pick her up?" He didn't miss the petulant glare from the Healer.

"Oh, shit. Yeah, we can't leave her here," Synjan said.

"What?" Daeson turned his glare onto his travelling companion. "She should go back home."

"As soon as the Authorities get their hands on her, she'll tell them you're a Healer," Synjan explained, rephrasing the information Hawke had already given. He didn't think that was what bothered the other man. It annoyed him that Daeson was short-sighted but he also liked that the Wanderer wanted to give Peri the best chance at returning home. He didn't know what it would cost him.

"They'll throw everything at us," Hawke said. "They won't stop if they know there's a Healer. They'll take me out, they'll take Synjan out, just to get to you. The moment Peri says Healer, that seals our fate. They've been after your kind for centuries."

The report he'd left behind wouldn't matter. Cayden would have no influence. Best-case scenario: he would be alive to face a treason charge. Or maybe that was the worst-case scenario—he'd be dead no matter what. There was no way Peri could stay here. He would shoot her himself if he had to.

He heard her clumping around upstairs and then a hitching sob. When he focussed on Synjan and Daeson, he was finally aware of the odd looks on their faces. Uh-oh. What had he said?

"How can you know that?" Daeson asked slowly.

How could he know what? That the Authorities would come after them? It was obvious. "How can you not know that?" Hawke threw the question back at him, unsettled that he'd given too much of himself away already.

"No," Daeson said firmly. He took a step forward. The height difference between them forced Hawke to look up at him. Standard intimidation technique. "How do you know the Authorities have wanted Healers for *centuries*?"

Ah, shit. It was knowledge he'd always had and never questioned. He'd learnt about Wanderer powers at Willets Academy. Being a shitty liar meant he would make more slips. He had no idea whether he was supposed to know something or not. What was common knowledge and what wasn't?

"It was something I learnt at school. But doesn't everybody know Authorities are after Healers?" He glanced from Daeson to Synjan but she didn't look willing to come to his defense. He looked back at Daeson to see if he'd convinced him but now the pair of them were staring at each other.

Synjan asked Daeson, "Do you think the Hunter's after *you*?"

So they knew a Hunter was after them but they didn't suspect that it was him. Hawke had trouble hearing over the whomping of blood in his ears. Spit streamed into his mouth at a ridiculous rate and he swallowed, feeling obvious. His eyeballs felt hot. He hadn't known that could be a thing. He felt vulnerable, like he was in the open. His skin itched and tingled and he shifted his weight, stepping back and putting space between himself and Daeson. He drew Synjan's curious stare as his hands fell limp at his sides. When he took another half-step back, he saw her eyes widening and her position shifted as well. She was ready to move in front of Daeson. They stared each other down, his hand near his holster, her hands drawn up in a defensive pose. There was an absurd familiarity to it. He recognised her stance because it had been taught to him by Kegan. Taught to her by Kegan.

"What is happening?" Daeson asked, looking between them. Hawke had reverted to his training and positioned himself aggressively. Synjan had reacted to that. He'd boxed them in to facing each other off. Thing was, he had a gun handy and she didn't. All she had were punches and kicks.

He had to diffuse the situation, and fast.

"How do you know there's a Hunter after you?" he asked, his voice sounding strange to his own ears.

"We got told on Femme," Daeson said. "Now you tell us

how you know about Authorities and Healers."

Even though Daeson spoke, Hawke's eyes never left Synjan. She was the one who could disarm him. In so many ways.

"I used to wear the uniform. I don't anymore." It was a gamble, implying he was an ex-Authority, because they might decide not to travel with him. If that was the case, they were staying here. If they were paranoid, he would have to hold them at gunpoint. Peri might get to go home after all.

"You used to be an Authority?" Daeson questioned.

"Well done, you've kept up with the conversation," Hawke replied, earning a frown from Synjan.

"What do you think we should do with this information, Daeson?" she asked. Hawke was impressed her gaze hadn't left him, either. If things went to shit, he doubted he'd be able to finish pulling his gun before she came at him.

"I don't trust him," Daeson said.

"Explain," Synjan ordered.

"I... I don't want to."

Hawke laughed, unable to help himself. "He doesn't like me."

"Why'd you leave them?" Synjan asked him directly, not pursuing the popularity vote.

"Try having Wanderer blood in the Authorities. I was never really accepted." He impressed himself with the bitterness in his voice.

"Tell Daeson why we should trust you."

After a pause, he listed a benefit. "I can make sure they don't get you." *Because I will.*

"How can you do that?" Synjan prompted.

It was as though his time on Femme being questioned by hostile blonde women had prepared him for this moment. "I know how they think. I know their procedures. I know they're bureaucratic almost as much as they're militant. And I can move faster than they do."

"How will that help us through this desert?" she continued.

He heard Peri moving across the room upstairs. She'd obviously finished crying and was preparing to make her entrance. He didn't want her walking into this shit-show and making things worse.

"I've gone through deserts before," Hawke replied. "How about you?" He made a show of folding his arms across his chest and Synjan dropped her stance. "So what's the verdict?" he asked.

There was a long pause as the three of them listened to Peri clomp down the stairs. Just before she appeared, Daeson gave his reply.

"Fine. You can help us through the desert."

Hawke didn't miss the very specific way he'd been answered; through the desert, nowhere else. It didn't matter. Once they got to the next world—Avaniero—he could contact Kegan and have them extracted.

"We should get moving before more Authorities come," Hawke warned. The sooner they left, the safer they'd be.

Peri surprised him by piping up. "You lot can go on ahead. I'll stay here and wait for them." She looked around herself, as if a chair would magically appear for her to sit on.

"I'm sorry, but you can't," Synjan said. Her tone wasn't

apologetic. Hawke glanced at Daeson, who turned his face, pretending to look out the window. Coward.

"I'm not coming with you. You can't make me," Peri said, her voice becoming more shrill.

"I think we can," Hawke said and, for the second time, his hands lowered to his sides. This time his right touched the weapon at his hip. Peri's gaze was drawn to it and when her expression changed into one of fear and despair, he hated himself with a singularity he hadn't experienced before.

He had become Eddie.

10

The Novice And The G.O.A.L.

TORIN LAWSON STOOD on the corner of York and Main. A chain-link fence loomed at his back, decorated with threatening signs. In front of him, dark warehouses lined York street, silent giants that stared through black windows. In spite of it being a warm and humid night, the teenager tugged his leather jacket more tightly around himself. He didn't know if he should be grateful the streetlight closest to him was out or not.

He listened to the faint sough of distant traffic and the night sounds of crickets and roosting birds. He spied a feral cat across the street, noiseless as it prowled along the gutter. Torin scuffed his sneakers against the pavement, expecting the cat to take off but it froze and faced him instead, eyes glowing. It hissed and then stalked away, not threatened enough to run but survivalist enough to leave.

Torin couldn't leave as easily. He'd caught an unfamiliar bus and got off at an unfamiliar stop. He'd passed a string of small houses with sagging porches and patchy front lawns. Some held ratty lawn furniture, others littered with bikes or toys. Even though it was so late that he'd snuck out through his bedroom window, many of the houses in this suburb were brightly lit. In one house, a couple had been screaming at each other about who'd last used the remote. Their voices carried up Main Street for a good distance before they abruptly stopped. Torin hadn't looked back, ignoring any slow-moving cars that trundled past him, blatting fumes or aggressive music as they rolled by.

Two kilometres later, the houses became storage lots and empty businesses. Another kilometre after that, he was in the warehouse district. He'd pulled out his phone to check if he'd received another message but, apart from noticing that he'd made good time, there was nothing else.

And now he waited, thinking he'd been trolled. Some asshole would do a drive-by, pointing and laughing at him. He would give them the finger and then walk back to the bus-stop, feeling like the fool he was. Except that didn't happen.

A car did drive past him. Not a cop car, though it had that kind of official feel. It was a heavy-looking black sedan with a menacing grill. He stared at it, unable to see who was inside. The driver had taken a good look at him, though. Torin had seen the light of a cigarette aimed towards him and felt the chilly sensation of assessment. His heart rate picked up—either in fear or excitement. Probably both. He couldn't help but think of those animals caught in headlights on country roads, staring at the bright lights bearing down on them, wondering what it was until it stole their lives away. Did any of them think something good was about to happen?

The car made a u-turn using the double driveway of a warehouse farther down the street. The car also used a great deal of footpath before rolling off the sharp edge of the curb. There was a *clonch* sound as the suspension compensated. It approached him again, this time from his side of the street.

Torin had the mad urge to take off, or to climb the fence that promised to prosecute him should he be found on the wrong side of it. He held his ground instead, even as the black car came to a stop in front of him. The passenger window whirred down and the driver—an older man in his forties or fifties—stared across the passenger seat at him, clearly dismayed.

"Go home, kid. You're too young."

"No!" Torin said, lunging forward and grabbing onto the door handle. He pulled but it was locked. He gestured for the driver to unlock it.

"How old are you? Twelve? Get on home."

"I'm seventeen, asshole," Torin spat. The driver grunted but looked unconvinced. It didn't matter, Torin knew that this guy had to take him to the meeting. With a push into his head, Torin learnt that the driver wasn't secure enough to come back without a passenger, though he was working up the courage to leave without him. Before that could happen, Torin reached through the open window and fumbled for the switch to unlock the door.

"Hey, what in the—? Back off!"

The driver reached out his meaty hand but Torin pressed the button and reefed the door open before throwing himself into the car. He shut himself in with a solid thunk.

The driver stared at him, cigarette hanging loosely beneath a salt-and-pepper moustache. Removing the cigarette from his parted lips, the older man used it like a pointer as he growled his warning.

"You can't make me take you anywhere but the nearest bus-stop, kiddo."

At 'kiddo', Torin pulled out his phone. He rapidly thumbed a message, moving the phone away to avoid the reaching grasp of the driver. It was difficult in close quarters but he managed to hit send before his phone was snatched away.

"You're a hobber, you know that?" the driver said, using a word Torin was unfamiliar with. He shrugged. "You're not supposed to bring your phone to the meet. You were told that, you fucking amateur."

The phone buzzed in the driver's hand and he glanced at it. Something on the screen made him look closer and his lip curled in disgust. Torin's heart hammered as he wondered what message had come back. He was too worked up to focus on what was going on in the driver's head. He had to calm down or he'd be going in blind.

"Hobber," the driver said, using that strange word again, this time in defeat. He tossed the phone at Torin who caught it awkwardly, and he read the message on the screen.

'Tell Snook he's been ordered to bring you.'

"It's just as well I brought my phone, Snook," Torin said. He felt smug but also relieved that Snook's boss believed in him. Was Snook's boss the mysterious 'Bourbon14' that he'd been chatting with online? He hoped so. They had a connection.

"You're making a life decision at seventeen, kid. You sure you want this?"

Torin was calm enough to connect with Snook's mind now. He scanned it lightly and wasn't surprised by what he found there.

"Your concern is touching," Torin said as sarcastically as he was able. "Don't underestimate me."

"Give me your phone." Snook held out his oversized hand, palm out. Torin stared into his hard gaze and handed it over after reading his intentions. Snook took out the SIM card and handed it back before making his phone disappear into the glovebox.

"This'll do for tonight because you're new but don't bring your fucking phone again, got it?"

"Got it." Torin pocketed his SIM and found the button that rolled up the window as the car pulled away from the curb.

Fifteen minutes later they parked in an alley behind a string of shops that had apartments above them. Torin got out of the car and looked up at the combination of fire-escapes and barred windows. Another shitty part of the city, then, with residents begging to be burnt alive. At least he heard no screaming matches, though the ever-present whisper of cars on a highway broke the silence. He counted six more vehicles parked in the alley; one of them was a chopper. He would get himself one of those as soon as he got his motorbike licence... though he'd have to keep it a secret from his mother.

"You memorising plates or something?" Snook growled, his eyebrows drawn together in a heavy frown. It was the same expression he'd worn the entire drive over. Torin was starting to think it wasn't a frown. Maybe it was just his face.

"Cool bike," Torin said. Snook grunted and headed for a battered green door. He pushed it open and a smell wafted out that made Torin think of mechanic's workshops and burnt wiring. He followed Snook, expecting to be led inside but they stopped after three steps and the green door shut behind them, trapping them in a short corridor. An amber light positioned on the low ceiling above revealed another door in front of them, a screen one.

"That's so dumb. Screen doors should be the outside door," Torin observed.

"Unless you want to see who's coming in," a woman replied in a lyrical accent. Torin looked beyond the screen to see who'd spoken. Her face was in shadow but he could see she wore a t-shirt and jeans over boots and carried a large gun—the kind of gun he'd only ever seen on TV. The kind only Authorities used.

"You going to stare at us all night?" Snook prompted, tapping the screen door so it rattled. Even though his words had the same flavour that Torin had experienced so far, his tone was warmer. He didn't need to use his Intuit talent to know Snook liked the guard.

She stepped forward and Torin blinked.

"Wow, you could be a model," he said. He'd never seen a beautiful woman in real life and she looked almost artificial because of it. Prettiness could be found in lots of places but he realised now there was a vast difference between prettiness and blazing beauty. Her glossy black hair was cut at an angle near her shoulders and her large amber eyes and bronze skin gave her an exotic, appealing look. Carrying an assault rifle somehow added to her attraction. Maybe because it made her dangerous. Her gaze settled on him and Torin found himself speechless.

"And you could be a fisherman, except you wouldn't catch a fucking thing on that line." She turned her intensity away from him. "You lose your keys again, Snooky?"

"They're in my pocket. Are you going to make me use them?" Snook asked. His tone was unusual enough for Torin to touch his mind. He detected a combination of frustration and amusement.

"Nah." The woman held the rifle in one hand, pointing it at the floor as she opened the screen door for Snook and Torin to pass through. "Is this kid supposed to be HypnoBeast?"

"He was at the pickup point."

"More like HypnoChihuahua," she replied without humour.

Torin looked around the room. It was a large, open space with iron support beams at regular intervals and makeshift partitions created out of chicken-wire. Amber lights dominated the room except for blazing spots of white in strategic locations. Against one wall a bank of computers sat on an arrangement of desks. It looked both erratic and neat, because cables had been tied together to contain tripping hazards, and the two people working there—a man and a woman—looked like they had everything within reach. They were both typing furiously. Hackers, likely.

Past them was a curved booth that held two dentist chairs, with straps for wrists and ankles. A trolley with medical equipment stood nearby and a shiver ran down

Torin's spine as he guessed he might be looking at a torture chair.

Voices carried from deeper within the room but Torin couldn't see the far wall. It was hidden behind one of the chicken-wire separators, with signs and boards strung up on it so nobody could see past. People were talking and laughing behind it but he couldn't tell what they were saying beyond a few random words. He heard four different voices, maybe five.

The wall opposite the hackers held a couple of workbenches strewn with circuit boards, tools and bits of wire. Beside each were open shelves filled with buckets, boxes and jars. It was like looking at a candy-shop for engineers, where various bolts, chips and fuses were squirrelled away. Unlike the hacker space, the engineer's space looked like a bomb had hit it—ironically.

With this thought, the reality of his decision hit him. He was no longer fooling around with the idea of hitting back at the Authorities. This time he was aligning himself with people who would do it. Who had done it. The shock hit him in two waves; one was emotional and numbing, the other cool and justified. He could feel them warring with each other. Something inside him recoiled at the idea of building bombs, planting them and detonating them.

Terrorist, his mind threw at him. It churned his stomach and made him want to ask for the bathroom. The other part of him recognised that he'd been conditioned by the Authorities. They took over worlds and brainwashed the people in them. Whoever didn't conform would be imprisoned or executed. And that wasn't the worst of it. Torin was their enemy—not by choice but because he'd been born into it. He had Wanderer blood, so they wanted to spill it.

Your eyes and your mind are open.

Torin cried out at the unfamiliar voice in his head. Snook and the exotic woman halted mid-conversation to stare at him, like they'd forgotten he was there.

"What? Someone spoke—" Torin began, but stopped before finishing his sentence. Someone spoke to him in his mind, but that couldn't happen unless he was actively listening, and it only worked between him and his mother because they were both...

That's right. I'm an Intuit. Like you.

The voice belonged to a man and Torin looked around in darting movements. The hackers were still typing. Nobody else had appeared, though some of the voices on the other side of the wall quietened.

"Must be Bourbon," the woman said. "C'mon."

As they walked the few steps that would take them around the makeshift wall, Torin sent out mental feelers, touching everybody's mind that he could reach but, as always, he could only touch the minds of those people in his sight. The hackers both had abstract math and stress in their heads, the exotic woman was filled with curiosity and disgust—mostly about him. He quickly moved onto Snook but there was nothing there except for an awareness about his sore knee.

They moved into a common area. Unmatched chairs and stools were gathered in a loose circle around a kitchen table covered by a blueprint. Torin counted seven people, five of them seated and two standing. One of the men standing studied the blueprint, the other studied him.

When they made eye-contact, Torin reached out to touch his mind and found himself in a mental grapple with the other man—though it was less like wrestling and more like a handshake.

Must be Bourbon, Torin thought of the woman's words. Did that mean Bourbon spoke to everyone that way? He'd never met another Intuit apart from his mother and she always alerted him to her presence in his head before she spoke to him in it. He'd thought it would be like that with every Intuit but now he suspected she'd been polite with her ability... knocking before she entered his mind.

"He's full blood," Bourbon announced. His physical voice didn't sound as deep as it had when in Torin's head. More importantly, Bourbon spoke as though he knew Torin was a full blood Wanderer—he couldn't have got that from him because Torin hadn't known himself. Perhaps Bourbon could tell by the strength of his power. Bubbles of excitement burst deep in his belly, threatening hysteria. Torin squashed it.

"Good, that'll be helpful," said the man at the map without lifting his eyes from it. He nodded at the blueprint, his hands splayed either side of it so he could lean over and get a close look. "Okay, people," the map-reader said at last, standing up straight and revealing his impressive height. His athletic frame made him look imposing but Torin knew he was the leader because the others grew silent so they could hear him speak. "This is HypnoBeast." Torin was gestured to and he felt the weight of many stares. He kept from wilting beneath them by reminding himself that he'd been invited to join these people. "He's a full blood Intuit like Bourbon, which means our communications won't be intercepted."

"Like the last fuckup," a woman growled. Torin looked at her—she was older, with greying hair and there was a hard look about her that matched her words.

The leader at the map-table replied, sounding agreeable and composed. "As you said, Rocket, it was the *last* fuckup."

Rocket, what a strange codename, Torin thought.

Not for a rocket scientist, Bourbon replied smartly.

Torin was caught between surprise and indignance. It was interesting that the hard-looking woman was a genuine rocket scientist and he was glad to know such a thing, but...

Stop barging into my head uninvited, Torin thought back.

You came through loud and clear, Beast. Pay attention now, you're about to meet the team.

No apology, no retreat. Torin balled his fists but lost his anger as different people around the room spoke up, telling him their codenames and what their specialties were. A few stood out. Snook was their gadget man. Torin figured that meant he made the bombs. The two scientists were both named after snakes; Python and Copperhead— though the latter's codename was likely more motivated by her ginger hair than the reptile. The exotic woman was named Cleo, after some Queen or other from a different world. She was their researcher and a fence for weapons. The tall man, their leader, called himself Preacher.

Might as well be Pope, Torin thought. Bourbon coughed laughter and Torin was stupidly proud. He knew he shouldn't care if the other Intuit found him funny, but he wanted to impress him. Bourbon had recruited him into this group and Torin owed him for that, if nothing else. Bourbon had something else going for him; being an Intuit as well. Torin was intrigued about meeting another of his kind.

He connected with Bourbon's mind. *Aren't they all Wanderers? Why didn't they tell me the power they had?*

Only a few of them have the blood, Bourbon sent back. *Cleo, Preacher and Copperhead, and Copper, well, she only has mixed blood. Can't even see the Portal. She's an Intuit like us, but if you want her to hear you, you have to do all the work.*

Torin could see and hear Preacher talking about the map and the mission it represented but he paid more attention to Bourbon.

What's Preacher, then?

Sensory.

What's that do?

You don't know? It's not a big deal for others, but it's good for him. He can see and hear better, run faster, is stronger than normal... that comes in handy at times. He's also a good tracker, can follow a scent like a dog.

Along with the words came a sense of hostility. Torin ignored it and glanced at Cleo, who must've felt his eyes on her because she looked over and frowned, gesturing for him to pay attention. He snapped his gaze back to Preacher.

And Cleo? What's she?

She, my friend, possesses the rarest of all bloodlines. She's a Catalyst. A full-blooded ticket to super-mega-fucking-powers.

Torin looked at Cleo again, impressed once more. He had

no idea what a Catalyst could do to his Intuit powers—maybe he could plant thoughts in people's heads, maybe he could broadcast to a whole crowd of people at once, maybe he could read people's dreams as they slept. Who knew?

I know, little Beast, Bourbon said in his mind. *I know.*

He would've asked for specifics, except Preacher caught his attention with a final statement.

"Wait, what?" Torin interrupted, attracting the looks of a few people around him. "I'm going on a mission the day after tomorrow?"

"Trial by fire, HypnoBeast. Best way to learn," Preacher said, grinning much like those brimfire ministers on TV when they asked for money in exchange for salvation.

11

Island In Their Stream

PERI AWOKE WITH a start, slapping at the itch burning into the back of her hand. Two things became apparent at that moment. One, she'd killed a mosquito. Two, she'd dozed off.

It couldn't be a dream.

Her heart plummeted to her toes and she fought off the wave of nausea that threatened to hurl itself out of her stomach. People didn't fall asleep *inside* dreams; they were already asleep. They searched for toilets that always had something wrong with them, they frequently got about naked in public and they always featured random people but dreams never featured falling asleep.

Tired. She was so tired.

She'd definitely been nodding off, hallucinating she was watering her garden with boiled oasis water, when the mozzie woke her. And the mosquito was quite real, too. She stared at her palm, where the bloody remains hung with grim determination, one skewiff leg spasming pathetically.

Holy shit. This was *real*. How the hell was she going to get out of it?

All through this very long and torturous day, she'd been trying to wake up. From moment to moment, there'd been blind confusion or pure terror with little room for other emotions. She'd ruined her lovely car, been caught in a gunfight—a gunfight! Like she was some sort of American school student!—seen murdered bodies, been forced to dress in a dead man's clothes and walk in a dead woman's boots.

All the chaos and fear had stupefied her with its surreality. She'd convinced herself she was dreaming.

It was only logical. She'd never been this scared except in nightmares. She'd always managed to get out of them when the going got too insane, so she'd thought she just had to wake up. Even if she was so tired her jaw hurt from yawning and her eyes were wet with tears... no! To wake up! It hadn't happened, so she'd rationalised that this nightmare was just... extra confounding. She'd persevered because that's what her students did when the going got tough and she was an excellent example to her students. Even tired.

Her real-life morning seemed like the distant dream. She'd woken up on her school holidays, seen Dave off to work and decided to do a bit of shopping to cook him something special for dinner. Better than marking the twenty-five Geography assessments she had on her desk. Better than planning for next term. Dave was always jealous he didn't get to spend her holidays with her, so she'd planned to make him the star of the evening.

Honeyed carrots and Scotch fillet steak followed by lots of cuddles and listening to him complain about the annoying guy he worked with at his game development job. That would cheer him up.

This was real, though. She wasn't there to cook or mark or even teach when school went back. She was gone from her life, just like that. The evening had come and Dave had returned home to a dark, empty house and a bewildered, meowing cat. No Persephone. She was vanished and gone.

The realisation filled her with a desolation so deep she wanted to lay down and give up. Contemplating his pain was far worse than her own, she couldn't bear thinking on it. He'd be so confused. Would he think she'd left him? Hopefully he'd believe she'd been murdered or that the story of her car disappearing into thin air reached him somehow. Any scenario where she hadn't willingly walked away from the man she adored was preferable to him thinking that she could.

It was the cat nap and the mozzie that finally convinced her that her perilous situation was real, because how could she *double* sleep? And why would a nightmare supply her with such inane information as there being mosquitoes near the oasis they'd reached? They were here because she was here. They were real. She was really here. This insanity was her new reality. If she kept thinking it, it would sink in. She wasn't much for swearing but damn could she have sworn a blue streak right about now.

"Are you hungry?" Prettyboy asked.

Peri looked at him, at his kind, attractive face and wanted to smear the dead mosquito on him. Instead, she wiped it on the Authority uniform pants she wore and did her best to smile and nod at him. He seemed happy with her answer, continuing to stir the soup they'd made by chopping up groceries—Dave's groceries. *Her* groceries!—on the fire they'd built. They'd shot a lizard to cook with her carrots. Dave's favourite, honeyed carrots, but the honey was at home, so sucked in! But Daeson was alright, really.

Not like Bitchface.

That woman should've died about five times today but, somehow, she'd managed to power through. The older Peri got, the more averse she was to labelling people things like 'bitch' but, honestly, that woman deserved it. If Peri hadn't had such a thing about the c word—even in her own mind—she'd have used it instead. That was how heinous that blonde piece of work truly was.

She knew her name was Synjan but Peri could not think of her any other way (she'd briefly considered nicknaming her Tits McGee but that had seemed complimentary so she'd discarded it). The little blonde had taken Peri's life from her when she'd accosted her at the shops and everything she faced now was directly attributable to her. Peri hated her with unrivalled singularity. Just watching the way she strutted about the camp made Peri wish many violent acts upon her.

Toughguy didn't mind the show. Peri saw him watching Bitchface with quite a lot of interest. She wondered how Daeson would take it when he realised. He'd been furious with Bitchface when they'd first arrived and he'd only calmed down because he was glad he wasn't dead.

It gave Peri an idea. If she could get Daeson to agree to leave the blondes, he might be able to get her back to

Earth. To Dave. To her world. Prettyboy didn't seem all that bright. He'd shown he was easily influenced when he'd healed Toughguy even though he didn't like him, so he was her best shot. How to get back, though?

Wanderers. That's what they said they were. Wandering through worlds and having adventures, tra-la-la. Couldn't go back, the Wandering (stupid name) only worked one way. Always forwards, never backwards. Sure.

Peri had gone along with their delusions at first, agreeing because it was easier than thinking about it. Plus, she'd been certain she'd wake up any second. Blood powers that made them uber... yep, she was pretty sure she'd read that book as a teenager.

Then she'd watched a bullet pop out of Toughguy's arm and the hole close up like magic, all because Daeson was touching him. Yeeeah. She had no real understanding of the powers the other two had because they were apparently in their heads (what a surprise), but she'd seen that healing thing. It explained why these nutjobs weren't all dead yet and why she'd walked away from her crumpled tin of a car wreck, but it didn't explain why Daeson wasn't ruling the planet with his megapower. He'd certainly have knocked Earth's major religions into the dust if they'd shown his power on television. Thousands of years of wars could've been nullified with just one papercut closing up. Dave would like seeing that. She'd have liked seeing that.

No! She wasn't going to start thinking like she was never going back! She had to get back to Dave. Her beautiful, soft-eyed partner of twenty years was her completion and her strength. Somehow, she'd have to find some within herself, without him. She owed him that; to fight with everything she had to get back to him. He deserved nothing less than her absolute best. She wanted to have his arms around her, to hear his voice but she couldn't even find her phone. His voicemails were gone, too. Peri started to cry, even as she started to plot.

The problem was *how*. They hadn't allowed her to drive her own bike today, probably because they thought she'd head in the opposite direction at the first opportunity. She wasn't stupid enough. Their bikes were all the same model; they had the same speed capacity and she was far heavier than Bitchface. She'd be caught and facing yet another gun in no time. Those cursed guns. One was hers. She had one. They didn't know she had one so she had to be smart about all of this. Driving away from them wouldn't work. She'd probably have to use the gun but she wasn't sure how and she wasn't ready. Not ready. Might never be ready to shoot them in their sleep. Maybe it wouldn't come to that, but she couldn't rule out the possibility that that was how it might fall.

None of them compared to Dave. She had to remind herself of that. Be ready, do it for him. He was worth twenty of them. A hundred! It wasn't right and it certainly wasn't kind but neither was stealing a person out of their happy life. They would reap what they'd sown. When the time was right, she'd make her move. For now, she'd keep her mouth shut and watch.

She would wait as long as it took.

"It's not good," Bitchface said, her sour expression matching her grim tone.

Peri's attention was snagged by the impending doom in

her words. They were sitting around the fire, Daeson prodding at the pot of food and the blondes looking like dolls as he looked at a map and she fiddled with her wet hair. They'd hunted the lizard when they first arrived, leaving Peri to watch Daeson set up his tent and collect plants for the fire. And try to wake up. Wake up!

Once the food was on, they'd cleaned up at the oasis. Peri hadn't liked being told not to use soap in it. She was filthy! She'd taken great satisfaction baring her stretch marks and jiggly belly alongside their crossfitruling-combatready-Wanderer-ninja bodies. Screw them. She'd found a small soap in the pack they'd given her so she'd scrubbed herself as clean as she could, keeping Toughguy glaring at her as she rinsed off on the sand, using a cup.

Daeson had Healed everyone after that because there was new water boiled (they still had plenty in their water cubes but Toughguy insisted they shouldn't touch any of that until it was necessary) and now Bitchface had had her share of the water to do... whatever she did. Peri didn't want to hear any word she said but that tone held everyone captive.

"What did you see?" one of the men asked. Peri wasn't sure who'd spoken.

"The Portal is North West. There are pockets of people between us and it but they're small groups. There's a city around the Portal with thousands of people in it. I think we'll be travelling through desert the whole way. If we walk... it will take us three months. Probably more. Sorry."

A nail of aggravation scraped down Peri's spine at hearing her say that word yet again.

"Through the desert?" Daeson asked in horror.

"From what I can tell, yes."

Peri sniggered, imagining herself walking through a desert. It was insane! They had to be joking. And months? No. Bitchface stared at her. She resisted poking her tongue out.

"Will we have enough water? Are there more of these?" Daeson asked, gesturing at the nearby oasis.

Bitchface shrugged. "I don't know. The map isn't big enough to show much beyond a week of travel." She gestured at the map on Toughguy's lap.

He cleared his throat. "There are ways to find water, even in the desert. We'll make it."

"Pity," Peri muttered beneath her breath. Only Daeson looked at her, frowning. She couldn't tell if he'd heard what she said or had merely picked up on her tone. "Is the food ready?" she asked pleasantly, nodding at the pot he was stirring.

It grabbed his attention as planned and then everyone was distracted by getting food. The lizard tasted horrific but Peri held her nose and swallowed, knowing she'd need the protein to keep up her strength. For Dave. For her. She'd barely finished her bowl when her stomach began to gurgle, signalling that the unconventional meal was wreaking havoc in her digestive system.

"I need to go. Toilet," she mumbled as she scrambled for one of the fold-out shovels nearby. It was where she'd left it, beside her roll of toilet paper—one of the supplies she'd insisted they find in that town of death. She grabbed her handbag as well, tucking it underneath her arm and hurrying as far away from the camp as possible.

Peri had never suffered the humiliation of shitting in a

hole until she'd been dragged to this desert world. The greatest indignity by far was in knowing that Bitchface was watching her while she did it. She'd made it very clear the first time Peri had needed to go—it had been before they set out into the wild and sandy unknown. Synjan had said she could see her 'pattern' in her mind, no matter where she went. Her eyes had threatened her, promising she'd be hunted down if she tried to run, so Peri hadn't bothered. She believed her. That was why getting around Bitchface was essential.

By the time she'd cleaned herself up and got back to camp, Bitchface and Toughguy had opened up A4 sized zippered cases and sat near the fire, cleaning their guns. Her gun might need cleaning! She wasn't sure if Bitchface had used it before she found it in the desert but there had to be lots of sand in it that needed to be cleared out. She had a gun. One gun. They had lots but Peri thought that what mattered was how and when she used it, not how many there were. She'd be smart, so smart for Dave.

Peri settled down where she had a clear view of what they were doing, watching intently while they pulled the menacing steel mechanisms apart and stuck bristly brushes and oily rags into every crevice. She considered asking questions but couldn't bring herself to talk to the blondes willingly. She needed a good look at her gun and also to look in the pack they'd given her. Was there a gun cleaning kit in it? She hadn't even known that she'd need to look for one.

"Want help setting up your bed in the tent?" Daeson asked.

He wasn't interested in looking at the gun cleaning or

listening to the dolls natter about different weapons like she was.

"I'm not sleeping in the tent," Peri answered off-handedly, not looking at Daeson.

Her words were the sound of secret things moving through the underbrush like when Biscuit prowled around the back yard. Everyone stopped what they were doing and turned to look at her. Her heart leapt into her throat, fuelled by panic.

"I'm claustrophobic!" she declared.

Frowns wrinkled foreheads and Peri realised she'd made a terrible mistake. Going into the tent away from their prying eyes would allow her to assess the gun, fresh after seeing Bitchface and Touguy do it. She'd be less likely to forget what they'd done or make a mistake.

"You'll be warmer in the tent with Daeson," Bitchface said slowly.

"You just want someone close so I don't wake up in the middle of the night and steal a bike," Peri snapped.

Toughguy clicked his gun and slid the top of it. The noise was very loud. "It doesn't matter where you are. I'm a light sleeper and I have all the keys."

His cold gaze flustered her further and Peri couldn't stay beneath his scrutiny any longer. She gathered up her handbag and scurried towards the tent.

Prettyboy's voice followed her into the fabric structure. "She's not claustrophobic," he insisted.

Peri stuck her head out and gave them a haughty look. In her teacher voice she told them, "It doesn't mean the same thing on my world," and zipped the door closed behind her.

While she rustled about setting up her bedding with one hand, she dug the gun out of her bag with the other, inspecting it as best she could in the muted light. She was certain they'd leave her alone for a short while but she wasn't taking any chances. She needed to know if she had to work 'Steal a gun cleaning kit' onto her agenda tomorrow... the gun seemed sandy but fairly well oiled. The weapon felt lighter than she'd expected and not as terrifying when it was in her hands. It was empowering more than frightening. She'd never handled a gun before but she'd watched a lot of movies. They were detailed enough for her to have a basic understanding of how a pistol operated. It fit her hand snugly and was comfortable to hold.

Through the material walls of the tent, she heard her dungeonkeepers muttering and whispering amongst themselves—about her, no doubt—but she didn't care. The gun had bullets and it was ready to fire once she cleaned the sand out of it. She'd be home with Dave in no time.

12

Nightmare

DAESON WAS WOKEN by a woman screaming. It came from right beside him, the sound of Synjan being tortured. Her body and hands pressed against the tent, making whispery sounds against the material in between her cries.

"No! STOP!"

Fear leapt in his mouth and crowded his heart as he fought his way out of his sleeping bag. He knew bringing Aron along with them had been a bad idea. What was he doing to her? Daeson thought he knew but he refused to imagine it. He rolled to his feet, standing the instant he exited the tent, unsure what he was seeing.

Aron stood nearby, sweeping his pistol around their campsite. At his feet, Synjan whimpered in between sobs.

"What did you do to her?" Daeson shouted, trying to decipher if Aron had attacked Synjan in her sleep. It seemed unlikely but it felt good to yell at him.

"Nothing," Aron said calmly, backing away.

Daeson hated the way Aron made him feel unreasonable with a single word or look. It wasn't normal to be woken up in the middle of the night by a woman screaming. It was Aron's fault, somehow.

He knelt beside Synjan, pleased when she sat up and clung to him. He could help her feel safe—in this he was useful. She would never be scared of him or threatened by him. He wasn't that kind of man and he knew she appreciated it... even if she didn't say so.

He made shushing sounds and murmured comforting words to her, knowing it didn't matter if he repeated himself with his *it's okays* or *you'll be fines*. He stroked her head and rested his cheek atop it. He willed his heartrate to slow and hoped hers would match it. Holding her this way made him feel better as well—he missed her smell and the familiar way she nestled in his arms. She was partly composed when the hitching sobs returned.

"They're all dead. I killed them, I saw them, I can't... I didn't want... I'm so sorry!"

He felt bad for ever thinking she was ruthless. Before this world, he hadn't seen her kill and he'd been concerned that it might end their friendship if he ever had to face it. Now that he'd seen it play out and her guilt after doing what she'd had to do to survive... it relieved him. As he'd realised earlier that day, she wasn't a cold-blooded killer. Her regret absolved her. Synjan's participation in violence damaged her and it was his job to put her back together. If she could do *that* for them, he could do this for her.

Not like Aron, who seemed unmoved by what he'd done. Where had he gone, anyway? Daeson shifted, looking for him, but he couldn't see him anywhere. Maybe they'd got lucky and Aron had left, deciding being woken in the night by a screaming woman was too much.

"Let me look after you," Daeson whispered after Synjan's sobs softened once again. She relaxed into his arms.

"I'm sorry I woke you. I get nightmares w-when I... kill."

"It's okay. They're gone now. Nothing's going to hurt you."

There was a pause before she spoke in a small voice. "You're not mad at me?"

"For having a nightmare?" he asked, thinking she felt bad about disturbing his sleep.

"Well... because of the shooting. And everything."

It was the 'and everything' that gave him pause. What was 'everything'? He thought of the way she'd campaigned to take Aron along with them. Was she finally seeing the error in that? Had her nightmare featured him somehow?

"You mean Aron?" he asked, wanting her to say it.

"No, Peri."

He couldn't hide his disappointment. Good thing it was nighttime and she wouldn't see it.

"It's done. It's done and it's over."

Synjan squirmed in his hold and Daeson was forced to sit back so they could look at each other. He was surprised how much of her face he could see. She looked hopeful.

"You forgive me?"

He nodded. "Yes, of course."

She threw herself at him and clung to him in a way that made him laugh softly in surprise.

"Thank you, thank you," she said and lifted her face. He moved his head sideways to look at her and received a peculiar kiss to his chin. It was all she could reach. He smiled and readjusted his hold to see if she wanted to kiss him properly, when somebody grunted dissatisfaction behind him.

Daeson turned awkwardly to see Aron perched atop a rock close by. Uncomfortably close, in fact—he was barely a metre away. Aron would've heard every murmur and whisper between them. How had he even managed to move into that position without making a single scuffle? Daeson felt his anger and frustration flaring up again. Why was Aron so close? It was weird and encroached on their space. He felt Synjan leaning to peer around him but she didn't seem as bothered. She took his hand and squeezed it.

"Thank you for checking on me. You should probably go back to Peri."

He wanted to say more to her, to offer to sleep beside her, but a quick glance at the bedding near hers told him that Aron was already there. Heat travelled up his neck and stuck in his jaw.

"Do you think you can get to sleep again?" his words sounded tight and awkward to his own ears.

Synjan didn't seem to notice. "Yes, but... I just hope I don't wake you again."

"I wouldn't want to sleep through your needing me," he said, wanting her to know that he was her protector and that Aron was nothing. Nobody.

"Thank you. I love that you care about me."

The heat left his neck and travelled into his chest, where it buoyed him enough to feel comfortable about going. He shuffled away, crawling around the corner of the tent and in through the flap. He was pleased Synjan had set up her bedroll near the tent wall where he slept. There was only a thin piece of fabric between them.

He worked his way back into his sleeping bag when he heard Aron's soft landing onto the sand from his perch on the rocks. In three steps, he was with Synjan.

"Sorry I woke you," she said.

Daeson was irritated that she felt it necessary to apologise to him as well.

"I checked for predators," Aron replied.

"Yeah, there's nothing big around."

"You didn't really communicate that to me."

Synjan chuckled at his sarcasm. "Sorry about that."

"It's alright, you'll do better next time."

Daeson seethed at the shitty way Aron was treating Synjan. His curse prevented him from speaking that kind of nonsense but he had no doubt that Synjan would've argued her case to him. Why was she different with Aron than she was with him? He didn't understand.

Peri shifted and muttered under her breath. "She didn't say sorry to *me*."

Daeson huffed and closed his eyes but sleep was a long time coming.

13

Ahead Of The Competition

D AESON WATCHED AS Aron screwed the last bolt onto the bike and then tried to start it again. Still nothing. It looked like a new machine but it had only lasted one day of hard riding.

"Nope, I can't get it going. It's dead."

Spiteful pleasure surged into Daeson's chest, even though it was to their detriment that they lost a trike. Aron, the superstar, wasn't good at everything.

"Looks like we're sharing," Synjan said and Daeson's heart dropped. He should've seen this coming—with Peri refusing to align herself with anybody except for him, it stood to reason that Synjan would share with Aron after she lost her trike.

"Do you want to drive? You're the one who knows the way," Aron said. Daeson's insides flopped, in the mild way it did when someone was telling a half-truth. It didn't make sense for that sentence to have been a partial lie, though. Synjan did know the way. Maybe his nausea was from needing the toilet. He hadn't been able to do anything but urinate for a couple of days now.

"I'm not that familiar with—what did you call them? Trikes?"

"I'll drive, then," Aron said, grinning. Daeson had a strong desire to wipe the smile off Aron's face.

"We better figure out what we're culling," Synjan said, walking away from the foursome and gesturing for Aron to join her. It was a conversation Daeson hadn't been a part of nor invited to. Apparently only Aron and Synjan were the decision-makers about what was important enough to keep.

"Don't worry, I'll still vote with you at tribal," Peri said beside him, then gave a strange tittering laugh. Daeson looked at her but she was staring at Synjan and Aron walking together towards the trailer with their backpacks. Peri often said peculiar things that he considered were not meant for him but for herself. His father had been a bit like that, muttering under his breath or making a confusing statement to Daeson before chuckling. The memory renewed feelings of ineptitude and anxiety.

"What do you mean?"

"She didn't ask your opinion. I would've."

He grunted, acknowledging that it bothered him. Synjan apologised and apologised but she kept on doing the same thing. Her sorries had no substance because she wasn't changing her behaviour. It didn't even matter that she meant it. Now she was sidelining him, putting more effort into growing a relationship with the newcomer than mending the cracks of her friendship with him.

He'd been angry initially but he'd forgiven her after the

shootings, acknowledging that she'd had to make hard decisions. He'd also allowed the stranger to travel with them even though Daeson sensed there was something off about him. Had Synjan asked his opinion then, or forced his hand?

"She's done that a few times," he admitted, gratified that Peri both recognised and acknowledged it. He knew he shouldn't drive the wedge further between the two women but it wasn't like Peri would ever be Synjan's friend. Speaking about Synjan to someone else gave him a kind of release, he'd discovered that when talking about her to Roman. It lightened him, somehow. It made his issues with her seem not as important.

"Why do you put up with it?" Peri continued.

A fair question but he was far from perfect, and Synjan had been gracious in the face of his flaws.

"I make mistakes, too," Daeson replied.

"Not like her mistakes," Peri hissed, proving that she wasn't going to be diplomatic like Roman had. Why should she be? Synjan had threatened this woman's life and changed it in an extreme way. Now they were all stuck together. His silence prompted another question. "What do you see in her?"

He watched Synjan speaking animatedly with Aron, her smile growing before they both laughed. She'd made a good joke, apparently. He missed her smile. Tension had muscled itself between them in a way he didn't know how to unwind by himself. Now there were strange people around, changing their dynamic.

"She's a good person who had to do bad things to stay alive. Now she's trying to change herself for the better. She still makes some bad decisions but she wouldn't have hurt you."

"The gun in my face really gave that message."

Discomfort sat in Daeson's stomach, an uninvited guest. He lifted a hand to his damaged ear, tracing the creases and bumps between his finger and thumb.

He watched Synjan and Aron move pieces of equipment around, listening to their voices but not their words. Off one trailer here, onto another trailer there. A couple of items came out of one backpack while a more important item replaced it. All of the spare jackets were dumped onto the sand, along with some of the weapons. Daeson itched to help but had the notion that he'd be waved away or told they had it under control. Whenever Aron turned his cool gaze on him, Daeson felt stupid.

"What was she squealing about last night, anyway?" Peri asked, interrupting his thoughts. He remembered the scream that had made him feel cold to his toes.

"She had a nightmare because of what happened to you," he said, hoping Peri would feel ashamed. He shouldn't have bothered.

"Good," she said. The vehemence in her voice caused him to drop his hand from his ear and he turned his head to assess her. He'd considered her a plain looking woman but, at times, she could be ugly. He pondered telling her that when he'd left his world it had come as a shock, that he'd entered a place he didn't understand—not even the language. He'd had nobody with him to explain what had happened. At least Peri knew what was going on. She could cope, if she wanted to cope.

"I know you're angry... I know you have reason to be

angry, but holding onto it won't help you. It'll just make you feel bad."

Peri turned her intensity onto him, her burning eyes the same colour as the blazing desert. "You think I can forget about it just like that? Look around you. This is not my life. This is her fault."

And there it was, the truth, vindicating him and burying Synjan. It was how he felt as well, he couldn't deny it. It was a relief to hear it from Peri's lips.

"I know, but—"

"But you're happy to pretend it isn't, just so you can keep the peace. Now she's being a bitch to you and you're *still* not saying anything. You can't let her walk all over you."

He had no idea what Peri was talking about. He wasn't pretending it hadn't been Synjan's fault. He'd blamed her for it multiple times in fact, more than he'd needed to, and in front of Peri. He'd even accepted some of the blame because neither of them had known the car would come with them.

"She's not walking all over me. And she isn't being a bitch just because she isn't asking me how to split the equipment. She's just doing what she does, like she always has."

"So she's always ignored you?"

Daeson took a moment to consider, blinking at the sudden turn in the conversation. Peri had a strange way of interpreting his words.

"No, she asks my opinion."

"About what?"

He was grumpy with Peri's badgering and demand for examples. It wasn't like he could give her any without long explanations about the kind of worlds they'd been on. She wouldn't stop unless he made her stop and he disliked that she was pushing him. He'd wanted to talk about Synjan, not badmouth her. He felt rotten that he'd fallen for it at the start—that he'd wanted to complain, if only a little.

"Just stop. I'm not going to talk badly about Synjan and I also don't want to hear you do it."

His hand stole to his damaged earlobe where he pinched and stroked, even as he left Peri behind and made his way to Aron and Synjan. As expected, they refused his help.

———————— •❘• —————————

Lulled by the rhythm of the bike rolling across the desert and fitful sleep from the night before, Synjan fought to stay awake. She was pressed against Aron's back, her cheek upon the smooth fabric of his shirt and her arms draped about his trim waist. He'd offered her control of the three-wheeled vehicle but she was glad she hadn't accepted. It was more comfortable to lean on him.

Aron was an interesting man. His past didn't fit the expected profile of a Wanderer and that intrigued her. He 'used to wear the uniform'. What did that even mean?

She wondered if he had a goal world he wanted to find, like Daeson did, or if he was just in it for the travelling. His ability to look after himself was undeniable and his raw sexual appeal would ingratiate him anywhere he went, so he shouldn't have too much trouble getting what he wanted.

His attractiveness was a matter of preference but she'd known from the moment she saw him laying on the sand that he appealed to her. His face wasn't beautiful like Daeson's—she'd examined Aron's features and acknowledged numerous flaws—but there was just *something* about the way he was put together that captivated her.

Though her nightmares had begun as they always did—on a train, with her family falling to their deaths—and ended with stomach-churning images of Daeson and Peri being shot by the same Authorities she'd killed the day before, it was Aron who'd infused her dreams after she'd screamed the camp awake. She couldn't remember the content exactly but she knew her interest in him had caused her dreams to take an amorous turn. She'd had to force it out of her mind so she'd stop blushing every time he looked at her that morning. Pressing herself up against his hard body on the bike had been an enticing challenge after that.

Oddly, she no longer thought about Daeson in such a fashion, yet she had two days ago. Things had changed so quickly. Everything was upside down. She was grateful he'd forgiven her for Peri's presence and that he'd been appreciative she'd used her guns to save them. It should've been enough to restore her feelings for him but... it wasn't. Forgiving wasn't accepting and it *definitely* wasn't approving. His words of comfort had felt conditional; like he believed that if everything went smoothly from now on and she didn't make any more mistakes, he could probably bring himself to be intimate with her.

Probably.

It left a sour taste in Synjan's mouth even though she told herself she was overreacting. Daeson's words of forgiveness and caring about her were true and they should be enough to revive her devotion to him. He couldn't help that she'd made choices that had ruined someone's life. That was all on her. It was reasonable to condemn her. She was lucky he'd found forgiveness in his heart.

Of course, if Peri wasn't protected and pandered to, Daeson would probably lose his forgiving mindset. Even Aron had shown some care for her around camp and he barely knew her.

Synjan knew that, no matter how hard she tried, she'd never be able to make her misjudgement up to Peri. That was reasonable, but the looks the older woman gave her were increasingly disquieting. Neither of the men noticed how Peri never responded to anything Synjan said with a tone other than snappy. She wasn't sure what to do about it besides persevering with being kind and reminding herself that it was fair for Peri to be unhappy. She was out of her world and had been severed from her life unexpectedly.

Peri's face appeared between the handlebars of the bike and when she opened her mouth to speak, the roar of an engine was all that came out. Synjan pulled her cheek abruptly away from Aron's back and she sat up a little straighter, inhaling vigorously. She had to keep it together and stay awake.

Turning around, Synjan noticed that she and Aron had significantly outpaced the other bike. It was little more than a speck in the distance. She tapped Aron's shoulder and lifted her mouth towards his ear, yelling over the noise of the bike engine.

"We have to stop!"

Aron eased off the bike's throttle and braked. "What's up?"

"We're way ahead of Daeson and Peri. You should probably shut it off while we wait."

He nodded and did so, finishing her thought in the silence that rose around them. "Save fuel."

"Yeah," she agreed, marvelling at his acquiescence. Daeson would've asked multiple questions and probably *still* not stopped the bike. Frowning at her disloyal thoughts, she climbed off the seat and performed some stretches. Her backside was numb and she rubbed it as she stared into the distance.

Aron also stretched before sitting sideways on the seat, looking thoughtfully at their approaching companions. "We shouldn't have put the two heaviest on the same bike."

"Good luck prying her off Daeson," Synjan muttered.

Aron gave her a direct look. "She does know you *both* took her, right?"

Synjan sighed, appreciating that he'd picked up on Peri's animosity towards her. Perhaps her earlier thoughts had been unduly harsh. "I'm not sure either of them know that," she replied.

Aron didn't comment on Daeson's blame or his forgiveness the night before but his next question showed he was thinking about the event.

"So that nightmare last night...?"

Synjan looked at Aron, searching his expression for hints about his thoughts. She supposed she owed him an explanation about why she'd screamed him into an impromptu perimeter sweep in the middle of the night.

"Killing gives me nightmares. Always has. I usually get through it by finding someone to sleep with and get the tension and emotions out of my system but, uh, the options are a bit limited out here," she admitted, laughing awkwardly after her revealing statement. She found it difficult to breathe after what she'd just said, waiting for him to voice an opinion.

Frustratingly, he didn't say anything. He just looked down at his boots, wiggling them from side to side. Her mind raced. Gods, could he have thought she was hinting she wanted to sleep with him? It wasn't beyond imagining but he probably expected she and Daeson were sleeping together if they were travelling together. Or did Aron realise that wasn't the case? He seemed very insightful with most things to do with her. She was impressed that he could remain so impassive.

He looked up and caught her staring anxiously at him. He nodded. Though it was a tiny gesture, relief flooded through her. She felt he understood. She was glad she'd opened up to him. He wasn't judging her.

"Yeah, that doesn't work for me but I don't get it as bad as you. I've never woken myself up screaming," he reasoned.

Synjan's mouth twisted. "I hate killing."

"It's anticlimactic."

She blinked. It was difficult to define what he meant, as every kill she'd ever made always happened at the height of a battle, with emotions and expletives and bullets flying. It was the epitome of climactic. How were his kills the opposite? They had enough impact to give him bad dreams but not enough to raise his emotions? It didn't make sense.

"That's a really weird way to put it," she mused.

Aron looked like he was tasting his response before he gave it. "Some people get off on killing. I'm not one of them."

Synjan understood. She'd met some truly repulsive humans that had lived for the kill shot—Kate's abusive boyfriend, Ren, came immediately to mind. He'd been Ellis' assassin so death had been his art and obsession. "Did you think you might be?" she asked Aron warily, aware that she didn't really know him all that well, despite feeling a connection with him.

"Once."

She raised her eyebrows, surprised by his honesty. And impressed. At some point he'd obviously wanted to kill and thought it would be enjoyable to him. She wondered who it had been, imagining that the people whose deaths you found anticlimactic were likely the ones you built up in your head. The ones you really *needed* to die, so that you felt better about living; the ones who'd done you a wrong so heinous you looked forward to ending them. She thought of McGaw.

"For revenge?" she guessed, lifting her chin in a way that signalled her understanding of the notion. She was also relieved that he *did* find killing anticlimactic. Enjoying it was something she couldn't fathom.

Now it was Aron's turn to frown. He looked momentarily confused but then he nodded.

"Was that when you were with the Authorities?" She wanted to know more about how that had come about and what his life with their mutual enemy had been like.

It became clear she'd asked the wrong question. Aron's expression and demeanour shut down and he instantly closed off to her. He looked away instead of maintaining eye contact and she followed his gaze.

"Daeson and Peri are here," he announced as the other pair drove towards them. Aron straightened on their vehicle and started it again.

Synjan got on behind him and they pulled away in silence. She no longer had any difficulty staying awake.

14

The Novice And The Mission

TORIN MOVED AROUND his bedroom, shoving clothing and items into his backpack before reconsidering and taking some of them out. His mother clung to the doorway like she didn't have the strength to keep herself up. Maybe she didn't. The argument they'd had before he'd gone to pack had been draining for both of them and he couldn't face her tears. After a brief respite, she started Round Two.

"What about school?"

"I'm not going back to school." Two tee-shirts went into his bag.

"But you only have six more months and you're done!"

"I'm done now."

"But your future—"

"This *is* my future, Mum. I don't need school for this." Four jackets stayed in his closet as he shrugged on his favourite, the leather one.

"What'll you do for money?"

"I don't need money," he said, hearing the lack of conviction in his own voice. "I can get odd jobs."

"Nobody will hire a terrorist."

And there it was, that word. It haunted him because he knew that was how he would be painted. The nerve she touched twanged hard enough for him to spin and face her and he watched with horror as she recoiled. It made him angrier, that she would shrink from him like she thought he might hit her. He'd never raised a hand to her and had always done as she'd asked. Maybe that was why she found it hard to let go of him now.

"The *Authorities* are the terrorists," he hissed, not wanting to raise his voice and let the whole neighbourhood know what was on his mind. "The *Authorities* are the ones who invade worlds. The *Authorities* are the ones who bully people to conform to *their* laws, *their* culture, even their religion! You take me to church on Sundays but you kept your books about the Wanderer gods, and you read them a whole lot more than you read the Authority Bible."

His mother recovered her composure during his speech and folded her arms across her chest. "Where did all this hate come from? I didn't teach it to you."

"No, the Authorities did, when they murdered your sister and my father."

Her cheeks flared pink before the colour took over her face. Her hands dropped to her sides and she glared at him.

"Carmen and Jerrom paid a high price for a mistake we made. Don't copy that, don't copy what we did."

"I'm not copying you. I'm not Wandering."

"What you're doing is a million times *worse*! If you want

revenge, just live your life."

"That's exactly what I'm doing, Mum. I'm living my life." He had her with that one, he could see her struggling for a response. He finished packing and picked up his bag.

"You're a minor, you can't leave."

"I could've signed up with the Authorities at fourteen," he shot back, walking towards her. He had to stop when she refused to move out of the doorway.

"You're not an adult here until you're *eighteen*!"

"My birthday's in a couple of months."

His mother stepped forward and hugged him tightly. At first he tolerated her awkward hold but then he relented and hugged her back. It didn't feel like this was going to be the last time he saw her.

He gently reached out to touch her mind, feeling like an asshole as he did because he was looking for information rather than making a connection. He felt the whirlwind in her; missing him before he'd even left, feeling abandoned and alone because all of her family was either dead or doing their best to die (his thoughts soured when he sensed this in her mind) and then he found it—her resolve not to betray him. She would let him go, even though she hated who he was going to. She wouldn't call the police because she didn't trust that he wouldn't be gunned down with everybody else. It seemed to be her only reason but it would do. Her mistrust of the Authorities, both local and throughout the worlds, wouldn't change. His affiliation with GOAL was safe.

"I have to get my laptop." He extracted himself and moved to his desk, unplugging his charger and discarding it before holding the computer under his arm.

"You talked to them on it," she guessed. "They'll want to destroy it."

"Probably, yeah."

When he walked to the doorway the second time, she stood aside. He heard her footsteps moving after him down the corridor. When he opened the front door to leave, she spoke again.

"I want you to come back. When you see who they really are, when you see what they really stand for, you come back."

"Okay," he said, though he doubted he would. She was making herself his safety net, so it was only fair that he protect her in kind by not returning ever again. The realisation hit him full force and he felt himself trembling under the blow. Before he could change his mind, he hurried out of the door and down the path to the waiting black sedan.

I love you, she said into his mind. He wanted to say it back, to let her know how grateful he was; for raising him, for teaching him his talent and being there for him. Even now, even though she hated what he was doing, she was there for him. But he couldn't return the simple message of his love and appreciation for her because he knew that a residue of tainted emotion and resentment would go with it. It would be crueller to reveal that he'd chosen to leave even though he knew she was scared of being alone.

He opened the back door of the sedan and tossed his backpack and laptop onto the bench seat before bundling in. Snook was at the wheel and Cleo sat in the front passenger seat, both of them looking at the house where he imagined his mother standing on the doorstep. He didn't dare look.

"Get out of here," Torin growled, slumping down in the seat. He watched Snook glance at him in the rear-view mirror but he drove away without saying anything. In spite of not intending to, Torin looked out the back window, expecting to see his mother but he only caught the front door closing. Disappointment welled, forcing the corners of his lips downward. His eyes stung and felt hot and he blinked rapidly, berating himself and battling with emotions that threatened to choke him. He was grateful Bourbon wasn't here. Some things should remain private.

"That's a hard thing to do, kid," Snook said. Torin didn't reply, not trusting his voice.

"He's not a kid anymore, Snook," Cleo replied, surprising Torin enough for him to sit up and look at her. She half-turned in her seat so she could meet his gaze and winked at him. Butterflies flew in his stomach and the threat of tears vanished. "Still a Chihuahua, though." She faced the front and laughed at her own wit. The butterflies fell in a graceless heap inside his gut, heavier than expected.

Snook looked in the rear-view mirror again, checking on Torin but not saying anything. His eyes weren't smiling and Torin grudgingly appreciated that.

"So why d'you call yourself HypnoBeast? Is it because you're an Intuit?"

"Yeah."

"But you can't hypnotise people, right?" Snook sounded like he was clarifying for himself rather than trying to prove Torin wrong.

"No, but hypnosis is used to get at hidden memories, you know?"

"Oh, I get it. That makes sense." Snook nodded and Torin heard the question in his head before it even came out of his mouth. "So where did the beast part come from?"

The reason behind it felt lame and childish, now. Beast came from 'beastmode', something he'd announce about himself whenever he thought he'd pulled off a brilliant move in gaming, or a tricky hack. He didn't want to explain it.

"Forget that, why are you called 'Snook'?" Torin threw back at him. Cleo briefly glanced over her shoulder at Torin, her expression cool like he'd said something wrong. Her action had him scanning Snook's mind but he was distracted when the car made a quick turn and his backpack slid across the seat and bumped into him.

"My wife. It was her pet name for me."

Snook's voice was the same as always but Torin wasn't fooled. He met Snook's gaze in the mirror.

"The Authorities killed her, didn't they?" He didn't have to guess because he'd plucked that knowledge out of Snook's head. As soon as Snook thought about his wife, there were visions and memories of her superimposed upon each other. The clearest one was of her on a slab in the morgue.

"There was a peaceful protest at the hospital where she worked. There was a flu epidemic and the Authorities were taking almost all the vaccines. Nobody was dying of anything but the Authorities were being selfish, so the public wanted that to be noticed. She was a nurse and when the soldiers started arresting the protesters and dragging them away, she got involved. One soldier smacked her in the head with the butt of his rifle. It knocked her unconscious, put her in a coma for six days and then she died."

"Fucking assholes," Torin spat.

"There was an inquiry," Snook continued. "If that soldier had been arrested or even discharged from service, I would've thought that enough and gone on with my life, mourning her and being a father to my son. But her actions to protect the people around her was considered criminal and interfering with Authority business, so the soldier who murdered her was found not guilty. The blame shifted to my wife. That's when I joined GOAL and my son joined with me. He was twenty-one."

Torin sat quietly in the back of the car. The engine purred and traffic around them was hushed because the windows were up. He stared unseeing through the windscreen, wanting to ask about Snook's son but also not wanting to know because he hadn't been introduced to anyone who fit that description. There were a few reasons why Snook's son might not be with their faction but the most likely one was that he'd died—killed on a mission, probably. When he'd met Snook on the street corner last night, he'd resented his concern. Now he felt ashamed.

"Sorry," he said, looking at the rear-view mirror. Snook met his gaze and grunted. Cleo became a living statue, facing the front. The silence reigned for most of the drive.

"My mum and dad used to Wander, along with my aunt."

Snook's gaze found his in the mirror once more and Torin couldn't read his expression. He thought he might not expand on his statement, except when he pushed into Snook's and Cleo's minds, he found them both curious for more information... yet neither of them asked. There was a respectfulness about it, that he wouldn't be pressed to speak about something unless it was on his own terms. No wonder Cleo had frowned at him for asking about Snook's name. She probably hadn't spoken up because his question hadn't meant to pry.

"They were young. Younger than I am now. Well, Mum was but her sister was eighteen. They hooked up with a guy who wanted to make a Fold."

"What's a Fold?" Snook asked.

Cleo explained, "It's a myth where Wanderers can make their own portal to a fantasy world."

Torin blinked. He'd not known that other Wanderers didn't believe in it. He'd read the books his mother had, the ones about Wanderer powers and the lore. He'd always thought they were true.

"Um, kind of. Anyway, even after they settled down, an Authority Hunter found them and killed my aunt and my dad. Then, a decade and a half later, he came for my mum and me."

"What the fuck?" Cleo exploded. Snook flinched at the wheel, surprised by the outburst. It would've been funny except Cleo shifted in the chair to turn her ire on Torin. "You have an Authority Hunter on your ass?" she screamed, spittle flying from her lips.

Because he'd been half-scanning their thoughts, he was blasted by her fear. Funny that he didn't sense anger because it was clearly on her face. His Intuit ability proved anger came from fear. It took him a moment to respond.

"No, he... he's done with us, now. He got what he wanted from my mother."

Cleo's voice dropped to a hush and her demeanour

changed. "You mean he raped her?" she asked. Torin blinked at the sudden change. Why had she gone there?

"What? No. They had words."

Cleo stared at him, her eyes narrowed as though he was a puzzle she was trying to figure out. He'd retreated out of her head after her outburst and now he was too rattled to check back in. He had a water bottle attached to his backpack but it was empty. He wished he'd thought to fill it before leaving because he was getting thirsty.

"Do you know who he is? Do you have his name?" Cleo prompted. He thought he understood what she was really asking.

"His name is Hawke Aron. I'm going to find him and I'm going to kill him."

15

Partnerships

HAWKE LIFTED THE gun and assessed his target. It would be a difficult shot but not impossible. The rifle was strapped to his back but he had so little ammunition for it that he didn't want to use it until he deemed it necessary. Beside him, Synjan held a finger to one ear and huffed before she spoke, her voice a whisper.

"You won't make that shot with a pistol." He could've turned her statement around, telling her not to judge him by her own skill, but then he'd have to make the shot.

"Let me try."

She lapsed into silence and he took a breath, releasing it as he pulled the trigger. The bullet created a puff of dirt a metre away from the large lizard sunbaking on a flat rock. The crack of the gun caused it to dash off, disappearing into the cluster of rocks behind it. Hawke thumbed the safety and re-holstered his weapon as Synjan smirked at him.

"I was close," he told her, not missing the way her

eyebrow quirked at his words. He wondered whether she would agree and encourage him—like Brita would've—or if she would boast that she could've done better. He wouldn't respect either of those reactions.

"You didn't even hit the rock."

He grinned at her teasing. "Not all of us has a fancy guidance system inside our heads," he said, tapping his temple. Synjan laughed before picking her way down the slope that led into the dry river-bed they'd followed out of camp. He moved easily beside her.

"You sound like Freddie."

"Who's Freddie?"

"My trainer."

Kegan Frederickson, who Hawke knew as Kegsy. It was bizarre to think of him having some other nickname. "You called him Freddie?" he scoffed.

She gave him an odd look before returning her attention to where she was stepping. "That's his name."

"Right, right." He wondered which nickname Kegsy—or Freddie—liked better. Since he'd been Kegsy with the Authorities, Hawke figured he'd changed his nickname with Synjan to protect his own identity. He couldn't have Synjan telling anyone she'd trained with Kegsy, after all. They reached the river bed and headed for the rocks where they'd sighted the lizard. They were on the lookout for water and food—where there were animals, there was both.

"He's an Authority," Synjan admitted.

"So we're not all bad?" Hawke grinned, forgetting.

"Says the guy who left them, but no, they're not all bad. Freddie's the best of them."

The sentiment wasn't anything he would argue. They fell into companionable silence, their footfalls the only noise for a long moment. He thought about Kegsy. If Hawke had gone missing, would he have gone to her to find him?

Synjan had something different on her mind. "I have to ask, why'd you join them?" She looked at him plainly and without condemnation. He didn't want to talk about his hatred of Wanderers.

"Because they opened up the worlds for me... and not just for me, for everyone. They actually began as a kind of military explorer for the pioneers, the first people to be sent out of Utopia—the first recorded world—into unknown danger. They recruited whenever they needed a role to be filled. They added training or rules and regulations whenever they were required." He paused, wanting to give Synjan a chance to respond but she kept her silence. For some reason he'd decided to start with a history lesson. "Um... I don't like that they strip worlds of their resources or take over the less-established worlds but, while they crash the culture, they also bring a standard of living that most people want. I mean, running water out of a tap is impressive when you've had to drink from a well or shit in a hole."

"Is that the kind of world you came from?" she asked after a moment.

"No, um... well, yes, but I..." He'd been privileged but didn't want to tell her that. He'd been a little asshole on Boronia and the transition to common child on Varrell hadn't been smooth. "I was in Authority care before I learnt much about the greater part of my world. I joined because I didn't see any other option. I mean, I did have options but the Authorities was the best one. They make it sound great. Like, everybody has equal opportunity to be whatever they want and that's true... but if you're a Wanderer, you're always going to be looked at with suspicion because a Wanderer will never be an equal."

"They think they're that much better?"

"No, a Wanderer has an advantage they will never have. The Authorities allow Wanderers to sign up and they welcome them with open arms, but that lack of equality... it creates this undercurrent of resentment and mistrust. It's in the way someone smiles at you and when they find out you have Wanderer blood, the friendly light leaves their eyes. They're wondering if you can see their secrets or set them on fire."

Synjan gave a surprised little laugh. "Huh. I never thought of that."

Hawke blinked at her reaction. He'd thought Ellis would've put the fear of Authorities into her but she didn't seem intimidated. He remembered every conversation he'd ever had with the man, and the Authorities had been condemned every time. Hawke thought hating on the Authorities would help him bond with Synjan but she wasn't jumping on board.

"Wanderers can be just as bad. I was treated much worse on Femme than I ever was—" *by the Authorities*, he was going to say, but he thought of the DOME and the experiments he'd endured as Authority scientists tested his shield. Now, they only required his blood as a standing request, one that he was obligated to fulfil.

"What happened on Femme?"

He wiped the grit from his palms against his jeans. "I was

locked up."

"That's awful," she gasped. "What did you do?" He waited a beat before looking back at her and was surprised to see her cheeks were pink. Was she embarrassed by her outburst? He sensed an apology was about to pour out of her mouth so he answered before the conversation became awkward.

"I was on my own and that bullshit's not allowed." He shrugged, wishing he hadn't brought up Femme. At least it made sense to her that he would've been on that world. He had to be careful which worlds he talked about. It wasn't like he could tell her that Avaniero was next.

Synjan pulled a face. "But didn't they assign you a diplomat?"

"I was walking into Ning when the local Authorities grabbed me, zapped me with head-glue and shoved me into their plane-car-thing."

He anticipated she would drill him for more details but she went in a different direction.

"Didn't you arrive in the Round?"

"The round what?"

"The circle of twelve Wanderers and their slaves. I thought everyone arrived in the same place."

"The Portal does change now and then," he said warily, forced to rely on his Hunter experience.

"It did on J'Bdyamn but I thought it was always the same on Femme."

The J word that poured out of her mouth was one he couldn't recognise nor pronounce. It was proof she'd been to a world before Femme, the one unrecorded after Trent. He'd suspected for a long time that there were worlds in between because so many Wanderers had dropped out of sight for months before they popped up again. Was this why there was a regulation for Hunters not to pursue flares on certain worlds? It wasn't just flares from Trent or Femme, there were more worlds; Halstrom, Alpha Four and others he couldn't remember the names of.

The Authorities had to know... they'd captured Wanderers before. They'd had to have seen the signs of Wanderers who disappeared off one world and never appeared in the next. They'd had to have captured some and made them admit it, or got an Intuit to look into their minds. The Authorities had been around for thousands of years... of course they must know.

It had to be unofficial knowledge. Or perhaps marked secret, only available for those of the highest ranking. Wait. Did Cayden know? Hawke had never mentioned his thoughts of worlds in between the known ones, even though he'd heard similar theories presented to him over drinks or other get-togethers. Certainly not in an official capacity. What had Cayden said specifically during those conversations? He struggled to remember.

He was aware Synjan had asked him a question.

"I beg pardon?"

"Where did you wake up?"

"On which world?"

"Femme—but look, if you don't want to talk about it, we can let it go. You obviously didn't have a good time there. Neither did Daeson."

He was curious about what Daeson had gone through, but he had too good an opportunity to drop the topic. It was so riddled with traps and potential for self-incrimination that it was wiser to follow her lead.

"Thanks," he said. There was nothing left to add once they arrived at the rocks and they resumed their search for food and water.

Peri pressed a hand into the small of her back and arched over it, wincing. Pulling out plants to burn in fires was painful work. She was certain Bitchface and Toughguy had given her and Daeson the hardest jobs.

"I always thought the desert was nothing but sand," she mused as she looked around at the scrubby bushes and patches of grass surrounding them. "Maybe that's just Earth. There are a lot more plants here than I expected."

Daeson didn't answer so she looked over at him. He was twiddling with the weedy tree in his hand and looking off in the direction Bitchface and Toughguy had disappeared. He probably hadn't heard her—hopefully, considering he hadn't bothered to respond. That was a pet hate. He was just like Dave, tuning her out in a housework argument, or one of her students, too wrapped up in chatting to pay attention to what she was doing at the board.

A pang of despair stabbed her heart, making her feel weightless and out of control. Her arms felt liquid and empty, her legs uncertain and her abdomen hollow. She missed them all so desperately she had trouble sleeping, despite the exhaustion that accompanied an impromptu smuggling through the desert.

Oh, Dave. I need you so much.

Tears welled and she drew in a savage breath, stamping

down her feelings. She was not going to cry about what she couldn't change, she was going to stay focussed and change what she *could*. She would get back to him. She *would*. Daeson hadn't responded positively to her disparaging remarks about Bitchface earlier but—*just testing the water*—she was confident she hadn't found the right angle yet. She needed more information. She walked up beside him, looking in the same direction.

"Are you worried she'll cheat on you?" she asked casually.

Daeson looked at her sharply. She felt it, but didn't return his gaze immediately. She watched a bumpy rock in the distance, counting the seconds until he spoke. Everything was stagecraft now, she had to play smart.

"Cheat on me?"

Now she looked up into his eyes, her expression deliberately sympathetic. "Yes. She's your girlfriend, isn't she? And you're worried he'll make a move on her."

Daeson frowned. "She's not my girlfriend."

Peri's heart found new wings and tried to escape through her ribcage. "Then why do you stay with her?"

His expression darkened and she sensed his resolve weakening. Hope jangled, so tart it flooded her mouth like she'd bitten a lemon.

"She's my friend. And my Navigator."

Friend? She's a psychopath. You're a blind idiot. What the hell are you waiting for? Get away from her!

"So it's not going to bother you if she hooks up with Aron?"

"What do you mean?"

"She's just a friend so it'd be okay if those two get

151

together. But where does that leave you?"

Daeson's face stiffened. He spun on his heel and strode back towards the camp. Peri hastened to keep up with him, relieved when he stooped to pick up the plants they'd collected. It allowed her to keep pace and deliver the point of her message.

"From what I see, *I* think you should give them your blessing and leave them to it. They suit each other. They're nothing like you and me. They both like guns and violence and I know you're no fan. I also know you didn't have anything to do with abducting me in the first place—none of it was your idea."

I have her gun. Just one gun but one was enough to get me here so one will be enough to set it all right again. C'mon. Work with me.

He nodded curtly, tugging on his ear. He still didn't seem prepared to speak.

"You're a good guy. You should put this right. Help me. Come with me. Tell those two you don't want to stick around. Rescue me and get us both out of this nightmare."

Daeson stopped and looked at her. "Rescue you?"

"Yes! Those two are *not* nice people, they don't give a shit about us. They couldn't care less that my partner came home to a... dark, empty house and that I... apparently l-left him," she beseeched, annoyed that she'd started to cry when talking about Dave.

Oh, my love, you're everything the poets and the singers ever wrote about.

But she was unable to stop. She missed him with every cell in her body, pining for him was to be expected. She swiped at the tears in an effort to regain her composure and argue coherently.

"How do you think I can rescue you?"

It was a fair question, well asked. "Us. Rescue *us*. We'd have to be obvious about it. Tell them you want to split up and that you're going to take me back."

For the first time, his expression softened. It set Peri's nerves on edge.

"Peri, you can't go back."

"So you all keep saying! But those Authorities could do it, you all said *that*!" Her temper was fraying along with her argument. Daeson was supposed to be the nice one. Why wasn't he agreeing with her logic? What was blinding him? "This isn't impossible, I know it!"

The kindness cleared from his face. "I will never go to the Authorities. I wish I could help you, but I can't."

"Why *not*?" Peri snarled. Her emotions had become a rabid dog fighting against its leash. "Because you're a miracle healer and you can make everyone on every world well? I'd have thought you'd *care* about sick people, that you might like being a part of curing cancer and saving sick babies from lives cut short! Why are you so *selfish*?!"

Daeson's mood shifted to meet hers. He threw the plants on the ground and squared up to her. "It's not that simple. They would lock me up and do experiments on me."

"Like I said; selfish! You don't give a shit about me either, you're just out to protect your own skin!"

"I *will* help you, somehow. Just not like that. We'll find a new world, a nice world where you can start a new life—"

Everything inside her was a colliding, roiling mess— waves crashing and sirens screaming, children wailing and buildings collapsing. She was being torn apart, the

153

sensation starting in her brain and unfolding rapidly through her whole body like the sickest domino display ever.

"I DON'T WANT A NEW LIFE! I WANT MY *OLD* ONE!"

Daeson rocked back on his heels as she shrieked at him, blinking at the venom and power in her voice. She yelled across noisy playgrounds for a living. One selfish, imbecilic man in her face was no match for her power and fury. She knew she was ugly crying at him but she didn't care. He was resisting her and she was tired of feeling like shredded cardboard, curling up and flying away on the wind, one rip at a time.

By contrast, his voice was quiet and calm when he responded. "That's over. You can't go back. Yelling at me won't change it."

She let out another primal scream of rage, wordless and jagged, then she stormed into the tent and threw herself on her bedding to cry it out. She didn't know what came next, everything around her was a yawning chasm of blackness and hysteria. She wouldn't accept it, couldn't bear to, but it was clear nevertheless.

Daeson was not the way. She'd been wrong. He'd scooped her insides out as ruthlessly as she'd anticipated the others would, leaving her a husk. He wasn't the way back to Dave.

So who was?

16

Cayden And Kegsy

RMED WITH A bottle of wine, Division General Irian Cayden pressed the doorbell, hearing it chime melodically inside the house. He put on his best broad smile. It had been well-practised throughout his career as he'd hosted parties for superiors he didn't like or shook hands with peers he didn't respect.

The early evening air was brisk and he wore a tan sweater over a white tee-shirt and jeans. The clothes were new—he hadn't packed before arriving in this shithole world. Its only saving grace was the fireglass mined out of the mountains that separated Gredann and Bardon City. Fireglass had the unique ability to remain perpetually warm and was found only in this world. A hundred times more expensive than diamonds, it had funded a great deal for the Authorities. The crystal had been wasted on the docksiders, who'd been so short-sighted about its use, they'd made trinkets out of it.

The door opened, interrupting his reverie. Cayden reestablished his smile for the redheaded woman before him. Tiln. He'd met her twice but she always had little to say. He suspected that she disliked him and it frustrated him as to why.

"Tiln! Lovely to see you again," he lied with warmth in his voice. She smiled through her confusion and glanced to her left. "I brought wine," he continued, pretending that he wasn't bothered by her inability to greet him and invite him in. He held out the bottle.

"Um. Hello." She looked from the bottle to his face and didn't move. Cayden took this as a sign to be more proactive.

"Is Kegsy in?" he asked as he stepped forward, forcing her back lest she be trampled. He put the bottle very close to her face and she took it grudgingly, throwing him a resentful look as he passed the threshold. He wondered if Hawke had been welcomed with the same hostility whenever he portalled into Oceangate to visit them. His relationship with Kegsy had grown worryingly strong if he was going off-book and doing favours for his ex-mentor.

Kegsy appeared through a doorway from a room farther inside the house. "Irian?"

"I thought I'd bring wine if I was staying for dinner." Cayden gestured at Tiln but didn't look at her. He wanted to keep eye-contact with Kegsy, who stared thoughtfully back at him. Unlike Tiln, Kegsy wasn't obviously displeased to see him but he didn't look ready to host a parade, either. For a brief moment, Cayden thought he was going to be dismissed—that an excuse would be made and he would be forced to accept it. The moment passed when Kegsy grinned and gestured towards the sitting room.

Dinner was so delicious that talk naturally suspended. Tiln's skill in the kitchen surpassed even the talents of Cayden's personal chef—a necessity because Mary abhorred cooking. Cayden had guided the conversation around the inanity of small talk and prodded topics that Kegsy was interested in; mostly sailing but also the latest advances in military gear. Tiln was silent throughout it all. As soon as the last forkful was eaten, she excused herself to clean up the plates. Cayden didn't miss the look she threw past him to Kegsy, her eyes wide and her expression stern.

Cayden remained seated but Kegsy stood and picked up his empty plate and glass.

"You go pour yourself a drink while I help with the dishes," Kegsy said, using his chin to indicate the direction Cayden should go before disappearing into the kitchen after his woman. Cayden imagined there would be a hushed discussion about his presence.

He moved through the arched doorway and returned to the small sitting room that he'd started the evening in, chatting about how Mary and the kids were faring as Tiln set an extra place at the dinner table. The room had two armchairs in one corner and a small bar in the other. It wasn't perfectly rectangular because a bathroom on the other side of the wall encroached on the space. In the nook that it created was a tiny desk to suit one person. Cayden tried to visualise Kegsy's bulk seated at that square table, but the result was exaggerated and cartoonish.

Because they were on Trent, there was no computer or portal fax—only a landline. The Authority rollout for integrating technology had been slow because of docksider resistance. The rich folk who lived in Hill End had cameras, closed circuit security systems and computers to run them on, but nobody had television and only some of the Authorities carried mobile phones as far as he knew. The first thing Authority Pioneers did when they arrived at a new world was to set up an Authnet beacon so they could communicate.

Cayden's gaze kept dragging to the fat file on Kegsy's desk. Very few files ever looked as full as the one he had there. Hawke's file was that large—there was a lot of paperwork on him from assorted sources; Willets Academy, the DOME and every Hunter report he'd ever given. Now there was that tome of a contract from Nakhari Base and all the reports that had come from there. Once Cayden was promoted to Division General Superior, he would have access to those files. He was burning to know what had happened to Hawke.

Cayden heard the distinctive sound of a knife scraping food off a plate and the plastic rustling of the receiving bin. While Kegsy was otherwise occupied, Cayden moved to the desk and looked at the large file upon it. It was held closed by a thick red rubber band. Instead of sliding it off, he rolled back the corner of the folder, not wanting to crease it and leave evidence of his curiosity. He saw the standard 'Priority One Secret' stamp emblazoned in red at the top right corner, above the names of the people who were allowed to access this file. Division General Morgan's name was on there—the woman who oversaw the different Interword Tactical Response units—but Kegsy's name wasn't, even though he was the ITR Division Lieutenant. He wasn't supposed to have this file.

"You alright? Need more time?"

Cayden jumped when Kegsy asked his question from the doorway. He chuckled self-consciously, smoothing down the corner of the file that kept rolling up. "I'm good," he said apologetically, then headed for the opposite corner of the room to sit in an armchair—the same one he'd taken when waiting for dinner. Kegsy took the adjacent one and watched him expectantly. Neither of them had poured themselves a drink.

He could tell Kegsy was waiting for him to get to the point. He'd been avoiding it all night, unable to say anything in front of Tiln and wanting Kegsy in a position where he could read his expressions as they came. In all the time he'd known him, the man had worn his face openly. He had no artifice.

"I almost lost Hawke," Cayden said, wondering if he'd been monitoring the off-book mission.

Kegsy tensed. "What? How?"

"He was held captive on Femme."

During the pause that followed, Cayden watched him struggle not to react. His next words were spoken in a peculiar tone. "Why was he on Femme?" Cayden blinked slowly and Kegsy sighed. "It was worth a shot. Is he okay?"

"He was well enough to stay on mission if that's what you meant. So what's going on?" He expected Kegsy to stall some more but he answered frankly instead. It reminded Cayden why he liked him.

"I need Hawke to bring someone back."

"You sent my best assassin to *save* someone?"

Kegsy's smile was wry, showing that he appreciated the irony. "Yep."

"Isn't that your speciality? Why not use your own unit?"

Kegsy folded his arms. "It can't be official. But you knew that."

Cayden did know that, but he wanted Kegsy to say it to get it out in the open. Despite knowing, he detected a tension in the air that only came when someone was holding back. Cayden wondered if Kegsy knew both of them were hiding something. He had the wary look of a hunted man. He wouldn't show his hand just yet; first he wanted to know how far Kegsy's loyalty to him extended.

"Does Hawke know what you've got him into?" Cayden asked, choosing his words carefully.

"He knows everything."

Cayden voiced a chuckle, though he wasn't amused. "I doubt that." He waited, hoping Kegsy would fill the silence. Silence was a tool he often used during tense conversations. A lot of the time the other party would feel obligated to fill it. He often learnt more from others filling in silences than when he asked questions. Kegsy wasn't the type to fill silences for the sake of relieving tension, so Cayden continued. "I think I know more than Hawke does, at this point."

"Oh?" The dubious look on Kegsy's face irked him.

"So which one is he bringing back?" he asked.

"All of them."

Cayden frowned. Kegsy was playing dumb. He disliked dumb. "There are only two."

Kegsy sighed and threw himself back into the soft

160

cushions of the armchair. It made a *ploomp* sound. "Both of them, then."

"Who was the original target?" Cayden pressed.

"How much do you *know*?"

The astonishment in Kegsy's tone filled him with the kind of pleasure he assumed his wife's cat felt when she stroked it and tickled its chin. If he had a motor like that cat, he'd be purring right now. He settled for a smile. "Let's pretend I know everything and—"

"No, let's not, and tell me what you know instead of fishing around like I'm one of your fucking puppets!"

It wasn't often that Kegsy raised his voice or demanded things of him. He was usually softly-spoken and subservient. He was the kind of man that everybody loved because he cared about everybody's bullshit little lives. It was exactly what Cayden hadn't managed for himself and knew he never would. Breaking out of character revealed how defensive he was.

"Synjan or Daeson?" Cayden prompted.

"I want Synjan."

Cayden contained his excitement even though he wanted to jump up and yell out a cheer. He felt electric because of Kegsy's answer. Everybody could be happy with this outcome. Kegsy could get his girl back and Hawke would bring in the Healer. Cayden would get his Division General Superior status as well as a massive bonus... as long as Hawke delivered the goods. If he had no idea about the Healer, it was likely he'd shoot Synjan's travel partner in the head to lower the threat to him when he grabbed her.

"Does Hawke know what Daeson is?"

Kegan's eyes widened and he slumped in his seat. Under

161

his breath he mouthed, 'fuck'.

Cayden was relieved. It now made sense why Hawke had readily abandoned his time with Brita. He'd been put on the trail of a Wanderer Healer! "I'll take that as a yes."

"How do you *know* all this?" Kegsy demanded.

"I have my sources."

"In Gredann?" Kegsy had that dubious look on his face again. It shuttered and changed to something stiff and wary. "Is this an official visit?"

And there it was. The favour Kegsy wanted from him. The favour Kegsy would eventually owe back.

"Of course not," Cayden said with a winning smile. A genuine one.

"Nothing is in the system?"

"Nothing that wasn't already there before." Now that he understood what Hawke was doing for Kegsy and what was at stake, he could move on to the other topic that niggled his curiosity. "I was surprised when I read about Howard Ellis. Moreso what I *didn't* read on his record." Cayden watched as fear passed over Kegan's face. It was unmistakable. He'd seen its match on Nick's face just last night. Nick had been powerless, though. Kegsy wasn't. "Why the hell didn't you issue a kill order on that freak? What does he have over you?"

Kegsy massaged his knees. "I need a drink," he said hoarsely. He stood and walked to the bar, looking much older than usual. He grabbed the whiskey bottle and a glass and poured himself a double. To Cayden's astonishment, he skolled it. For a man Cayden had only ever watched drinking beer, this was new. He'd expected excuses or a confession, maybe. Something that they could clean up together. This was something unknown.

Kegsy cleared his throat as he grabbed a second glass and poured another double into each of them. When he returned, he thrust one in Cayden's direction, causing the liquid to slosh dangerously close to the edge before settling.

"He doesn't have anything over me," Kegsy said when he sat down. "But up until recently he was an inactive Wanderer and I didn't see the point."

Kegsy rolled the glass around in his hands before taking a light sip and then fiddling with the glass some more. He was no master at the art of deception but Cayden thought he wasn't even trying. Kegsy looked anxious and maybe he didn't know how to continue.

"What do you need from me?" Cayden prompted.

"Do you have to put his talent in the system?"

"His talent?" Cayden repeated with a smile. It was a word he'd never heard associated with a Wanderer ability or power. A talent was something earnt, not inherited. "I can keep his *talent* out of it if you want."

Kegsy's shoulders relaxed but his jaw remained clenched.

Cayden could've let it drop and ended the conversation there, but his curiosity got the better of him. "Why do you want this? Why is he so important to you?"

Kegsy startled him when he slammed his glass down on the side table, the crack of the connection loud enough to make Cayden jump, even though he saw the movement in its entirety. "Fuck it, I didn't say yes!"

Cayden sipped his whiskey, studying Kegsy over the rim of his glass. "But he's still important to you," he said eventually.

"Not enough to sell my... not that important."

Sell my soul, like Cayden was the devil. It made him laugh. "We're still friends," he said. It attracted a sharp look from Kegsy but no protest came. Cayden set his whiskey down and leant forward, lowering his voice. "You shouldn't have asked Hawke. You should have come to me."

"I didn't want to compromise you. I knew Hawke could get it done."

The answer was quick and placated him. Kegsy could be playing him but he was one of the good guys and good guys were thoughtful. "How is he supposed to get them back to us?"

"I'd planned to play that by ear."

Cayden frowned. "Playing by ear isn't a plan."

"I can't plan where he'll reach them," Kegsy shot back.

"Isn't she on the run? Isn't he going to have to bring them back by force?"

"It's complicated."

"Ellis. He's gone after them, too, hasn't he?"

Kegsy nodded and Cayden saw the worry in his eyes. 'Complicated' was no longer potent enough to describe this fucked up situation.

"So, *should* I put a kill order on him? If he beat your mistress to a pulp, what's he going to do your... what *is* Synjan to you? She's a bit young for you, isn't she?"

Kegsy pulled a face. "She's like my daughter."

"You put your 'daughter' in the hands of a Controller?"

"He's looked after her. Since she was six."

"And he raised her as a criminal until she ran away. Good job."

"Much like you raised Hawke."

Understanding dawned. He'd always thought Kegsy intelligent—if a little naive—but now he thought that some of his 'good guy' nature was a facade.

"So she's your asset."

Kegsy's eyebrows rose. "Like... Hawke is yours?"

Cayden laughed. "I've spent a lot of time developing him." He'd been the only one to see the potential of a Wanderer Shielder—someone who could hide from Wanderer powers—and who despised Wanderers to his very core. They'd taken everything away from him. That kind of fury would be powerful motivation in the Hunter division. Hawke had been another lightning strike that others had passed on. Bringing the boy into his family, defending him against others, cultivating his rage against Wanderers— years of moulding and shaping the boy had paid off. Hawke's success was now his success. "He's the best Hunter I have."

"Hawke's more than that, isn't he?"

"Of course."

There was a pause before Kegsy barked a short laugh. He didn't sound amused and Cayden thought he heard something hard in it. "How did you get Nick to talk?"

It was a good guess on Kegsy's part, but Cayden knew he'd dropped too much information. Depending on who knew what in this incestuous little cesspool, it could've been easy for Kegsy to figure out who Cayden's source was. He saw no point lying about it now that he had the upper hand. He grinned.

"It wasn't hard. The Controller laid the groundwork for me. Logan couldn't wait to get off-world."

"You got him off-world? Where?"

Cayden laughed. "So you can get to him? I think not."

"Okay. Goodnight, then."

And just like that it was over. He was surprised by the abrupt ending but the night was getting late and he and Kegsy were the type to rise early. He set down his whiskey, mostly untouched, and got up to head for the door.

He paused. "Should I say goodbye to Tiln?"

Kegsy shook his head. "She's gone to bed."

Cayden imagined the comments his wife would have about someone who went to bed before their guest was seen out. Kegsy could do better. Many women swooned over his muscular frame and gentlemanly manners. He couldn't see anything special in Tiln that kept Kegsy tied to her and this shitty world. She wasn't even that attractive.

Never mind. That ignorant bitch couldn't spoil his good mood. "Take care," he said to Kegsy on the doorstep. He had a lot to feel good about; he'd got everything he wanted.

Almost everything.

He wanted to know more about Howard Ellis. And he had one more person to ask.

17

Undercurrents

E VERYONE SLEPT, EXCEPT him. Hawke had never needed a great deal of sleep and it was often to his advantage. Instead of prowling around the confined space of their camp, he lay on his back and stared at the stars, identifying the constellations. It was a way of centring himself after all the half-truths and careful words. He'd taken too long to react to his name at one point tonight, forcing Daeson to repeat it three times before he'd remembered that 'Aron' was him.

His gaze travelled the pinpoints of luminescence. They looked powdery due to sheer quantity, visible because of no backwash from city lights. He wasn't a fan of this kind of environment. Snow would've been better; at least more familiar. Even a marsh would be an improvement, though the constant itch of biting mosquitoes was on par with sand that got into unfavourable places.

Whimpering broke him out of his reverie and he sat up. He could make out individual words now, soft whispers of protest that would build up into a scream if he didn't act fast. He didn't want to witness the sickening lovefest between Synjan and her big lug again, so it was better that she didn't wake him or the Earther.

He leant forward and reached out, gently swiping her cheek to wake her, dismayed that his hand came away wet. He shouldn't have been surprised to feel tears; he was fairly sure her dreams were better described as night terrors.

Her eyelids fluttered open and she sat up, wiping her cheekbones with the heels of her palms. Maybe to wipe the tears, maybe to hide her embarrassment. He couldn't really tell by the light of the dying fire. Silence lingered between them as she composed herself and he felt it growing heavier with every breath. He remembered the cure she had for nightmares.

"Did you need to get it out of your system?" he asked with a grin, shifting position so she could see his face. Unfortunately, it put her expression into shadow.

"You're offering?" she asked with a chuckle and a sniff.

"It seems rude not to."

She laughed but held most of it in, lowering her head to contain it and not wake the other two.

"Is that a no?" he asked.

"Well, you are my type."

She surprised him by saying so. She was both forthright and demure, a heady combination. He liked that about her, though he imagined it got her into trouble at times. Nothing she couldn't handle. He liked that, too.

"So I'm your type. In that I'm here?"

"No!" she hissed, glancing at the tent though her whisper

168

wasn't that loud. "Authority."

He stared at her blankly, wondering what she was accusing him of when he realised she meant she liked men in uniform. Or was it just Authorities? Did she get off on the idea of sleeping with the enemy?

"If you're hot for the uniform, I can borrow Peri's."

She cackled and clamped a hand over her mouth, muting herself. The two of them laughed softly together but she didn't speak again until they wound down.

"I don't need you to be clothed," she hinted.

Hawke complied by unzipping his jacket. Synjan watched but didn't say anything. He moved onto his shirt and was halfway done unbuttoning it when she spoke again.

"You'll get cold," she sang playfully.

"I'll be quick."

"Way to sell it."

"I thought you were already sold?" He reached the bottom of his shirt and looked at her, expecting she'd tell him to put his clothes back on, or say some other words indicating the joke had gone too far. She didn't say anything and he found himself wishing that he hadn't positioned himself where he couldn't see her face. The air between them changed and electrified. He started to think she might be serious.

"Your bag or mine?" Synjan asked, her voice lower and huskier. Desire zapped through his body. With it came the memory of what Woy had predicted about them, that he would have sex with Synjan. Had she seen this moment? This half-hearted joke that hoped to be serious, the chill in the desert air that would make dipping into Synjan's warmth all the more pleasurable? Imagining her entwined around him had him moving forward, rolling onto his knees even as she met him in the middle. Their bodies pressed together as their mouths connected and he found himself lost in the sensation of a new experience. With his shirt already open, her hands explored first his chest then went around to his back. They were cool on his skin, sending waves of delight across his spine. He felt her nipples, hard and prominent against his chest, and his hand lifted to explore them but he never made it. The striking sound of a zip filled the air, rending them apart like they were naughty school-children stealing a kiss in a classroom.

They both watched Peri crawl out of the tent, the folding spade clutched in one hand. She didn't seem to notice them as she struggled to her feet and moved away from camp to do her business. The idea of the Earth woman digging a hole to defecate in killed the mood.

Hawke buttoned up his shirt and zipped his jacket, taking some quiet, calming breaths. He watched Synjan run a hand over her hair and work to compose herself in much the same way. Finding himself squinting to see her more clearly, he decided it was a good time to rebuild the campfire.

As he climbed out of his bedding and headed for the fire pit, the cold night air brought him to his senses. His infatuation was unnatural. He saw things in Synjan that weren't there; pushing for an attraction because he'd been told it would happen—and because he'd been curious about her for years. He'd built her up in his head like he was the fan to her celebrity and he'd become so starstruck that he wasn't paying attention to who and what she really was.

Short and blonde; nothing he normally gravitated to. Athletic instead of graceful—another step away from his preference. A Wanderer. A kidnapper. Even as he thought it, he could feel himself internally justifying her actions. True, the circumstances were different, but he doubted Peri would care.

When the flames licked greedily at the scrub he fed into it, he walked back, pleased that he could see Synjan's face by its light. Peri returned just as he sat down. If she was curious about them both being awake and staring at her, she didn't say. She returned to the tent and closed it after herself. They didn't speak until they heard her breathing drop into the long slow rhythm of sleep.

"How come Daeson's not stopping your nightmares?" Hawke asked.

She examined him like she was looking for some sort of message in his face. By the time she answered, her words were carefully measured. "We're... friends. I wanted more but he doesn't."

"What's wrong with him?" he teased. She obliged him with a smile, but he wanted to know more. "You haven't been together long."

"Is it that obvious?" she asked.

"He stifles you. I can't imagine you'd last long like that."

She took in breath, like she was shocked. "He doesn't stifle me," she countered. "He just doesn't like... when I—"

"Think for yourself?" he finished.

"No!" She dropped her voice. "We're just very different and he doesn't understand the way I've been raised. He doesn't like the violence. And I'm trying to be more like him."

"What? More like him?" Hawke questioned, failing to see how that would work. It made more sense the other way around. Shouldn't the big lummox be asking her to train him to shoot and fight?

"He's kind. He's gentle. He helps people."

He thought he understood now. "You mean he Heals them."

"Exactly."

"Don't get the power mixed up with the man."

"He saved my life."

He thought of what they did together at the training zone. "So did I."

"He's not a killer like I am."

She condemned him at the same time as herself. It was maddening. He'd been forced to defend himself his entire life, being told he wasn't good enough because he wasn't the firstborn son, then because he had Wanderer blood, then because he had no family. The list went on and on and everyone in his life had judged him. Except Kegsy. He'd thought Synjan was on that list, too, but now here she was, stark and minimal, hating herself for the same things he did.

"Not a killer like we are," he corrected. "But for men like him, we'd be dead."

She frowned. "That's very cryptic."

"Not so. Throw your guns away and show me how being like him makes you better."

She gave him a lofty look. "That's not fair. You'll see."

He huffed and left her, refusing to be defined by his

172

ability to pull the trigger.

———————— ·◦· ————————

When Synjan opened her eyes, she awoke to a sky shifting from the murky grey light of pre-dawn to one pierced by racing streaks of rose and peach. The sand beneath her was radiating cosy heat and the air was crisp with promise. It was her third day in this world and the second morning she'd awoken this way.

Then Aron's voice floated to her from somewhere beyond her line of vision and everything came rushing back with sickening clarity.

She'd *kissed* him! Her cheeks burnt with the memory and her heart-rate picked up. Delicious pulses rippled through her, reminding her of the ache she'd fallen asleep nursing. They hadn't ended the night on the best of terms but that hadn't stopped her thinking about what might have happened if Peri hadn't left the tent when she did. Those thoughts had flavoured her dreams and she hadn't slept properly until Aron's dream-hands had brought her to a throbbing climax. She furtively sniffed her fingers, wondering whether she'd touched herself or whether it had been a dream… just her imagination, then. Unless he'd touched her while she slept. The notion sent a thrill of longing through her.

What in the worlds was wrong with her? She'd meant every word she'd said about Daeson but Aron had such a way of undermining her feelings that they were all twisted inside. Was it just because he appealed to her physically? Did he seem like a good idea because her relationship with

Daeson had shifted yet again and she'd be able to forget about Aron once things settled down? Was she actually wasting time worrying about boys like a lovesick teenager? She was too old for this sort of nonsense. She sat up with a huff, wrapping her bedding around her shoulders and looking at her companions through sleepy eyes.

Aron was showing Peri how to siphon fuel into one of the trikes with a hose. Daeson sat in front of the tent, scowling at them as he ate some of the lizard and vegetable soup from the night before. There was no fire so he had to be eating it at a very uncomfortable temperature but he barely seemed to notice.

Synjan could see both men's faces from where she was and she couldn't help but compare them. Daeson's beauty was marred by his disapproving expression but his face was still dear to her. With a secret burst of relief, she acknowledged that just looking at him warmed her heart. She really did care about him and she missed waking up beside him with such intensity that it curled her toes.

Looking at Aron warmed her in entirely different places and she exhaled shakily as she watched the muscles of his arms and shoulders flex beneath his shirt. He spoke patiently to Peri, smiling seductively at her over the top of the red cube. He made a joke that was reflected in his pale eyes and elicited a rare smile from the Earth woman for his troubles. Synjan wondered how pouring fuel could be so entertaining. What had he said?

With a snort of disgust, Synjan got out of her warm bedding and pulled on her pants and jacket. She headed in the opposite direction to her travelling companions and found a place to relieve herself, wishing they were near a water-hole again. Washing hands and bodies would be a luxury until they found another source and she was already annoyed by it. Some things were best left unscented.

She re-entered the camp to find the only thing that had changed was that the second vehicle was now being fuelled and the sky had continued to lighten. On a whim, she moved to Daeson and wormed her way into his lap, snuggling against him and pressing a kiss to his cheek.

"Mmm, you're so warm," she purred, nuzzling his throat.

"And your nose is cold," he flinched away, but then he wrapped his arms around her, somehow not spilling any of his breakfast. He tipped it into his mouth over her head.

"Says the man drinking cold soup. Can I have some of that?"

"There's more in the big pot," Daeson replied distractedly, watching Aron and Peri.

Synjan frowned, unimpressed by his selfishness. "Is it icy?"

"Not under the layer on the top."

She shook her head and sighed, drawing his attention at last. "What?" he asked defensively.

"You'll eat anything as long as it's labelled 'food'."

He grinned and it flowed into her like the sun's warmth. "Mostly."

She laughed but it stopped when Aron spoke from nearby.

"Nice of you to finally wake up," he announced.

Synjan turned her head to look at him, resisting the urge to sit up and move out of Daeson's lap. Instead, she forced a yawn and wriggled closer. "Sorry," she lied. "I didn't sleep well." She fluttered her eyelashes and smiled coyly, unsure why she was antagonising Aron. His sour expression likely had a lot to do with it.

"When you're done warming up tonight's distraction, you might want to pack," Aron told her coolly, his gaze flicking to Daeson to reinforce his point before he looked back at her. "The bikes are fuelled and Peri and I are ready to go."

"Hey!" Daeson objected.

Synjan could only gape at Aron as he turned and walked back to where Peri was arranging things in the trailer. She was glad Daeson couldn't see her face because she could feel a blush colouring it.

She was mortified. It wasn't just the implication that she would use Daeson to get her bad dreams out of her system, it was Aron's weary tone. Like he was thinking about their kiss from the night before and thought less of her now; like he believed she didn't care who destroyed her demons, as long as they got the job done. As if their kiss hadn't meant anything to her.

"I don't trust that guy," Daeson muttered, interrupting her train of thought.

"I know," she sighed and got out of Daeson's lap. "Do you want help getting ready?" she offered once she was on her feet. She frowned, feeling agitated and impatient for an answer so she could be doing *something* besides standing.

Daeson frowned too. "What's wrong?" he asked.

She fought the impulse to answer quickly, knowing he'd interpret anything dismissive as a lie. "I didn't like what he said. But I also don't want to talk to you about it."

"Why?"

Because I kissed him last night and I really liked it but when he saw me with you he implied I was fickle and now I feel weirdly guilty.

She swallowed. "I don't know who to feel loyal to."

Daeson's jaw set but the hurt that flared in his eyes reflected directly into her heart.

"Are you going to leave me?" he asked tightly.

"No!" Synjan cried, crouching down in front of Daeson and gripping his forearms firmly. "I don't mean it like that! I mean *I* like him but you don't trust him so it feels like I'm caught in the middle and I have to choose between you. I don't *want* to choose!"

Daeson stared at her so long she began to suspect he wasn't going to say anything. "You should be loyal to *me*."

She nodded and hugged him, unable to speak around the lump of emotion in her throat. Even if she'd been able, she didn't know what she'd say.

It was odd to be so conflicted after such a short amount of time. She understood the distance between her and Daeson came from uncertainty about Peri. The shootings had a residual effect between them as well. She couldn't as easily reason away her attraction to Aron. She didn't think it was the flirting or the kiss or the fact he'd challenged her relationship with Daeson. She was inexplicably drawn to him, to the point where an offhanded remark had cut her. She was entirely out of her depth yet something in her yearned to hurl itself into that dark abyss and fall until he caught her.

Ridiculous.

To avoid further conversation, she left Daeson to go and

organise her gear. Once her bedroll was re-attached to her backpack, she shouldered it and returned to the pot of soup. She finished what was left, swallowing quickly so she didn't have to taste it. She was the last to arrive but Aron didn't say anything as he helped her get everything stowed in a trailer.

"I'd like to ride with Aron today," Peri declared to no-one in particular.

Synjan looked at Aron. There was a breathless moment where their eyes met. She had the distinct impression he was waiting for her to make a decision but it passed as he straightened up and smiled at Peri. "Sounds good," he agreed.

When Synjan looked at Daeson, his expression was contemplative but somehow disapproving, like he wanted to object but wasn't sure how. He didn't say anything but his eyes narrowed as he watched the other two get on their vehicle.

Synjan sighed and waited for Daeson to get on the driver's seat of the trike before settling in behind him. She hoped she wasn't going to be lectured about how evil Aron was the whole way but she also couldn't imagine what she'd say if she'd been riding with him instead. She'd only embarrass herself if she addressed his quip but she *really* wanted to make him apologise.

As they pulled away from their camp, Daeson spoke to her over his shoulder. "Maybe she'll get him to drive away with her and solve both our problems." He sounded pleased to have come up with this idea.

Synjan merely frowned, wondering what in the worlds had given him that notion.

18

Seduction

PERI HAD A song stuck in her head. An earworm. It wasn't the whole song. It wasn't even the whole chorus, just two lines kept repeating. She couldn't remember the rest.

I wasn't ready, to let go
I wasn't ready, to say goodbye

It was something she'd recently heard on the radio a few times and she liked its beat. The woman's voice sailed smoothly into a stratospheric register on the last word of each line—probably thanks to autotune—and Peri recalled laughing as she tried to sing that note, driving home from school. *Just because I can't sing doesn't mean I won't sing!* She loved that meme.

She wasn't laughing now. There was nothing to laugh about. All the laughter had died the day Bitchface had abducted her from her life. Bitch of a bitchfacing Bitchface sucked the goodness out of everything.

I wasn't ready

It had been three days but it felt far longer. More like three months since she'd slept in a soft bed and ohhhhhh, had a shower. She missed indoor plumbing like... like a lot. It was at least three years since she'd seen Dave's face or cuddled Biscuit. Three hundred years.

to let go

Have a plan, they said. Set some goals and harness your inner tiger, then go out and smash them, they said. None of that was any good when a blonde upstart waved a gun in your face and forced you off your path. There was no planning for that business. Now she had to concoct a new plan every day, because every day she tried something new and she failed.

I wasn't ready

Daeson was not the hero of this story. He was just a whiney kid with no testicular fortitude and a level of selfishness that she rarely saw outside her class of eight-year-olds. So what if he would be imprisoned or experimented on if they went back to the Authorities? She couldn't bring herself to care. Besides, he could still do the planet a whole lot of good and live a fulfilled life in a lab. They bloody *owed* her, after what they'd done! He wasn't even sleeping with Bitchface. Peri couldn't understand why he was still here.

to say goodbye

Well, forget him. She'd moved on and forged a new plan that involved Toughguy. Initially, she'd likened him to one of the male Physical Education or Design Tech teachers at school, swaggering around with his popped collar and flexing muscles, showing the world what a man's man looked and acted like. They were often nice guys when you got to know them but she remembered the time one of the P.E. men had delivered an entire professional development presentation bouncing a volleyball off his foot and catching it. And dropping it. And kicking it up and catching it, all while monotoning his forgettable message. She'd been mostly focussed on the way the tendons in his shoulder bulged alluringly. They were strange peacocks, P.E. teachers.

She'd realised Toughguy wasn't like that at all, once she'd had some time to observe him. He was older and wiser, in his early forties, she thought. Closer to her age. More like an experienced Science teacher, exuding a quiet confidence because he had intimate knowledge of fifty untraceable chemicals that could kill you swiftly (and twenty more that he could use to dispose of the body without a trace). Toughguy had a casual menace borne of genuine danger, rather than posturing machismo.

And here she was, hanging onto his narrow waist as they rolled through a never-ending desert, waiting for her chance to woo him. Such was life, right, Ned? She'd been psyching herself up to the task since Prettyboy had let her down the day before. Frankly, her options had been severely limited from the beginning and she felt like a reverse Goldilocks as she reviewed them. Daeson had been the best chance, Toughguy had been a slim chance and Bitchface was a no chance. She'd started at the top and was working her way down the one step she had.

What would tempt a tough guy like Aron? She'd struck out with Daeson and Aron was only going to be less malleable. He had appeal, though. He'd already been an Authority so he knew a lot about them. More than the other two dingbats. Peri had got a weird tingle in her spine when she'd watched him sitting at the fire. And whenever he'd picked up his gun. He had this way of *looking* at everyone that was just like a teacher. He scanned, he assessed, he chose his words carefully. He never said anything incriminating but it was what he *didn't* say that had her suspicious. He was way too alert to no longer be an active Authority. She strongly suspected he'd done a runner and was currently A.W.O.L.

Bitchface and Daeson watched each other and her. Toughguy watched *everything.*

It was like he expected an attack from every front at once and he was always ready for it. Unless he was busy sneaking peeks at Bitchface when she was talking to Daeson, then she was all he cared about.

Was this suspicion about his current military entanglement enough to get Peri what she wanted? She didn't feel like he was the type to suffer blackmail. The behaviour management gurus said

I wasn't ready

nobody was ever punished into better behaviour. She needed honey, not vinegar, but she saw the kind of honey he was drooling over and Peri knew she didn't compare. What else was there, though?

Peri's chance came when the terrain changed. Instead of being mostly flat or sandy, it became heavily eroded and filled with rises and gullies that Toughguy had to slow the bike down to negotiate. He stopped before it really began, letting his bike idle while he looked for a safe way through. Peri peered over his shoulder.

"Are they very deep?" she queried.

"Not too bad but we'll have to go slowly, especially with the trailers." He turned his head—probably to yell that exact message at Daeson, who was driving the other trike—and swore as the other two roared by. Peri could hear Bitchface squawking at Daeson, causing him to slow marginally.

"Idiots," Peri agreed as Toughguy released his brake and trundled after them.

He stayed a safe distance back and followed their path only if they had no trouble getting out the other side of the chasm they'd entered. Mostly they went their own way, reassuring Peri that the conversation she had planned would remain private. Their bike's burble was loud enough to stop the others from hearing if they got close and moderate enough that she could be sure Toughguy would hear her if she leant to the side.

to let go

"Are you sure the Authorities are going to come after us?" she queried.

It took him a while to answer. Whether it was because he was concentrating on driving or was too surprised to come up with a quick answer, she couldn't be sure.

"They've found the bodies by now," he finally said.

"So it's only a matter of time before they track us?" The question sent a thrill of excitement through her. This group of misfits was clearly her damnation; the Authorities would be her salvation.

"Mmm."

"Do they have satellites in this world? I haven't seen anything moving in the sky."

"Don't think so."

"They'll find our tracks though, right?"

"Synjan would notice if anyone got too close."

Peri's stomach was a cauldron of venom, bubbling poison into her oesophagus. "And she'd just kill them, too, I suppose?"

Toughguy slowed the bike and turned his body so he could look Peri in the eye. His expression was wary and calculating. "She's going to protect Daeson at all costs."

"What about you?" Peri challenged.

He raised his eyebrows.

"You two don't get along. You don't owe him anything. Surely you'd get a nice kickback if you turned him in to your people?"

He turned back to face the front of the bike and accelerated. "They're not *my people*," he spat.

She doubted it, but she wasn't going to call him a liar straight up. "No, but they would be if you brought them a Healer, right? All your past sins would be forgotten and you'd be set for life—a *much* better life than this one, crawling through deserts and killing your own."

"What the fuck are you on about?" he snapped. His entire body was tense but she wasn't sure why. He might be angry she'd figured out he and the Authorities hadn't parted on good terms or he might be tempted by her words but couldn't bring himself to walk away from Bitchface—for a reason based only on sheer lunacy. She chose to proceed as if it was the latter.

"I'm saying your loyalty is misguided. You barely know them! If you took me back—"

"I have the blood, you dumb bitch, like they do. Why would I turn them in? I'm taking you exactly nowhere."

Peri flinched back into position behind him, her face hot. She'd been wrong about that temptation. Sooooo wrong.

I wasn't ready, to let go

She needed to regroup and switch tactics. She'd been prepared for pushback and she needed to be less sensitive about a bit of name-calling and anger. Just because he terrified her at the best of times and the amplitude had been cranked didn't mean she should give up. She summoned Dave's presence, closing her eyes to look at his face and imagine how he'd soothe her after such an attack. Thoughts of his love filtered through her, settling her nerves.

I wasn't ready, to say goodbye

"Look, I didn't mean to upset you," she said in an even voice, opening her eyes and leaning sideways to speak to his profile once more. "I'm sorry."

He grunted acknowledgement, keeping his eyes forward.

"I just see lots of benefits for you if you take me back and I don't know why you care about Daeson so much. Those two hardly seem like your squad. They're young and stupid, you and I are old enough to know better. Maybe there's some benefit to them that I just don't comprehend, otherwise what use are they? You've been travelling without them up 'til now, what can they offer you?"

"Fucking shut up, would you?"

"I could, but I won't. I don't belong here. This is not how my life is supposed to be. I need your help to get... out, to get free."

A muscle ticked in his jaw. She knew it wasn't a good sign but she had no choice; she had to persevere. Hope was fading and she felt trapped in a pool of quicksand; the more she struggled, the faster she sank. No point prolonging the agony.

"I'll do anything you want. Be anything you want," she offered, sliding her hand around him and along his thigh, heading for his crotch. He went rigid again, glancing down as if he had to see for himself what was slithering towards his junk. "I know you like her but she seems prissy. I'm not much to look at but I know my way around a man's dick. I give great head, too—"

"Peri. Don't."

"No! It's true! I'd say ask Dave but, well, that will have to be when you get me back to him," she laughed brittly.

Toughguy repeated her name but she ploughed right through that warning tone just like she'd driven away from the police with Bitchface's gun against her arm. Her heart fluttered at the use of such crass language but she swallowed and told herself now was not the time to back down.

"I'm open to anything. In my mouth, my tits, my pussy, my ass, anywhere you want to stick it, anytime you wa-OW!" she screamed as he reached down and snatched her hand off his zipper, squeezing it so mercilessly that the bones ground together. Sobs poured out of her but he didn't let go.

"Get your fucking hand off my cock and stop embarrassing yourself," he snarled and threw her hand away in disgust. Peri cradled it above her other arm against her body, infuriated and humiliated in equal measure.

"You've got no idea what it's like to be forced out of your life against your will, you asshole!" she yelled, her tone matching his in viciousness. "To be lost and alone with *no-one* willing to help you! You're as bad as them! You *could* help me, you *could* just drive us away right now and get us to the Authorities or leave me here in the desert but nooooo, you'd rather I remain your *hostage*, trapped in this goddamn *nightmare!*"

He stopped the bike and swivelled around to glare at her. His face was an angry purple colour she noted through her tears. Anything mildly attractive about him was overshadowed by his lack of empathy when he spoke.

"I am *never* going to be desperate enough to fuck you and you are *never* getting anywhere near the Authorities. I will kill you first. You will not be taken home or left alone. You will endure this fucking nightmare and you will stop thinking about your past as a possibility. It's gone. Your only job now is to survive—and if you don't shut your mouth and stop groping me, even *that* won't be an option for much longer." His eyes were soulless chips of grey, describing with stony certainty how amenable he was to murdering her where she sat.

Peri sobbed harder, finding it difficult to catch her breath in the face of such ominousness. Toughguy glared at her until he was satisfied her heart was entirely broken, her will thoroughly crushed and then he turned back and continued driving.

I wasn't ready, to let go
I wasn't ready, to say goodbye
... but I have to?

Even in the deep trenches of despair that swallowed her for the rest of that day, she made sure to maintain a sliver of distance between his body and her own.

19

The Novice And The Network

TORIN SAT IN the front passenger seat, staring at a nondescript concrete building. It housed the bank of servers that hosted the Authority telecommunications network, AUTHNET. The building was an anonymous block surrounded by paved stone paths and neatly trimmed hedges. It was early in the morning but the sun had been up for an hour, already bright and promising a blazing summer's day.

The vehicle he and Snook sat in was a black van with the Authority logo stuck on the side, in the same style as the technician vans. Bourbon had stolen a similar black van a month ago and stashed it. In that time it had been done up to look like a service vehicle. Becker had forged four personnel IDs for the team going on the mission. Torin didn't have one, so his cover story was supposed to be that he'd joined his dad for the day—played by Snook.

Security at the gate had waved them through without even checking their IDs. Torin's stomach unclenched as the boom-gate lifted but clenched again when Snook parked and Preacher, Bourbon and Stalker got out, all three dressed in light blue tech uniforms. Stalker carried a box that advertised itself as a motherboard. Inside were Snook's bombs. Her ponytail swung from side to side matching the bounce in her step. It surprised Torin—he would've walked with more care.

My home world, he thought. *We're going to blow something up on my home world.* It didn't seem right that Baxter would be targeted first. Their headquarters were on this world. Wasn't that like shitting where you were eating?

It had felt like hours since they'd gone into the building.

"How long's it been?"

"Should be they'll come out soon," Snook said.

Torin gave him side-eye. "You have a weird way of talking."

"You're seriously coming at me with that?" Snook asked as he raised an eyebrow but he grinned. "You didn't say anything to Cleo, and that woman talks in highs and lows."

It was true—sentences that came out of Cleo's mouth made everything sound like a question, her words cut-off and her pronunciation strangely rounded. It was different enough that Torin had to pay close attention when she spoke. A few times he'd wondered if her accent was fake— like she was having a joke at everyone else's expense—but it had a rhythm to it that he got used to after a bit of conversation. He'd been surprised to find there were a few people in the group that still struggled to understand her.

"Cleo's not open to criticism."

Snook laughed. "And you think I am?"

"What's taking so long?" Torin asked, sticking his head out the window for a better look.

"Don't do that, you hobber. You'll attract attention," Snook growled, smacking Torin on the arm. He sat back down in his seat.

"What does hobber mean, anyway?"

"Uh... there's nothing that captures its essence, here."

"Try."

Snook fell silent and Torin thought he was ignoring the request so he went back to studying the building—though there was only so much concrete and hedge that he could look at. The Authorities liked things sterile.

"Kind of like an anarchist," Snook said, momentarily confusing Torin until he remembered he'd asked for a definition. "But self-absorbed as well. They don't really stand for anything other than not following rules just because they resent anybody telling them what to do."

"That's... fucking insulting."

Snook chuckled. "It's more light-hearted than what it sounds. Like when you call a friend a bastard."

"What do you call people you don't like?" Torin mumbled.

"Hobber," Snook said, then boomed laughter as Torin eye-rolled and stared out the window again. Still no movement. There wasn't even anyone patrolling. Nobody was walking around. Sure, they'd come early to avoid most of the workers but Torin hadn't expected it to be as dead as it was.

"How many bombs are they setting up?"

"Eight. The server rooms are long and separated into four quadrants, so to take everything out they've got to put the explosives into the centre of each quadrant, on both floors."

"If there's only two floors' worth of servers, what are the other floors used for?"

"Offices, like. Support staff and the sort." Snook shrugged.

"So why—"

Get ready to jet, we're coming fast.

Torin blinked at the message in his head, received as clear as if Bourbon was talking beside him. He looked around but couldn't see his mentor anywhere. He'd have to learn that trick—speaking into the minds of people he knew but couldn't physically see.

"Um, start the van," he told Snook. He expected the older man to question him, to want to know the reason why he was instructing him but Snook turned the key and the engine grumbled to life. He liked that Snook listened without question, it confirmed that he'd made the right decision joining. He was genuinely part of a team, not someone sidelined.

Snook checked his side mirror. "Here they come."

Torin leant forward to catch a glimpse using the mirror on his own side, but he could only see Preacher and Stalker running. For every long step Preacher took, Stalker took three but what she lacked in height she made up for with energy.

Bourbon? Where are you?

He tried to connect with Bourbon's mind but found nothing, as though his mentor wasn't even there. A thick sensation formed in his throat, hot and gluggy. He'd gleaned that missions had gone wrong before and now here were two of a three-person team running back to the van like something was amiss. Needing to make a fast getaway implied something had gone wrong.

He jumped when the side-door of the van slid open and Bourbon launched himself into the vehicle, rolling out of the way when Stalker and Preacher caught up. With the wash of relief came the understanding that Bourbon had been out of view from the side-mirror when Torin had looked.

"Go go go!" Preacher ordered as he stepped into the van, doubled over and awkwardly sliding the door shut. It didn't make a heavy clunk when it closed and rattled in its frame as Snook accelerated away. A bonging noise floated out from somewhere in the dash, warning that the door hadn't been properly closed. Nobody bothered to correct it.

"How long we got?" Snook yelled, reversing so quickly that the three in the back tumbled into each other. The van launched down the long driveway that led to the boom-gates. The security guard was a dark blue stick-figure in the distance, growing fast.

The noise of the explosion behind them was so loud that Torin ducked in his chair. He was positive the whole building would rain debris around them but when he looked in the mirror, it showed only a plume of dust covering a few of the middle floors.

"Not long," Bourbon replied, then laughed. Stalker and Preacher joined in but Torin was transfixed by the lowered boom-gate.

"They'll put up the spikes!" he warned, concerned that the Authorities would catch them. One mission, a few blown computers, four shredded tyres and he'd live the rest of his life in prison. The incessant bonging twanged his nerves.

"Shut the fucking door!" he screamed over his shoulder.

"Cover your face," Snook instructed. Torin only had time to turn around when Snook drove into the boom-gate. He expected the van to stop—the boom-gate wasn't just wood, there was metal pipe there too—but other than a jolt, they continued through. Torin heard a few pops, like champagne corks had gone off, and then someone thumping on the van wall. He turned to see what the trio was up to in the back. Preacher and Stalker were both sitting on their backsides but Bourbon was crouched and had a hand on the van wall for support while he opened and shut the side door. The nagging bonging finally halted. Three round holes in the back of the van above Preacher's head let light into the dark space. Torin stared at them, his stomach roiling when he realised what they were.

Bullet holes. The pops had been gunfire and bullets had punched through the van; that was what had made the thumping noise, not somebody knocking on the side. They'd been shot at as they'd sped away. Nobody had been wounded but they very easily could have been.

Torin slammed into the door as Snook turned a corner. There was a horrible moment when it felt like gravity would pull their vehicle onto its side but then it righted and they sped away.

Ten minutes later they parked in a mechanic's workshop where Pockets waited for them. He pulled the rattling garage door down once they were inside. Torin recalled that Pockets was the thief of the group, the kind of guy who could pick locks and disable alarms. He was an average-looking guy but his gaze would always dart around like he was searching for something.

There were two other vehicles in the garage apart from the van, which had a smashed front as well as bullet-holes in the back. Snook and Bourbon grabbed some fluorescent orange vests and put them on before hopping into the cab of a tradesman's truck. They left first. Stalker stripped out of her clothes (while Torin pretended not to watch but discreetly spied her in her underwear), and put on a pink tee-shirt and denim shorts. Preacher had also changed clothes, though Torin only noticed when he appeared in jeans and a polo. The pair of them looked like they were in a relationship and Torin supposed that was their cover. They left in the compact car with Stalker driving and Preacher folded into the passenger seat, his knees almost at his chest.

"You have a better chance with Stalker than you do with Cleo," Pockets said as he moved past Torin, heading for the back door.

"What?"

"I saw you looking," Pockets said, opening the door and gesturing for Torin to go through first. "I figured that meant you were interested. Unless you're the kind of guy that jumps at any opportunity."

"What?" Torin said again, knowing what Pockets was talking about now but not wanting to engage.

Outside was a mean-looking silver sportscar. Pockets pulled out a key and waggled it at Torin.

"I saved the best for us," he grinned then hopped into the driver's seat. Torin ran around to the passenger side and slid in, thinking his life was super-cool right now.

———————•┃•————————

Torin and Pockets parked the sportscar on a suburban street and caught a bus that took them close to headquarters. Near their stop was an electronics store that had just opened for trading. Torin barely looked at it but Pockets grabbed his arm and tugged him inside. Annoyed, he followed him in, wondering what was so important. They walked past an aisle of microwaves and coffee machines to stare at a wall of television sets—most of them showed the same channel but they'd been muted so the store could play crappy ballads over their speakers.

Images of the Authority building—that had only plumed dust when their van sped away—showed it was now fully collapsed on one side. The news helicopter was flying over it, zooming in on the damage. A marquee ran along the bottom of the screen, announcing two people were confirmed dead and nine more were missing. As an unbroken outer wall came into view, Torin could see four letters spray-painted on the side of it in red paint. 'G. O. A. L.' His heart hammered and he looked at Pockets, feeling a mixture of shame, euphoria and responsibility.

"I hate those fuckers," a voice spat behind them. Torin jumped and whirled around to see a staff member glaring at the televisions with his arms folded. "They think they hurt the Authorities but all they've done is taken the fucking services down for a couple of weeks, crippling businesses like mine. You think I can sell phones right now? Can't sign anybody on! I hope they blew themselves up. Dumb fucks."

Torin blinked at the venom pouring out of the storeman's mouth. He caught Torin staring and became aware that he had potential customers. His scowl instantly turned into a beaming smile. His arms unfolded and opened out, like he was ready to receive a hug.

"Hey, but never mind those assholes, you probably came in here for a new television. These—"

"No, thanks," Pockets interrupted and hurried towards the door. Torin looked from him to the salesman—who'd gone back to scowling—and followed Pockets. He had an overwhelming urge to say sorry but he squashed it. Damned if he was going to feel guilty for killing people who thought it was okay to hunt him and his family down.

He caught up to Pockets in the street, though he had to jog to catch up.

"Preacher won't like this," Pockets said as Torin joined his fast walk. "This mission was set up not to take lives."

Torin didn't say anything.

They entered headquarters, let in by Copperhead. She walked them over to the illegal portal—what Torin had initially thought was a torture chair—and he was struck by how large the space seemed without people in it. It had felt small before but, then, there'd been fourteen of them.

"You're the last to arrive. We've already sent everyone ahead to Mwavey. It's just me and the two of you now. You're on cleanup, Pockets. Let Python know when you're ready."

"Will do." They hugged one another and Torin watched them, feeling awkward. Pockets noticed him and slapped him on the back. "It's okay, Hypno. We'll do better next time. Talk to Preacher about it, okay?"

"Sure," Torin said, though he didn't know what he had to talk to Preacher about. He ended up peeking into the other man's mind and was surprised that Pockets was devastated about the deaths they'd caused. He'd assumed Torin was horrified as well. He could've laughed. Copperhead gave him a peculiar look before taking his hand and leading him to the machine. She was twice his age but the touch had him reassessing her. Was she interested in him?

She indicated for Torin to sit down on the chair that would portal him to a different world. After she strapped him in, she leant over to whisper into his ear.

"Just because a woman talks to you or touches your hand doesn't mean she's attracted to you."

Torin felt heat rise into his face. Bourbon had warned him that Copperhead was an Intuit but he'd said she was only partial. Apparently, it had been enough for her to glean his immediate thoughts about her.

She sat down in the chair beside his and the balding Python came over to strap her in. He rolled over what looked like two floor lamps on a trolley and plugged each lamp-machine into the sides of the chairs. He moved away to collect two syringes, injecting Copperhead first and Torin second. As he felt the cool liquid spreading along his arm and across his chest, his eyelids grew heavy. It was a strangely underwhelming concept, to travel into a new world while unconscious. It wasn't the first time he'd left a world—his mother had Wandered with him when he was very young—but it was the first trip he remembered.

20

Damning Evidence

DAESON PARKED THE trike and turned it off. "I think we should camp here, tonight," he announced, looking at Synjan over his shoulder.

She glanced at the nearby terrain. He'd found an area of soft sand in the lee of some scraggy rocks with numerous small plants growing out of them. This desert had an eerie habit of shifting lethargically from day to night and back again. Dusk and dawn lingered far longer than they had in Gredann. Synjan judged there to be an hour of light left before proper nightfall; enough time to establish camp, gather firewood and hunt some meat for dinner.

With Aron. A quiver of apprehension clenched her gut but she nodded and offered Daeson a smile.

"Good call," she agreed, swinging her leg over the seat and standing beside him.

"I wasn't asking for approval," he said, still on the trike.

Synjan frowned at him, noting the challenge glinting in his eyes and baffled by it. They'd had a pleasant enough day riding together, though she hadn't liked the way he'd barrelled headlong into the rougher areas. Perhaps he was still nurturing some resentment over the way she'd criticised his driving. Deciding that was his prerogative, she nodded again.

"Fair enough." She headed to unpack the trailer.

The strange undercurrents continued when Aron and Peri pulled up moments later and Daeson repeated his camp proclamation. Aron got off the trike and began unpacking. Synjan thought Daeson looked disappointed that Aron didn't argue. Peri made no eye contact as she hurried away, found a spot on the sand she liked and sat. She stared mutely into the distance, clutching her handbag. Everyone else unloaded around her, orienting the camp so that she'd be the perfect distance from the campfire but she didn't register anyone's presence. Her empty gaze was unnerving.

When they scattered to collect firewood, they came back and found Peri's preternatural stillness had broken. Instead, she was sobbing heartbrokenly. Synjan decided it was time to go.

"Ready to hunt?" she asked Aron.

"Been ready a while," he muttered, gathering the rifle and striding away from camp.

Synjan hurried to get one of her guns and let Daeson know they'd be back soon. He nodded, dumped his load of kindling and turned to get more.

Synjan jogged after Aron, surprised by his speed. Did he want to get away from her or Peri? Even though the exertion had been minimal, Synjan's heartrate didn't slow as she fell into step beside him. He'd been on her mind all day. She'd had countless imagined conversations with him, ending in a variety of ways. She didn't know him well enough to accurately predict the effect of what she wanted to say. She hoped for a positive outcome.

When they'd gone far enough away that they no longer heard Peri crying, Aron's steps slowed to a pace that was less manic and Synjan took her chance.

"Peri seems especially unhappy tonight."

He grunted his agreement.

"I guess everything's getting too much. Three days in this place is a lot for anyone, let alone someone who didn't expect to be here."

Aron glowered at her and Synjan got the impression he wasn't interested in talking about Peri. That was fine, neither was she. She swallowed and took a calming breath before she began with her well-rehearsed opener.

"I need to talk to you."

His gaze was wary but he looked closely at her, which she took as a sign to continue.

"I wanted to clear up what happened." He came to a stop and turned to face her. She mirrored him. "Last night... I liked kissing you. Too much, probably. But I didn't enjoy what you said afterwards or this morning."

"You defer to Daeson." He shrugged.

Synjan gritted her teeth, biting back an impulsive answer in order to find a more diplomatic one. "Well, it's more than that. Daeson and I are good friends, we've been travelling together for a while now and we're a team. We rely on each other."

"You're more capable than him," Aron scoffed.

"Maybe," Synjan said quickly, holding up a hand to stop

him saying anything more while she got out what she needed to. "At some things, that's true. But he's not incompetent and he has more good qualities than just being able to Heal. Right now, you two are like a rusted fishing reel, all you do is catch on each other. I'm hopeful that'll change if you can give him a chance but I *also* wanted to say that you owe me an apology."

Aron looked genuinely surprised. "An apology?"

Synjan squared her shoulders. "Yes. For what you said this morning. You made out like I lied to you when I kissed you, that I was warming up to Daeson so I could fornicate with him and get rid of my nightmares. I told you that we're just friends. I *didn't* lie to you."

Aron impressed her by not answering quickly. He appeared to be considering her words, possibly doing exactly as she had—not answering impulsively but trying to find a reasonable response. Gratitude washed through her, settling her nerves.

"I'm sorry," he finally said.

She grinned at him, the simplicity of his acknowledgement warming her heart and spreading outward from there. His easy gallantry wasn't dousing her feelings for him but now was not the time to worry about that.

"Thank you. I forgive you. Now, let's go find something for dinner."

Looking at Peri made Hawke feel like an asshole. Her shoulders heaved and her hands covered her face, unable to stifle her sobs. He tried to remember if he'd cried like that when he'd been taken. He remembered that he *had* cried and he'd tried his best to keep quiet for fear Eddie would beat on him. He remembered being taunted about his tears and how it had fuelled his anger and hatred. He'd been desperate to escape. If he'd been a little older, sexually active, aware of what a man might want, would he have tried to seduce Eddie? He didn't think so. Selling his body would've been a form of surrender.

He didn't believe it was any different or easier for Peri to have suggested this to him. She'd come at him pretty hard, thinking he was the kind of man who didn't care about anything other than gratification. She thought that about him, and had tried him anyway.

It wasn't the only surprise Peri had given him on the trike. She'd come uncomfortably close to the truth, speaking to him like he was still an Authority, behaving as though he could take her back. Something had given him away and now Peri was sitting on that information. She must have been feeling her way while she'd been feeling him up. He wished he'd had enough sense to ask her about her suspicions but he'd been battling his own rising panic at the time. He'd ended it with pain and humiliation because he'd wanted to inject enough fear into her that she didn't dare speak of it again. To anyone.

Peri had been quiet when Hawke and Synjan returned from their unsuccessful hunt. The first night without fresh food and the possibility of future failure created a sombre mood in camp. He suffered through a dry ration dinner, sipped water and chewed a multi-vitamin tablet for dessert. Synjan and Daeson did the same but Peri was fuelled by misery alone; she'd refused to eat anything and collapsed in on herself instead. Her crying was like an itch buried in his flesh, too deep to scratch, too irritating to ignore.

He glanced over at Synjan, who looked like she was peeling potatoes. He couldn't tell what she was really up to and he wasn't sure how to approach her. The potential for sex had turned into an argument last night, when she'd put her I-love-Daeson goggles on, and then he'd snapped at her this morning. The small conversation they'd had while hunting didn't feel like a resolution. He supposed he should be grateful that she'd given him the chance to apologise.

If he wanted her guard down, he had to make up properly with her. She had to trust him the same way she did the Healer, or his ability to scoop them up and return them to Kegan would diminish.

Return them to Kegan. Bullshit. He had to face the reality that it was Ellis who held claim to Synjan and Daeson. Hawke didn't trust the man not to hurt them for running away—he was a crimelord and runaways from his organisation would not go unpunished—but he did trust Kegan to protect her.

Hawke figured the best way to start was to sit with Synjan. As he grew closer, he realised she was whittling a piece of wood into a squashed sphere. On her knee lay a small wooden figurine of a cat curled up to sleep. She must be trying to copy it but the artwork was well-crafted and deceptive in its simplicity.

"Learning a new skill?" he asked.

She looked up at him with a smile and he took that as an

invitation to sit beside her. She was close to the fire, using its light. "My father made this for me. He used to call me Kitten."

He hadn't expected her to share such an intimate memory. He thought about all the items he could've taken and had chosen not to.

"I haven't kept anything from home. I don't know if that's good or bad."

His Boronian home had become a complicated world. When he'd returned, he'd understood exactly how insular the people were. It was backwards in so many ways. His family were self-important elitists, watching over the townsfolk like they knew what was best for them. It was like being caught inside a microstudy of how the Authorities ran things.

He was aware of Synjan looking at him but he didn't make eye contact until she asked, "Where's home?"

He chuckled. "A long way back."

"Did you leave it to join the Authorities?"

He couldn't tell her about being taken.

"I Wandered one world as a child. It ended up being into an Authority training world, much like this one. I got picked up pretty fast. They made me their ward and placed me into one of their boarding schools. Almost everyone signs up at fourteen so I did, too."

She gave him a thoughtful look. "How long did you stay with them?"

He thought about when he'd joined the Hunter Division, leaving behind the usual ranks. Cayden was already in charge by then and it felt natural to follow him. "I was twenty-one when I started travelling the worlds on my own," he said.

"And you've been through their portals?"

It was interesting that she would turn the discussion to the giant machines that the Authorities built. He hoped she wouldn't ask him to compare between the Authority one and the Wanderer one. He didn't remember the latter.

"Yes, lots of times. I portalled into worlds well ahead of this one and many back, as well."

"Do you know much about this world? What it's called? Do you know what's ahead of us?"

This world was Alpha Five but she didn't want to know the Authority name for it. He searched his memory for the original name.

"Um, yeah. The people who used to live on this world called it Kronn-Ska."

"Kronn-Ska," she repeated, tasting the name and exchanging a glance with Daeson.

Hawke regathered her attention by speaking again. "Their civilisation is long dead and buried so I don't know much about it. They were gone well before the Authorities found this place." He paused, thinking of the next world— Avaniero, another Authority world. It was extremely similar to Earth, except they knew about other worlds and had relinquished the majority of government and military control to the Authorities. It was the perfect world to contact Kegan and get this over with. Peri presented a more difficult problem. "Um, the next world is Avaniero. It's like Earth and after that..." he shrugged as if he didn't know. In reality, it was because he didn't want to talk about something Synjan would not be visiting. "What about you? Why'd you start Wandering?"

"Because if I'd stayed, I would have died."

The matter-of-fact way she said it chilled him. "You didn't regret leaving anyone behind?"

"No-one living. I thought they were important to me but they're not."

Hawke stared at her, thinking of how unsettled Kegsy had been at the idea of losing her. She'd been important enough to Kegsy for him to risk his career to get her back and she didn't rate him as important?

"What about Freddie?" he blurted, feeling like he was being obvious.

"He'd understand," she said.

He hadn't but Hawke wasn't going to argue that now. She would soon find out.

"Now our goal is to find a nice world we can live on in peace," she continued. Her I-love-Daeson goggles were back on.

"Our goal?" Hawke looked over at Daeson, who was staring at them, as per usual. "Or *your* goal?"

Daeson's gaze hardened and Synjan cut in.

"I like Wandering more than Daeson but if we find the right world, we'll stop."

They were interrupted by a dramatic wail. He expected Daeson to move over and comfort Peri, but the Healer rolled his eyes and kept his head down. Surprising.

"I'd suggest she learn to whittle except I wouldn't give her a knife," Hawke said.

Synjan smiled but it didn't reach her eyes. "I just hope she winds down before sleep. Actually, I've got something that might..." Synjan's sentence faded as she moved to her backpack and shuffled around in it before pulling out a folder. It was a document wallet that looked battered and squashed, a little torn around the edges but ultimately in good shape.

Synjan approached Peri with it, holding it out like a peace offering. Hawke supposed that was exactly what it was. It took her two goes to get the Earth woman's attention.

"Peri... Peri? This might interest you. This is all the information I have about Wanderers, given to me by my boss. It talks about their powers and what the Authorities know—"

There was more but Hawke couldn't hear it over the *whomp-whomp* of his heart in his ears and white noise in his brain. His focus narrowed to the two women as Peri first eyed the folder and then turned her suspicious gaze to Synjan. Her expression held elements of disgust and resentment even as she took it. Why was Synjan even bothering? And why offer the Earth woman information about Wanderers and Authorities? It was something Ellis had collected, which meant there was a genuine danger that it contained information about him. Would there be a photo? There'd been one of Synjan, taken without her knowledge. Snippets of Synjan's one-sided conversation entered his consciousness: "...I haven't read much of it... it might help you understand... there's stuff about different worlds..."

His insides felt sloshy, like he'd had too much to drink. Hawke shifted position but couldn't get comfortable. He wanted to get over there and snatch the folder out of Peri's hands but of course he couldn't do that. All she needed to find was one incriminating page about him and he would be forced to take a stand out here, where there was no backup and an arduous journey ahead.

He didn't want to have to hold them at gunpoint now. On each of the past two nights and again when they'd made camp tonight, Hawke had asked Synjan to check if they were being followed. He figured she'd use less water at night and under no stress. She'd reported movement in the training zone, but nobody had been sent after them. Yet. They'd celebrated quietly and individually but if the situation turned here, having no Authorities on the way became a bad thing.

Peri pressed the folder close to her chest, holding it like a security blanket. Her handbag was against it as well. Hawke stared until Synjan returned and spoke to him. He continued a conversation with her, half-listening and being careful not to look at the folder too many times. After a while, Peri set it down beside her without bothering to open it. If he was lucky, it would stay that way.

He wasn't his usual talkative self, matching Daeson's silence in camp. When the chatter died, Synjan declared she was going to have an early night and Daeson and Peri shuffled into the tent after they took turns with bathroom breaks. Nobody wanted to share the same hole.

If he was the last to go to bed and the folder disappeared, he imagined Daeson would throw accusations his way. It made sense to bed down and then get up later, once everyone was asleep. He cast a desirous eye towards the thick cardboard wallet but kept up his routine, doing a quick search around camp to make sure everything was secure and animals couldn't get to their supplies. He invigorated the fire, throwing more than he needed to onto it, to make sure it would blaze for a while yet. He prepared an answer about being cold but didn't need to use it because nobody seemed to care he was wasting material.

Eventually, he was wrapped up in his unfastened bag, listening to Peri and Daeson murmuring in the tent and willing them to sleep. Wasn't she exhausted from all the crying? Didn't he want to avoid talking to her? Apparently they'd found their second wind because they wouldn't shut up. He listened to Synjan's breathing; soft and rhythmic. He wanted to go to the folder now but knew his impatience would undo him.

Once he believed everyone had succumbed to sleep, he had every intention of counting to a thousand before he moved... he got to three hundred and couldn't take it anymore. He rolled away from Synjan and paused, knowing she would miss his body heat even though they weren't pressed together as tightly tonight. She didn't react and he continued out of his bag.

The fire continued to crackle as he reached the folder. He took it and crouched on the sand near the fire, facing Synjan and the tent. He opened the folder and slid the contents out, glancing at the huddle that was Synjan. There were a lot of papers bundled within and he went through them quickly. There were Authority maps and lists of worlds. A bunch of neatly handwritten pages that looked to be a kind of loose-leaf journal. As he flipped quickly past them, he saw the names Omerri and Freddie. He didn't recognise the woman's name, but now knew that Kegsy operated under the assumed name of 'Freddie' in Gredann. He wondered if Omerri was a codename too.

He continued on. He was already Shielded—as being defensive tended to do for him—but the next few pages made him rigid with tension as well. Authority Hunter Division letterhead. Orders. Was there a mole at Red Rock? He saw a portion of a paperclip on the next page before he flipped it over. In the orange glow cast by the fire, he looked at a photograph of himself. In uniform. A bit younger, but much older than twenty-one. Ah shit, he'd forgotten about his identification photo, which required everyone in uniform whether they wore it daily or not. And the stats page of his file. Fuck. Fuck!

He threw it into the fire—the whole folder. It wasn't until the wallet and its contents were burning that he realised he could've looked through the rest of it at least. There might have been something interesting or useful in there.

He watched it turn to ash before returning to his bag. At least now, if he woke up Synjan, she would think he'd just gone for a nightly toilet break. He zipped himself in and rolled to Synjan's form, feeling guilty when she murmured and cosied herself against him. He was enjoying their easy adventuring. She made for a good companion.

He would miss her when he turned her over.

———————— ·❦· ·—————————

Hawke pretended not to notice Synjan going through everyone's bags for the second time, even though she'd undone a lot of careful trailer packing to do it. He stayed busy putting everything back in order while she stalked over to the campfire and started poking at it, muttering to herself. He kept his head down as Peri returned from her final toilet visit, strolling blindly into the storm.

"Why did you do it?" Synjan demanded, springing into Peri's path and forcing the Earther to take a step back.

"D-do what?" she asked cautiously, readjusting her handbag on her shoulder before positioning her toilet roll and shovel between her and Synjan.

"You burnt my folder! That I let you *borrow*!"

The subtleties of Synjan's indignation were lost on Peri, who brandished her weapons of toileting bravely and sidled towards Daeson. "Did I?" she queried, her eyes widened appealingly at the big idiot heading nobly towards the women.

"What's wrong?" he asked Synjan.

"Peri burnt my Wanderer folder!"

"How do you know?"

"Because it wasn't anywhere this morning. It's not in any of the bags and I'm pretty sure this is burnt paper," Synjan clarified, her voice muffling as she crouched, presumably to lift some ashes for Daeson's perusal.

After a few moments, he straightened and turned to reveal Peri, who'd been hiding behind him. "Did you burn Synjan's folder?" he asked seriously.

The pressure of everybody staring at her became too much for Peri. She started crying. "I didn't! I... don't think. I mean, I didn't mean to, I just... I left it there, it must have blown in," she wailed. Daeson put an arm around her shoulders to comfort her, weathering Synjan's follow-up tirade by her side.

Hawke continued packing the trikes, awash with relief more than guilt.

21

Cayden And Omerri

VISITING HOURS HAD finished long before he showed up but Cayden didn't attract any overt attention as he re-entered Hill End Medical. The lights were dimmed, the facility already in night mode as he made his way up to Omerri Backhouse's room. He used the elevator, sharing it with two chatting nurses that didn't give him a second look.

The key was confidence. He moved like he belonged there and he had somewhere urgent to be—too urgent to waste time making eye contact. He slowed as he approached Omerri's room and grabbed an orderly to remove the chrysanthemums. He didn't want allergies interfering with the interrogation.

As he entered the room, he sensed her eyes following him and he was pleased she was still awake.

"I'm sorry about the flowers," he apologised as he moved to the chair on the other side of the bed. He positioned it so that, when he sat, they were able to maintain eye contact without putting any strain on her head or the equipment holding her in place. "I'm allergic. I asked the gentleman to bring them back when I leave." He smiled, gauging her reaction.

She watched him long enough for him to ponder whether she really was awake before she raised her eyebrows, encouraging him to continue. He launched into his prepared spiel on her cue.

"You don't know me, Ms Backhouse, but I'd like to be your friend," he said, smiling again. "I do favours for people and they do me favours in return. I'm not here asking you for anything, other than a few words scribbled on your pad there. Just a couple of answers that mean more to me than they do to you. I can repay you with the kind of favour you'll want."

He paused to let that sink in. This time, one eyebrow quirked. She was listening.

"I'm sure you'd like to know what happened to your lover, Nick Logan. I know he hasn't visited you for a couple of days and you know that's unlike him. I promise he's quite alright. He left because he felt unsafe here. He didn't want to be made to do anything against his will again. So I gave him some money and a nice house on a pretty world, and he told me all about Synjan and Daeson and Ellis."

This time Cayden got a reaction. Tears welled and rolled down the side of her face. He was surprised. Not only had he expected a woman in a powerful position such as hers to be more ruthless, he'd also assumed her relationship with Logan hadn't been significant. The third-rate criminal had sold her secrets and abandoned her without hesitation. Perhaps the feelings only went one way. It worked in his favour that she was upset.

She stirred from her melancholy and reached for the pen sitting on the rolling table. Cayden sprang to his feet and moved it into a better position for her to write, hovering patiently while she laboriously asked her question.

'What do you want?'

He looked her in the eye. "I want to know about Kegan Frederickson and Howard Ellis."

She blinked so he wasn't able to fully decipher the range of emotions that flashed through her eyes but what he was able to glean was raw and savage. Her lips pursed as she wrote her next query.

'What do I get?'

He wished he could tell if she was angry or hurt, it would make deciding how to play this easier. He followed his gut. "How about revenge, for a start? People are after Synjan and Daeson. Ellis has gone after them himself—an illegally Wandering Controller. Do you want me to put a kill order on him? I asked Kegan about it, but I didn't get a straight answer. Should I do it?"

Omerri's pen wavered. With a dignity he rarely witnessed in such a minute gesture, she placed it on the table and folded her hands on her crisp bedclothes, looking beyond him at the wall. The sentimentality he'd glimpsed earlier played out across her face now, allowing him to see that she was investing a lot of years and a lot of heartbreak into her decision. He'd have thought agreeing to eliminate someone that had beaten you almost to death would be quick; apparently the pool he was looking to dive into was far deeper than he'd anticipated. That couldn't be a bad thing.

Finally, she picked up the pen again. *'Kill him. What else?'*

Cayden gave an appreciative chuckle. The decision may have taken longer than he'd expected but it was still in his favour, so he didn't mind. Now the negotiations could truly begin.

"I could get you an official licence for your business. No more raids on the Queen of Hearts," he offered, watching her face. Her expression remained frustratingly impassive. "I know you operate an illegal nightclub and there are whispers of a gambling parlour. I can make it all legitimate and you'd have the only club and casino around. Since Ellis will have a kill order on him, everything he owns will be seized. I can make it all belong to you. That should be enough," he prompted, pleased with his own magnanimity.

A frown creased Omerri's brow as she wrote again. *'Why not off world?'*

Truthfully, he hadn't anticipated she'd want to follow Logan. He hadn't expected she had that level of sentiment. Perhaps she was only testing him.

"Because there's only so much I can do without an investigation. A lot of Authorities know you. Your absence will be noted. You're already well-established here. Let me expand your business for you," he enthused, touching her hand in encouragement. "I can get you a house in Hill End and a new manager for the Queen to replace Logan. Let your manager live in Dockside. You can live among the wealthy and successful."

Her gaze travelled from where he was touching her hand up to his eyes. It felt like she was assessing his value rather than his offer and he wasn't sure she rated him as highly as he deserved.

'Agreed. Ask your questions.'

It was Cayden's turn to blink and regather his wits as Ms. Backhouse decided to play. The thrill of potential answers thrummed in his chest and he did his best to hold back a grin. "What's your connection with Howard Ellis and Kegan Frederickson? What binds you together?" he asked eagerly.

Omerri paused again, her pen tapping thoughtfully against the notepad. Cayden watched her eyes, saw the way they scanned down the list of things she'd already written, like she was reviewing all the steps she'd taken to get her to this point. She began writing again but she didn't move her hand out of the way for him to read it before she tore the page off and screwed it into a ball. She stared at the new, blank page with an expression he read as anger, tears welling in her eyes as she scrunched the page tightly in her fist.

Cayden stared at the paper, wanting to know what was written on it more than he could remember wanting to see his children after they were born. He needed to know what was on it. It was the key to all of this. Gently, he reached over and pulled the crumpled page from between her fingers, surprised and relieved when she allowed it. When he smoothed it open and read it in the muted light he found that it didn't offer the answer he thought it would—it just raised more questions.

'We Wandered.'

22

Point Of No Return

PERI WHIMPERED AND collapsed on surprisingly soft sand once Team Bitchface had decreed it would be the site of their ninth camp. She breathed a tearless sob as she set about getting her boots off, cringing through the pain of blisters rubbed so raw her socks were bloody.

Daeson crouched in front of her, watching. "I'll Heal your feet as soon as the water's boiled," he promised quietly.

Peri didn't bother looking at him. Of course he couldn't inconvenience himself and just reach over and touch the foot twenty centimetres from his goddamned hand. No, that was ridiculous. Water first, relief when convenient. Peri was never convenient. Don't be like Peri.

The sun was too bright, low on the horizon but still up and annoyingly in her eyes because it was sinking. She turned from it and him, hunching over to inspect her feet. They'd stopped earlier than usual because there was water nearby. Praise be and happy days, they'd found *water*. Oh, but she'd been warned it wasn't as deep or broad as the last oasis, they should be very careful and conservative this time. It was probably not as clean, they should boil it before they drink it and where's an Elementalist when you need one? Hahahahaha, hyuk hyuk hyuk, we're so damn funny, listen to us laugh at our Wanderer cutesies!

Nothing any of those bastards said was cute. Especially Bitchface, with her nerve-jangling sorries and her stomach-churning whines of 'Peri' and her ire-raising 'why'd you burn my booksies?'. Forget her. Peri wished she could. Forget her and her face and all of these assholes into fucking oblivion.

Oblivion would be nice. Dave was so far away and everything was blurred with tears she couldn't even summon any more. They still poured from her soul, a waterfall of silent misery, unquenchable and inaccessible to everyone. On the outside she was just... fuzzy. And pain. Inside: desolately inconsolable.

The last bike had stopped working or run out of fuel or something two days ago, so they'd walked yesterday. The blisters had started yesterday. Today they'd bred like trashy cousins, festering and slicing, causing her to slip on rent skin and her own blood as she walked across the landscape she kindly referred to as Hell.

Walking! Two days of it! They acted like this was *normal*, like people rugged up in sweltering heat to fend off a voracious sun and just *walked* through deserts through the day for fun. It was too damn cold to go at night, she got that, but why move in the day?

Peri wasn't having it. She watched them from beneath

her brow and the brim of her hat, glowering at the way they split up and collected plants to burn and water to boil. They set it up near her, like they were considering her inability to move, but really it was just the flattest bit, with the softest ground surrounding it.

She'd remembered the rest of the song. Well, the chorus, anyway. It ran through her head in an endless litany that she was either singing beneath her breath or mouthing silently.

I wasn't ready, to let go
I wasn't ready, to say goodbye
I wasn't ready and you should know
I still won't be ready, on the day I die

Sometimes she got weird looks from the gang when her voice snagged and squeaked out something close to one of those high notes. She'd been asked what she was singing. She'd stared at them until they went away. She thought it had been Prettyboy but didn't care. Couldn't care less. Care less. Careless. Carless.

Words rolled and morphed in her mind, entertaining her as the days dragged on. She'd re-lived her favourite books and movies often in the last few days. She'd written letters of complaint, pleas for rescue and explanations of fantastical beings to a distant Prime Minister. She'd delivered some bloody wonderful lessons to her imaginary class. Truly inspiring, teacher of the year stuff. Teacher of the Planet? Probably. Who knew, who cared, life was only to be scared. Bared. Bored.

Her gaze moved to the whisperers. Bitchface and Toughguy hissing and snarking again, huddled in cahoots, talking about her. Looking at her. Lamenting her and wishing she was less of a burden but she was everything they deserved in their hateful, nasty lives. She was their punishment for being evil and heartless and not thinking about her and Dave.

I wasn't ready, to let go

They saw her looking and turned away, pointing. Swinging arms and checking the guns near their packs. Gun. One gun. Her gun. Peri pulled her arms free of the backpack she was still wearing and pulled her handbag out of it. She held it in her lap, patting the smooth leather, admiring how soft and supple it was, how well it was enduring Hell. Well, Hell, swell, fell, smell. It smelt better than she did but the fire was nice.

Oh, Toughguy was here suddenly, lighting up the pile of little trees and nesting the pot of water in it once it was big and flamey. He'd been over *there* only a moment ago. Ninja.

"Won't be long," he told her, like she was lining up for a bath in it.

She nodded and looked at the oasis, considering. When her feet were Healed, she would walk over to that and float in it for a while. Too bad if she stank it up.

I wasn't ready, to say goodbye

"Do you want to hunt now?" Bitchface asked, walking over and hunkering down beside Toughguy.

Peri turned her face away. She hadn't looked directly at the blonde demoness for days, couldn't bear to. She was the reason. Her. That was all there was to it. It was her and she was a bitch and she was hated with every cell in Peri's body and Dave's too. Prettyboy had failed. Toughguy had been an exercise in mortification and she still couldn't

220

believe the words of degradation that had come out of her own mouth.

There was just her. The indomitable. The unconquerable. She Who Must Be Disposed Of. How, though? When? Why? Howhowhowhow?

"Too early. Everything will still be underground," Toughguy answered.

I wasn't ready and you should know

Bitchface sighed and sat beside him. "Yeah. Fuck, is it actually hotter?"

Toughguy chuckled. "Yes. We're not moving, there's no breeze."

"Thank the gods, I'd rather be stopped anyway. Is the water boiling yet?"

"Man, you're impatient."

"I'm thirsty! And hungry."

"You have water in your canteen and rations in your bag."

"Yeah, yeah," Bitchface grumbled and Peri heard her groan and sigh as she got to her feet and tromped over to her bag. "Hey, Daeson, do you want a ration?" she called from somewhere not too far away.

"I do," Daeson answered from where he was setting up his tent.

"Of course you do," Toughguy muttered, low enough so that only Peri heard it.

Her gaze slid to him and she watched him from beneath the curtain of her lashes, her face impassive. He had less patience for Daeson every day and more time for Bitchface in response. Prettyboy saw it, he listened to them talk their nonsense every night but he didn't seem to know how to

221

counteract the natural chemical reaction percolating merrily before his eyes. Foolish child, what have you done? How have you failed? What will you become? Become of you?

"I'll put your stuff away," Daeson announced from above her and Peri cried out in startlement. Daeson flinched too, his hand on her backpack. "It's okay," he said.

"Sorry," Peri muttered, her voice an old, cracked strap her ears didn't recognise. She watched as Prettyboy carried her gear into the tent. She cradled her handbag closer, empty of malice for the moment.

It returned swiftly when Bitchface did. She sat beside Toughguy and when Prettyboy came back, he sat closer to Peri. Bitchface threw the ration at him and he caught it easily, looking at Peri.

"Do you want some?" he offered.

Peri shook her head. Good for the waistline at least; travelling through a desert eating food that offended your tastebuds on the way in and violated your rectum on the way out. She'd lost kilos, to the point where the soldier's clothes were loose. She'd had to belt the pants and she'd never needed to do something like that in her life. She wished she still hadn't because it wasn't healthy. She was wasting away, circling the drain, waiting to make her move and having no clue what that move would be.

I still won't be ready on the day I die

"We'll need to boil at least three pots of water," Bitchface observed, chewing repulsively on her food. "And fill up every container we can with it before we leave tomorrow. Take as much as we can all carry. Who knows when we'll find this much water again?"

Tomorrow? Leave? Lightning burned away the fur in her brain for good. Leaving the water was exactly what she wouldn't do. It was the only certainty in an ocean of sand, the last chance she had. The last stand. It was now.

She was ready.

Peri laboured to her torn feet, holding her handbag in front of her and drawing everyone's gaze. When the pain had subsided and she was standing firmly, she pulled her secret weapon out and tossed the bag. She pointed the gun at Bitchface, her arm a little wobbly though she felt calm. With her feet planted, she took a breath and lifted her gaze to meet Bitchface. The look of horror she saw there was truly heart-warming.

"No," Peri said calmly. "I'm staying here."

Hawke stared up at Peri. She had her arm outstretched, like she'd taken a part in a theatrical play and was now pointing accusingly at Synjan in a court of law—but instead of a finger, she held a silver pistol. He flinched. It was rare for him to be taken by surprise, but somehow this soft Earth woman had done it. He would've laughed at the irony, except all trace of humour had left him. He stood, thinking he would earn the gun's focus because he was more of a threat, but the gun remained on target—on Synjan, sitting cross-legged on the ground. Hawke felt his shield settling over his skin, hardening it even while his heart raced.

"Peri. Put the gun down," he said quietly, not wanting to spook her.

Peri's gaze flicked over to him but she didn't point the pistol away from Synjan as he'd hoped.

"You shut your fucking mouth and stop groping me," she said before cackling and he was filled with shame and fear. She'd reached her limit. He could see Daeson sitting off to one side, shocked and frozen in place. Hawke recognised that Daeson didn't have the wits to talk Peri down so it was up to Hawke to handle it however he could.

He stepped forward, putting himself in front of Synjan, calculating Peri's skill and how far he would be able to get. He noticed she hadn't moved the safety yet. He could rush her and force the gun into the dirt—but where the fuck had it even come from? It wasn't Authority issue.

"Stay *back*! You get *back*!" she screeched. The pistol swept upward, aiming at his chest. Her thumb stroked the safety off as she did so and he froze. It must be her handbag gun, something to protect her from muggers on Earth. He'd made assumptions about her that were wrong, so very wrong. He'd thought she'd given up but she'd only been biding her time.

Now, with a weapon hot and the woman wielding it out of her mind, he was forced to retreat. His hands went out from his sides in a non-threatening display but he had every intention of solving this problem. He moved farther back than was necessary, out of her peripheral vision and as close to his bag as he could manage. He had a solution in there.

"Easy, easy, I'm back. It's okay."

Peri turned to face Synjan and her expression of vicious satisfaction melted into one of despair and fury. The gun followed her gaze, wavering alarmingly as deep emotion welled.

"You're a terrible, awful person. I hate you. I wasn't ready, to let go, I wasn't ready, to say goodbye!" she sang, the tune wobbling as much as the gun. Now with the safety off, she was as likely to shoot Synjan accidentally as she was deliberately. "You *forced* me!" she shrieked, jabbing the pistol towards Synjan's body. Then the gun swayed upward, hovering in line with Synjan's eyes. "How does it feel to have a gun in your face? How do *you* like it, Bitchface, hmm? Not nice, is it? But that's what happens when you leave a person—an innocent, nice person like me and Dave—no choice! I should've fought you, why didn't I fight you then and there?" she beseeched and then she was crying, her voice cracking and breaking. "I should've done better for him, from the beginning. It never would've ended up like this. I should've made you shoot me or jumped out of the ca-*ar*," she wailed, swiping at her tear-streaked face with her free hand.

Hawke continued to sidle, drawing as little attention to himself as possible, glancing at Daeson and then at Peri's hand. Her aim wasn't as fixed on Synjan while she was crying. He hoped it continued.

"I let him *down*. I love him so much and he'll never know, he'll think I abandoned him but I didn't, it was YOU!" The tears were gone and the rage was back. "Everything is all about you. Both of them do your bidding, your majesty, Queen of the Cesspit, while you smarm around. Well, I've *had* it! You're the straw, lady! I am *not* going anywhere with you tomorrow! I am goddamn *tired* and I can't risk leaving this water. This is the best place, the safest place to be. They'll come here and they'll find *me* here and if you don't like it, well you just tell me so RIGHT NOW and this will all be over! Do you agree, bitch, or would you prefer to die? Because that's how it has to be. Yep! That's it. I've decided this time, it's *my* turn, tag, *I'm* it! I decide. You have to do what I say or face the gun! I'm sick of this desert rubbish, I'm sick of the pain and the heat and all of it. I'm staying and I'm ready to stop you. Somebody has to, you're a goddamned *menace*! Best eliminated. I can be like you. I have to, because this shit is seriously making me lose my mind. I. Will. Kill. You. Because I have to. Because you deserve it, because Dave said so, and Dave—"

"Peri," Hawke said.

She looked over her shoulder at him, her lips pulled back from her teeth in a snarl. The gun was still pointed at Synjan, but now he had one of his own and, unlike her, he didn't have to psyche himself up to pull the trigger.

———— ·◆· ————

Synjan's world narrowed to the few millimetres of darkness at the end of the gun barrel. She was frozen as she stared at it, contemplating what came next. Her mind told her body that she should move, roll away or throw herself forward and tackle Peri but... nothing happened. Her brain talked, her body ignored. She just sat. Terrified. Everything in her turned to water and all she could do was watch that black hole move and sway, jerk and jab, waiting for the explosion that would signal her death.

And think. She could still do that.

This was very different to every other time she'd faced danger. She'd never looked down a barrel wielded by a hate-driven enemy and just... *waited*. Waited for them to decide they had given her enough time. Waited to find out if she would survive someone else's rage. Waited for them to be done with her.

Other times she'd been shot or nearly killed, she'd been ambushed and too surprised to think much about her enemy or worry about death. The pain had been too intense and she'd fought against it with everything she had. Today, she had no pain and an abundance of time and it wasn't working in her favour. One half of her brain reminded her of Freddie's recounts of people loosing their bowels at the moment of death (and feeling like she already might have, in all the wateriness) and the other was actively calculating and screaming at her legs to run, *fucking RUN!* To no avail.

And then Aron stepped in and saved her. For a tiny, heart-stopping moment, she'd thought Aron's shot had come from Peri's

hers, it was hers and she'd be killed by her own fornicating gun and she flinched, expecting pain. Darkness.

It *did* go dark but only because her eyes squeezed shut. The peculiar sound of a bullet puncturing flesh, biting through bone and exploding wetly out the other side didn't accompany any pain. The garbled cry wasn't hers. When her eyelids lifted, Peri's falling arm caught Synjan's attention and she watched her gun as it swung down to the sand in front of her, still clutched in the other woman's hand. Peri's body was there too, mostly angled away so that all Synjan could make out clearly were her bare feet and her legs. The rest was a crumpled mass of hazy blue beyond the gun, the shapeless lump coated in Authority clothing that had fallen in a heap before her.

The moment she realised Peri was dead and that she was okay, Synjan wasn't relieved. She was livid. Rage bloomed inside her. How *dare* this woman decide she had the power to take away Synjan's life? Who in the worlds did she think she was? She was no-one! Just some accidental hostage that shouldn't have been here at all. Hot tears of fury leaked down her cheeks and she swiped at them, finally able to move.

Certainly, she'd stripped Peri of everything familiar, comfortable and loved but she hadn't *killed* her, she wasn't *dead*. Just alone and unhappy. Things would have got better! Other worlds would be beautiful and welcoming. Peri could have found a way to be happy again—people did it all the time, like when they had terrible accidents and lost limbs. Or when natural disasters swallowed homes and broke apart provinces. Or when almost entire families were killed, leaving small children behind that had no idea at all about how to continue on alone but they did it. Because people were strong and even if they thought it was impossible, putting one foot in front of the other got them through the tragedies of life and they survived.

But not Peri. She'd given up on the possibility of her life getting better. She'd been overwhelmed. She'd given up on surviving. Synjan had never seen that quality in her, the Earth woman had always fought so hard to get through the desert with them, had cried through her suffering and had seemed to be getting better. Pulling the

her

gun had been a betrayal on many levels because there

was intent to deceive and a false persona revealed, along with abandonment of survival. Perhaps it was hope she'd abandoned, rather than the will to survive.

Peri's final words echoed in Synjan's shocked memory and guilt washed through her, dousing the anger. The other woman hadn't wanted this outcome. She hadn't wanted to die, she'd just wanted the torture to end and she'd come from a world so soft she didn't comprehend that violent actions yielded violent consequences. Pulling a gun on those more skilled with using them was never going to be the way to achieve her goal. It was futile. How hadn't she guessed that?

"Are you alright?"

Synjan blinked, recognising that the concerned voice was directed at her and she looked up at Aron. She licked her lips, testing that she'd be able to speak. "Yeah, I... I'm fine. Thank you."

"You're *thanking* him?" Daeson cried. "She's dead!"

Synjan's head felt like an apple on a wobbly stick as she turned back to look at where the other voice was coming from.

Daeson was crouched over Peri, his hands on her chest. He looked at Synjan and Aron with revulsion.

Synjan scrambled awkwardly to her feet, feeling the blood run into her legs in an oddly emphatic way. They'd been on the verge of going to sleep. She felt like she might tip over and lifted her hands to help keep her balance. Aron gently gripped her upper arm to steady her.

Looking down at Peri caused Synjan to catch her breath. She swallowed the fear that threatened to undo her, forcing herself to exhale. Peri was definitely dead. Her glazed eyes were open to the bright blue sky like she was laying back daydreaming but the bullet hole in her forehead and the puddle of blood pooling behind her head ruined the illusion. The whole scene—the darkening blood corona, the dead woman dressed in Authority blue—sickened Synjan in a way she couldn't define. Perhaps it was the *waste* of it all; an avoidable death in a foreign land wearing the clothes of an unknown organisation that had necessarily wrought her end. To protect all of those still living.

It was a terrible, horrible tragedy that Peri was dead and Synjan was sorry it had happened. But she couldn't regret it.

"It was her or Synjan," Aron told Daeson, mirroring Synjan's thoughts.

Daeson surged to his feet, forcing Synjan to step back as he threw himself at Aron. The two of them thudded on the hot desert floor with such force that it vibrated briefly in the soles of Synjan's boots and made her wince. Aron's breath was expelled in a strangled grunt that she understood all too well; she'd been winded often enough to experience sympathetic tightening of her airway and a phantom pain flare in her midriff.

Because Daeson was on top, all she could see were his elbows pistoning as he pummelled Aron's torso, giving him no chance to get his air back. Aron was fighting for breath even while doing his best to block. He chose not to hit back or stop it and Synjan admired him for it. After witnessing—or not-witnessing, as the case was—invisible Aron taking down a trained Authority in a fight, she knew that he could've disabled Daeson, even while he was choking. He was letting Daeson vent. That didn't mean *she* had to stand by and let it happen.

"Daeson! Stop!" Synjan screamed, running over to the pair. She grabbed one of Daeson's arms and pulled it tight against her body, trying to handicap him. Unfortunately, she'd underestimated his strength and she was swung around instead of getting him under control, her boots offering her no traction on the pebbly desert floor.

"Get off me!" Daeson roared, using his free hand to shove at Synjan as well. He was so enraged that he batted her away like a giant flicking a fly. One moment she was clinging to him, the next she was sprawled on her backside in the red dust, blinking.

"That's enough," Aron declared and grabbed Daeson's closest hand, bending it backwards at a severe angle.

Daeson yowled and crumpled while Aron hauled himself out from beneath the larger man. He maintained his grip and loomed.

"Daeson, whether you know it or not, Peri was going to kill Synjan. Fighting now doesn't change it."

"Let go of me!" Daeson snarled, his nostrils flaring as he was held, incapacitated by pain.

Aron checked with Synjan. She nodded so he simultaneously freed Daeson's hand and skipped lithely backwards.

Daeson climbed to his feet, nursing his sore wrist. He stepped up to Aron, who stood his ground... warily. Daeson inhaled and glared down from his full height. "You are no longer welcome to travel with us," he hissed, twin spots of red colouring his cheeks. He was close enough that a few drops of spit landed on Aron's face but she noticed the blonde man didn't wipe them off until Daeson had spun on his heel and marched away.

Aron watched him to be sure he was leaving before he walked over and held out a hand to Synjan. She took it and allowed him to help her up, wrapping her arms tightly about him once she was on her feet. He returned the hug and rested his cheek atop her head.

"It wasn't your fault."

She sobbed, overwhelmed with gratitude and wonder that he would offer her such kindness. "It's my fault she was h-here," she argued, pulling back to look up at him, wiping her tears absently.

"Not on purpose... and that matters," he said. "And all three of us chose not to leave her at the training area. All three of us chose our lives over hers."

Synjan frowned, instinctively thinking that Daeson hadn't, he wouldn't... and then she recalled the discussion about leaving Peri behind. Aron was right. Daeson hadn't advocated for taking her like they had but he hadn't opposed them, either.

He'd said nothing at all.

23

Affirmations

ARON AND SYNJAN carried Peri's body as far from their oasis camp as they could, two fold-out shovels and her handbag balanced on her midriff. Synjan went first, situating herself between Peri's legs, facing away. It wasn't dignified but it gave Synjan a good grip around the body's thighs and a sound load-bearing position. Aron was at Peri's head, looking at her dead face and the hole he'd made in it. Synjan created yet another page of gratitude in the mental book of thanks that she was writing for that man because he didn't complain.

They found a place to dig as far from the water source as they could. Digging helped to numb the experience even though their hands and bodies ached. It seeped into Synjan's bones where it nestled with her weariness for life.

Finally, they stood at either end of an anonymous mound of sandy dirt, the last streaks of daylight dimming into the usual slow-dying golden glow around them. Synjan knew there was no rush to get back to camp. The heat of the day would linger while the light lasted.

There was a tiny puddle-cake of dried blood on the sand nearby, where the body had waited. Synjan couldn't stop glancing at it and then back at the grave. She stood at Peri's head now. They'd made sure she held her handbag and her eyes were closed before they covered her over, though they could do nothing about the hole in her forehead. Synjan imagined a little stream of sand trickling into it in the darkness and tightened her fists, trying to think about something else.

"This reminds me of my family's funerals. Funeral," she corrected quietly. She recalled the practical wooden caskets of her father, mother and sister lined up silently beside each other, waiting to be lowered into the communal family plot.

"What happened?"

"They were killed in a train accident. The tracks collapsed. On a mountain. I survived because my father tossed me out of their carriage before it fell. My nightmares always start with that moment, being caught by strangers, watching them fall."

Aron moved to stand beside her. He brushed his hand against the back of her fist and she loosened her fingers to grip his, still staring at Peri's grave as she spoke.

"They all went in one grave. I was only little. I thought they'd organised it that way, so they could be together forever. Ellis told me years later it was because the Authorities were being economical. The funeral was part of the restitution package for their railway killing everyone. Ellis could've paid for more graves but he didn't, even though he had plenty of money. I should've realised

234

then what he was like."

It had been annoyingly bright and sunny that day, though the weather before and after was typical Gredann rainy misery. Synjan had squinted, constantly turning her head against the sharp sunlight searing through rustling leaves. She remembered holding Ellis' hand tightly; he'd already discharged her from the hospital and taken custody of her, triggering the final act of her indenture.

The funeral.

She'd hated the words that were said without her permission. She'd hated that the ceremony was presided over by an Authority priest who pretended to know how wonderful her family had been—who'd tried to use words to fill a hole inside her that was far deeper than the one their bodies were put in. She'd hated that he said Authority words over them and didn't know the Wanderer rites like her mother had taught her. Ellis knew them and he'd said them with her.

Synjan didn't know what gods Peri had believed in, if any, but it was appropriate to say something over her grave. She decided to say what she wanted, this time.

"In darkness, the gods loved you and filled you with their divine light. In life, like the stars, you blazed across the worlds. In death, may your light return to the fold as your body becomes one with this world."

She released Aron's hand to make sweeping outward gestures for mind, spirit and body.

"What's that?" he asked, looking confused. It made her mutely angry that he, a Wanderer, didn't recognise the words.

"The Wanderer burial rites. She probably would have

preferred the Authority one about ashes and dust but too bad. She died a Wanderer."

"No, she didn't. She couldn't handle it. That's why she's dead." Aron looked down at the grave, not meeting Synjan's shocked gaze.

She wanted to argue with him but couldn't. She'd thought it herself, briefly, after Peri's death. The Earth woman hadn't been able to cope with the changes in her circumstances and process it enough to convince herself to hang on. That didn't excuse them for killing her but she supposed it was why the problem had escalated into a full-scale catastrophe.

Synjan couldn't ignore the fact that she was the cause for Peri being put into the situation in the first place. She took a breath, letting the guilt and grief wash through her and out with her tears. Ultimately, Peri's death was just another in the long line of deaths she was responsible for but it stung more because it had come *now*, after Synjan had made steps towards changing her circumstances. Daeson had been her example of all that was good, untainted by life like she was but, as Aron had pointed out, he was as culpable as all of them, even if he couldn't accept it.

Doing nothing wasn't the same as doing good.

She cried until a sense of calm spread through her, replacing the guilt, then she smiled at Aron and squeezed his hand in gratitude. He smiled back as he led her away from Peri's grave.

They headed towards the nearby oasis. The sky, the ground, the very air around them was awash with the same golden tinge of refracted late afternoon light. It didn't match the breathtaking beauty of a Gredann sunset but Synjan was charmed by the way it encased them and made it feel like everything negative was being held at bay.

The serenity wasn't complete. Small rocks clattered and rolled, scrubby vegetation shivered and scampering feet sounded as the inhabitants of the desert awoke. It was a brutal environment but far from barren. As they approached the water's edge, a small, furry creature with oversized ears and a long tail hopped into their path to get a drink but dived for cover when it spied them. A hoot echoed from somewhere far above Synjan's head, causing her to wonder whether the fluffy animal had been scared by them after all.

Aron's attention was caught by the bird and he looked up while they walked, relying on Synjan to steer him. After he was satisfied, he looked back at her curiously.

"Anything big nearby?" he prompted.

Synjan wondered if he wanted her to map for safety or because he enjoyed the sensation of being drawn to her, as all Wanderers were to an active Navigator. It didn't prevent her obliging him, though she stopped beside the water before she closed her eyes and checked the area around them. She began with the limits of the oasis and moved ever outward until she encountered a very distinctive blue pattern many kilometres away.

"Only Daeson and he's *still* walking," she sighed, opening her eyes to look at Aron. "Should I go after him?"

"Maybe after we get cleaned up," he replied, dropping the shovels he'd been carrying.

Synjan looked down and registered how foul they were. Aron was covered in blood and dirt, the lines of his face and neck creased brown where the sweat had run while he dug. Her shirt and pants were less bloody but no less covered in muck. She bent down and pulled the laces of her boots, toeing them off and kicking them away. She then removed her clothes, remaining in her underwear and carrying the rest into the water.

———————— •◆• ————————

Daeson strode purposefully into the desert, heading nowhere. His racing thoughts were less scattered if he focussed on the rhythm of his feet. There was something satisfying about walking in a straight line because his life was going in circles. It didn't matter the choices he made or which world he Wandered to, he kept facing the same situations, over and over.

Peri had become Marcus. Aron had become Nick. And Synjan was Synjan, as she forever would be. She wanted nothing to do with violence, yet every decision she made led to it. To protect her, someone had to die. Again. Marcus had never held a gun to her head, but his knowledge about her and Daeson led to his murder at Nick's hand. It had been nothing Daeson had asked for or wanted. He'd made that clear at the time. Yet Synjan had accepted Marcus' life in exchange for her own, arguing that Nick had made the right decision—he'd protected them. But when would it end? *Would* it end? At some point, she'd have to reconcile; she would either stop killing to save herself or conclude that her life was worth more than multiple others.

He thought he knew what course she would take. Maybe he was a fool for thinking she'd ever want to choose differently. What she said—what she *believed* about herself—was so far removed from what she was.

He found her attractive but had never been attracted *to* her, and it had taken him a while to understand why. They'd had a problematic beginning. The first time they'd met, she'd been dressed as an Authority officer. The second, covered in blood and dying. The third, warning him that he would never be safe, that he had to Wander again... and then she'd come with him, uninvited, unwanted, a reminder of the danger he'd tried to leave behind.

It was her fault. Everything was her damned fault. She'd forced herself on him, all while begging him to relinquish her world. He'd done that and she'd taken it with her, with *them*. And now she was his only way out, her power the only thing that could save him from this ongoing nightmare. He needed her and she owed him but he doubted she would see it that way. Not with Aron around.

He'd never despised anyone so much as he did the Shielder. Everything went through Aron now; decisions, equipment... survival. It was all dependent on him. Daeson had to get rid of him before the bastard decided Daeson was just another tagalong like Peri.

Look what had happened to her. She'd tried to make a stand but had only proved that she wasn't up to the task. She'd talked and talked, saying things he hadn't properly understood, but it was clear she'd been unable to pull the trigger. People who could pull the trigger did it right away. People like Aron. Or Synjan. They aimed, they shot. They didn't talk.

Deep inside his core he knew that if he got in Aron's way,

he would be sacrificed. Daeson didn't know exactly what motivation the Shielder had in joining them but there was something else going on. Something he couldn't see. Something Synjan didn't want to see.

The worst thing was, he could tell he was losing her to him but he didn't know how to stop it. The two of them had a natural connection that Daeson didn't belong to. Undoing that would be hard.

With Peri dead, who knew what the situation would be? The Earth woman had been a buffer for the problems between the three of them. She'd been something to focus attention on. Her death would change things again and he doubted Synjan would see things his way.

He should've chosen Roman. There was a moment where he'd considered it. He suspected that Roman had sensed it. *Leave her behind. Leave all her baggage behind.*

But he couldn't do it, couldn't abandon her to the Hunter, couldn't leave her without an explanation or a goodbye. Even though Roman was a better choice in many ways, the most obvious difference between him and Synjan was loyalty. If things got too hard, Roman would leave him. Synjan wouldn't.

Now, under Aron's influence, he was starting to wonder if she would. With the Shielder taking up all her attention, washing her in compliments, hanging on every word that came out of her mouth... he'd been seducing her from the start. Why? He was much older than both of them, used to travelling alone. What did he want with a woman ten years his junior? If he was as good as all that, they were a hindrance to him, not an asset.

Roman's advice came to him again: *The best pair to*

Wander together was a Navigator and a Healer. It made sense; someone to show the way to the Portal, someone who could fix wounds or illnesses. Aron didn't seem to care that Daeson was a Healer, he just wanted her. At first, Daeson had dismissed the favouritism as a result of his unfriendliness towards the other man but, while Aron had done everything he could to win Synjan over, he wasn't doing the same to him—which was even more confusing. Synjan had been Team Aron from the start. It was Daeson that needed winning over.

The light in the sky changed. Daeson looked up, though there was nothing to see. No clouds or streaks of colour to identify the lateness of the afternoon. His steps slowed—he sensed he'd been walking for hours, far from camp. A light wind ruffled his hair, threatening to cover any traces of his steps. The sand wasn't soft like the dunes here but he still sunk into it a little, like wet sand without moisture. He turned, seeing his footprints disappearing into the distance. He doubted he'd gone in exactly a straight line—getting back would be difficult if he didn't have his footsteps to retrace. Would Synjan come after him? Anger gripped his throat and chest, heating up his insides, making it hard to breathe. He should've grabbed a bottle of water, though his exit had been impromptu.

He hoped the wind wouldn't sweep his trail away, forcing him to need Synjan's help to return to camp. The wind, slight as it was, seemed to hear his wish and died down. Before it could rise up, he headed back, walking at double pace to make it before darkness fell.

The night was young but not quite as chilly as it could get by the time he got close to camp. He could hear soft murmurs and splashes; probably Synjan and Aron washing blood off themselves. If they were a little way down from camp, Daeson would be able to get back to his tent unaccosted. He didn't want another confrontation tonight.

Daeson circled around, pausing only to look at them from his higher vantage point, hoping they wouldn't see him. He stared for a long moment, watching them in the water. When disappointment and frustration overwhelmed him, he strode back to camp.

The fire had become a pile of ash. Daeson averted his eyes and crawled into his tent. Inside were a pair of Authority gloves and the bedroll and backpack Peri had used. He'd set them up for her. It seemed a lifetime ago. He could smell her in the tent with him, a putrid odour of sweat and madness.

Daeson rolled her bedding up and threw it through the tent flap, then pitched the bag and gloves out, one after the other. He saw the comb he'd given to Peri and threw that out, too. Anything that reminded him of her went.

In the end, he had only his pack and bedroll with him before he zipped the tent closed. He clothed himself in multiple layers and curled up, thinking of ways to get rid of the Shielder.

———— ◆ ————

The shallow oasis was almost as warm as a bath, having bubbled up from inside the ground to be heated by the sun. The swish of it around Synjan's legs and the gentle stimulation of the sand beneath her feet was divine. When

Aron waded in beside her and sat, she did the same. The water came up to her waist, tickling her stomach as she got comfortable.

In companionable silence they scrubbed their clothing, getting as much filth out as they could. She washed and wrung out her socks and pants, spreading them on nearby bushes to dry with Aron's. After cleaning her shirt, she used it to scour her exposed skin. She savoured the sensation of exfoliation and the dirt being vigorously swiped away but her bra was an issue. It was getting in the way of her cleaning under her breasts.

Oddly, she was self-conscious about taking it off in front of Aron. She recalled the first time she'd exposed herself to Daeson, changing in his tent on J'Bdyamn. She hadn't been interested in Daeson back then—she recalled with a twinge of sadness that her thoughts had centred more around Bo—so it had been easy. Even afterwards, when her feelings about Daeson had changed, she'd put very little thought into stripping in front of him. Now, she could no longer visualise him as a sexual partner.

Aron was an entirely different proposal. She wished that the sun would finish setting so he didn't notice her repeatedly washing her chest and blushing while she snuck peeks at him.

The problem wasn't baring her body. It was what that state might lead to. Aron made her giddy and the feel of his lips on hers had been a ghostly companion since the night they'd kissed. She didn't trust herself to show restraint. Their eyes met and heat radiated into her. It felt like he was looking into her soul. She blushed and broke eye contact.

"Do you want me to turn my back?" he asked, proving that he was looking into her mind, if not her soul.

Synjan laughed; it was too loud and brittle but she committed to it anyway. "It's fine," she demurred, prickles of awkwardness biting at her skin. Had she gone completely red? "It... won't offend you if I take it off, will it? To get clean properly, I mean." She smiled, feeling like she was baring all of her teeth at him.

He nodded, puncturing his serious aura with a tiny smile. "I will not be offended," he vowed.

She laughed more naturally, chastising herself for causing the tension in the first place, as she unhooked her bra. Aron didn't stare or do anything weird like Daeson might have, he just continued scrubbing his shirt. Synjan peeled her bra off, dropped it and stretched. With a happy sigh, she doused both breasts with water then lifted each in turn to wipe her shirt beneath them. She rolled over onto her tummy and wriggled, awash with the unique joy only a woman released from the suffocation of a bra after a stifling day could understand. The grin she exchanged with Aron was very comfortable until he frowned and leant towards her.

"You've got..." he shuffled closer so that he could cup the side of her upturned face, dropping down onto one elbow to get close to her position. "Blood," he muttered as he swiped her forehead gently near her hairline.

His fingers and his thumb were callused where they contacted her soft skin, causing her to think about what they'd feel like sliding down her body. She looked up at him, willing him to read her mind *now*, aware that his face was so close she could kiss him effortlessly. His heat pushed towards her and his breath fanned her cheek but their previous psychic connection failed.

"It's in your hair. Can I?" Aron requested, lifting her plait. He was all business.

"Oh! Sure," she agreed, rolling onto her side so that she was leaning up on her elbow, her back towards him. He sat up and moved to accommodate her.

Aron methodically unwound her braid and swished it underwater to clean it. The gentle tugging paired with the occasional tweak of a pulled hair had her nape prickling. When she sensed he needed to clean higher than the length that was in the water, she rolled back only to find her head cupped in his hands. She closed her eyes as he lowered her into the water and cleaned away the last of whatever he'd seen. He then began massaging her scalp with tender fingertips.

Lightning chained across her skull, puckering her nipples and raising bumps on her skin. She covered her breasts with her hands, enjoying the contradiction of warm, soothing water and hypersensitive flesh as Aron's attentions wandered. His thumbs worked the muscles and tendons of her neck before kneading their way outward. He squeezed and pressed, his fingers describing delightful circles over her collarbones and digging into the hollow above them, moving along her shoulders and pinching her muscles until she shivered and released a quaking breath.

His hands felt even better than she'd anticipated. Half submerged in warm water, all she could hear were swirling splashes and the thudding of her own heart getting faster with every brush of his rough skin. She was suspended out of time and place, alive with desire that stemmed from him. She anticipated his touch beyond her neck and shoulders, imagining it fanning across her chest and to her breasts, moulding them—

Her sensual bubble burst rudely as he released her and shifted away. Cooler water rushed in to fill the warm void, causing her to shiver and sit up with a gasp, her arms still crossed over her chest. His expression was devastatingly neutral.

Synjan cleared her throat, not trusting herself to speak straight away. "Thank you."

"I can braid it for you later, if you want."

It took her a few seconds to realise he was talking about her hair. She glanced at some strands stuck wetly to her shoulder. "You'd braid my hair?" she queried. That was *not* the way she anticipated him touching her again. It was almost paternal, leading her to think of Ellis. She rapidly squashed it, pleased when Aron chuckled at her disbelief.

"I had a sister. *Have.*"

All thoughts of her personal demons vanished as he surrendered a personal detail. She yearned to know more; her craving for him was boundless. "Where is she?"

"On Boronia. Our home world. She has no idea about..." he waggled a finger at their surroundings, indicating the desert and the dimming sky above, "...this."

Synjan was baffled, interpreting his action as a general reference to Wandering. But how could his sister—who had to have the blood as well, unless she was only his half sister—not know about Wandering? Was his whole family therefore ignorant? Perhaps he hadn't understood his own ability beforehand, like Daeson hadn't. The thought was illuminating. "Oh! Did you Wander accidentally?"

His smile twisted. "Something like that."

His elusive response gave her the feeling he was regretting this line of conversation.

"How does that work?"

"Um..." he began, trailing off as he looked up at the sky.

She watched the way the light played upon his unshaven skin. Glints of gold flickered in his days-old beard and his eyes took on the aspect of silvery ice as the twilight pierced them. His lashes contrasted them in dark, elegant curls. His throat bobbed as he swallowed, drawing her gaze downward. He had a beautiful body, sinewy and taut with well-exercised muscles, covered in a swirl of chest hair that speared to his navel. She longed to run her hands through it. He was lithe and powerful, bronzed by the light and held captive by her question, like a wild animal tamed only as far as it suited him. His magnificence took her breath and she was startled when he finally answered.

"I didn't know what I had until I left it."

"Ah. Yeah," she replied, having lost the thread of the conversation when she'd allowed herself to be absorbed by his physical presence. What he'd offered was a common enough Wanderer sentiment for her to respond. "And then you Wander on and it's gone."

"It's not really," Aron argued, turning to look at her. "It's just something you've left behind."

"Isn't that the same thing?"

"What, out of sight, out of mind? It's not the same as solving a problem, no. It's leaving it for someone else to deal with."

She was struggling to keep up with him, aware of subtext that only he understood and wary of overstepping the boundaries he erected with his vague wording. She sensed a condemnation of Wanderers in his phrasing and a cynicism with their kind that she couldn't fathom. It was clear he'd left his family behind and he had regrets about it. Perhaps that was why he nursed the resentment she was sensing?

"So... you do your best to leave absolutely no marks on the worlds you go through?" she hazarded.

This time he looked down, patting the water in front of him, making ripples. "Nobody will notice if I die."

Synjan was alarmed by his statement and a feeling of darkness too powerful to name washed through her at the thought of burying *his* body in an anonymous hole. She reached out and gripped his forearm. She hadn't known him long enough to warrant such powerful emotions, but everything they'd been through had heightened her awareness of him. "I'd mourn you," she vowed. "You've had a huge impact on my life."

Aron met her gaze, his eyes haunted by something she couldn't define. "I'm... I'm not..." He shook his head, unable to continue.

Ready, her mind finished for him. He wasn't ready for her to push him, she was coming on too strong. "I'm sorry," she apologised, letting go of his arm. "I don't mean—"

She stopped speaking abruptly as he reached out and grabbed her hand, squeezing it. "Can I stay? Daeson told me to leave but... can I stay?"

His question was so earnest, his tone so intense that she didn't have any difficulty in reading more into it. He was asking to stay with *her*.

"I want you to," she whispered, feeling like there wasn't

enough air in her lungs.

"Mmn," he said and a smile ghosted around his lips as he returned to patting the water and making ripples. "We work well together. Have you noticed?"

"You know I have."

"Why do you let him make decisions for you?" Aron looked up at her. "You're better suited for leadership."

She shook her head. "I'm no leader. I don't always make the right decisions."

"Nobody does. But he hangs them over your head."

Synjan sighed, her shoulders drooping as Aron reminded her exactly where they were. And why. It had been so lovely, immersing herself in him and shutting out reality. Daeson was still gone and Peri was dead and everything was just... waiting for them to face it.

Aron was right about Daeson punishing her for her bad decisions. A spark of weary realisation flared in her as she recognised a less than stellar trait in herself, buried in this pattern of behaviour; it had felt right for Daeson to continue punishing her for her mistakes because it was the way Ellis had trained her. There was nothing so strong and twisted as a relationship built on reprisal and restitution.

"The Gods only know how we'll get past this because it's going to be my fault again," she mused.

"Just because he doesn't accept his part of the blame doesn't mean you have to wear it all."

She gaped at him, stunned into silence. She'd been conditioned first by Ellis and then by Daeson to bear blame automatically. But he was saying she shouldn't? Initially, Aron telling her things weren't her fault or prodding her to not always defer to Daeson had seemed like an encouragement to slough responsibility, but now she was seeing it in a different light.

He wasn't championing irresponsibility or offering absolution for her misdeeds; he was saying that they were all flawed, that they *shared* responsibility. She wasn't alone. She suddenly felt lighter. Free. She launched herself at him, hugging him fiercely.

Aron hugged her back. "It's alright. You're alright," he soothed. He kissed the top of her head tenderly and she felt cherished.

She rested her cheek on his chest and relaxed against him. "Thank you. You make me feel so good," she confessed. "No, more than that. You make me feel *worthwhile*."

"You shouldn't be with anyone who doesn't make you feel worthwhile," he growled and she marvelled at the way his sincerity rumbled his chest, beneath her ear.

Synjan tipped her head back so that she could look up at him. Feeling her shift, he looked down and met her gaze. Their breaths mingled and the look stretched, taking on new dimensions of meaning. "*Be* with?" she queried huskily.

"Yeah," he said, his expression soft and fathomless.

"I should be with you."

The look he gave her was so heated she felt it in her toes. "Are you sure?"

She leant up and pressed her mouth to his. "I am," she said against his lips but anything else she might have added was swallowed by his kiss. Their position was awkward and they shifted, stretching out on their sides, front to front.

He kissed her like there wasn't anything he'd rather be doing in all the worlds; his reverence was intoxicating. His tongue entered her mouth with just the right mix of curiosity and boldness, coaxing hers into a complex dance. He tasted like the light dying around them; hot breath and confidence.

Everything in her quivered and burned. His hand whispered across her face, down her throat, over her shoulder and onto her breast, lighting blazes on her skin wherever it contacted. She arched into him, whimpering beneath his attentions. When his hand braced on her lower back, she became boneless and hazy, wrapping her thighs around his leg and squeezing out a message he couldn't fail to interpret.

He pulled away from her lips only as far as was strictly necessary to deliver one of his own. "I haven't got protection," he said.

Synjan put a valiant effort into thought and calculation, coming up with a conclusion that was frightening. They should stop. The risk was high. She moved until she could see his face, doing her best to ignore the slippery feel of him wedged against places that really wanted to be speared. "I think... my cycle might be due soon. I was in Femme, last time, it's been... weeks, it's probably—"

"You can't get pregnant. I'm infertile. I was thinking about diseases."

Laughter bubbled out of her, giddy and bright. "What diseases? Daeson's Healed us both."

Wonder dawned upon his face and she was freshly smitten.

"Satisfied?" she queried, wrapping her hand around him in a manner that confirmed for both of them that he certainly was not.

His answering grin was slow and predatory. With deliberate care, he spread his hand across the small of her back again. She released him before writhing mindlessly against him.

"That's not fair," she gasped.

"It was my discovery," he murmured, tilting his head and pressing light, unapologetic kisses to her throat. His beard scratched her tender flesh as he moved.

"You kn-know my weakness," she sighed and squealed as his fingers quested, seeking the exact boundaries of her vulnerability.

"Mmm-hmm," he purred beneath nibbles.

Synjan clasped his hand and pulled it over her hip, turning it and pressing it to where it would be put to far better use. She sighed as his seeking fingers slipped beneath her underwear and obliged her silent command.

"Mmm, warm," he slurred.

She was just as drunk on him and lucidity was fading fast. She opened her eyes to fight it and looked at the buttery sky above. It was tinged with silver blue and the scent of approaching night cooled her lungs as she inhaled, bringing a moment of clarity.

When his thumb entered the fray, she was lost in him once more.

"You really *don't* fight fair," she muttered, turning her head and latching onto his earlobe, suckling the soft nub of flesh while she held it between her teeth.

Aron flinched and an unexpected noise escaped his lips.

They both froze.

"Did you just... *giggle*?" Synjan asked.

His response was swift and caused her eyes to roll back in her head.

She did her best to fight him with swirling tongue and clutching hands but he was as skilled in this warfare as he was with a gun. Their clothes disappeared, his mouth replaced his hand and electricity cavorted through her veins, leaving her limp and floating.

When he kissed her afterwards, a primal surge of possessiveness overtook her, opening her to impulses she'd never experienced—the need to own and brand this man as hers.

"You're amazing," she whispered, her lips burning deliciously from the ravages of his whiskers.

"You're not so bad yourself," he responded and claimed her in one smooth stroke.

A seismic wave rippled through Synjan, stunning her. He didn't just fill her, he *connected* with her. Her eyes sprang open and her fingers dug into his shoulders as she clenched around him. It was the only way she could tell where she began and he ended. She'd never felt anything like it.

The sun was gone and stars twinkled in the infinite darkness above them, suspending her in this moment with him. Every cell in her body opened independently and vigorously to Aron, like a flower to the sun.

He whispered something; it resonated against her skin more than she heard it over the noises their bodies were making. She thought it was, *"You're beautiful,"* but she couldn't be sure. She kissed him and he tasted like a perfect blend of the two of them. It was exhilarating and terrifying. He made her feel frantic in a way she'd never experienced.

This time, it was more than waves of pleasure; she was thrust over the edge and into the everyworld. She exploded into a million fractions of stardust around him. Infinity opened momentarily inside her then closed back into one condensed, vibrating whole, leaving her trembling and weak in his arms.

Awareness seeped into her gradually but the chill of night made moving increasingly urgent. She looked at Aron, smiling before she kissed him again, tenderly, then pulled away. She had no idea what to say. He was more than she'd ever experienced and infinitely more than she'd expected. Her brain was happy to let her body sing with repletion and not bother her with the details necessary for speech.

They cleaned up hastily, gathering their clothes and wringing them out. They were too wet to bother wearing but her pants and socks were dry enough; she pulled them and her boots on for the walk back to camp. As Aron came up beside her similarly attired, she mapped.

"Daeson's back. In his tent," she told him, clutching her wet clothes to her front and trying not to shiver as night sank its icy teeth into the desert at last.

Aron looked at her thoughtfully and nodded. Then he took her hand and they walked back, uncertain about what came next but allied in their resolve to face it together.

24

Moving On

SYNJAN WAS COMPLETELY enervated by the desert. It had been tolerable when they'd had vehicles to navigate its vastness but multiple days on foot had created new levels of hatred for this environment.

At first, it had been a place of shifting features and unexpected secrets. The long dusks and slow dawns gave time an intriguing aspect, offering relief from blistering days and freezing nights.

Today, they'd walked away from the last oasis they'd see for who knew how long. The days ahead stretched before her like the desert itself; dry, unpredictable and unrelenting. It was a land of extremes and she was devoid of the emotional fortitude to cope with any of them any more.

She missed Gredann. She missed walking up and down gusty streets that carried the fine mist of the ocean to her, rejuvenating her spirit with every breath. She missed the clangs of the trawlers coming in from a night's fishing when she visited the docks, the calls of the fishermen and the pungent odour of old fish. She missed Baltham and his efforts to marry her off. She missed rain. There was plenty to not miss about her home but she found it difficult to recall exactly what that might be in her current, depleted state.

Synjan looked over her shoulder, checking on Daeson with her eyes because she couldn't afford to map. He was refusing to walk with her and Aron, preferring to stalk along behind them, throwing them dark looks if they glanced at him. She wasn't sure if his fury was all about Peri's death or whether she and Aron had done something else to antagonise him when they'd returned to camp the night before. He'd dumped all of Peri's gear out of his tent and hadn't come out to eat. Synjan had called for him but he hadn't responded. They'd cleaned up Peri's gear— burning most of it—just like they'd taken care of her body. Without Daeson's input. She was too weary to fight with him, it was too hot and there were too many kilometres for them to walk.

Aron was also content with his own thoughts but they didn't seem sullen. If she looked at him, his expression lightened. Even if he didn't smile, his eyes glistened in a way that was familiar and thrilling. He was happy to catch her looking at him. He seemed to have no expectations after the night they'd shared and no regrets, either.

She supposed she should. Her whole life in Gredann she'd spent her time with itinerants just so she wouldn't be forced to lie about her work. Locals posed the risk of attachment or wanting more than she could give. *That* had scared her, yet she'd slept with someone she was

Wandering with? Someone that had no intention of leaving. Someone she was already far too attached to.

Her past self wouldn't recognise the woman she was now. All in all, that didn't seem a terrible thing but she was at a loss as to how to proceed from here. Aron was the best lover she'd ever had. Most skilled, the absolute sexiest and hand-to-heart the best orgasms of her life. Just looking at his hands got her tingling and his mouth and eyes... she couldn't look at him too much lest she implode with lust. What did it all mean? And how was Daeson ever going to be okay with it? She thought she might be able to keep things platonic with Aron if it meant Daeson gave him a chance and they could travel in peace, rather than tension. It would be very difficult but she'd do it, for the sake of harmony—

"What?" she said. She stopped walking and Aron did, too.

"Pardon?" he asked, confused.

The Portal had disappeared. It was a distinct feeling, striking her in the solar plexus. Without mapping, it was like a noise she could hear in her subconscious but if she concentrated, she couldn't hear it any more. She focussed instead on her breathing until the Portal finally landed. When she felt its intensity, she closed her eyes and risked a quick confirmation map that took minimal energy.

Daeson stopped on her other side just as she opened her eyes. "The Portal moved *closer*," she announced turning to look at Daeson. "That fucker did us a favour!"

He grunted. "How much closer?"

His expression muted her joy. Her smile crumpled in the glare of his grim tone. "We should reach it tomorrow afternoon, if we don't slow down."

"Then we won't slow down," Daeson said and continued walking, the rapidity of his strides the only change in his demeanour.

Synjan sighed, fighting off a wave of hopelessness. Sensing Aron looking at her, she summoned a smile and began walking with him again, brushing his hand with her own in gratitude because he didn't say anything about Daeson. He was a weight on her heart that she couldn't dislodge.

After they'd settled into a faster walking pace, Aron proved that he wasn't thinking only about himself.

"That 'fucker'?" he queried. For the first time that day, Synjan laughed.

———————•❦•———————

The fire was as cheerful as Synjan's mood. She and Aron had taken extra time on their hunt that evening, setting snares near some burrow entrances before the sun went down. When they went back to check on them, they had a selection of fat, fluffy things to kill and eat, along with another big lizard. They'd also gathered multiple armloads of desert scrub to sacrifice for their final meal in this inhospitable environment.

They butchered and spitted their meal away from the camp, neither of them ready to expose Daeson to any triggering violence. They returned to find he'd set up his tent and was squatting in front of it. Under his watchful eye, she and Aron built up the fire and roasted the different meats. The delicious smells soon had them all salivating. Even Daeson became interested in the cooking process, willing to turn or lift to prevent the meal from getting burnt.

There was too much for just the three of them but they continued cooking to create a few rations. They had no idea what sort of world they'd wake up in tomorrow evening. Synjan silently prayed to every god in existence that they not land in another desert.

"This reminds me of a Mukake feast," Synjan mused as they sorted the leftovers into containers for packing. "Not enough beetles, though," she grinned conspiratorially at Daeson, hoping the abundance of food and the roaring fire had cheered him up enough to accept her gesture of peace.

A smile flickered around his mouth, not ready to land just yet. "At least I didn't have to spend six hours weaving one plate."

Synjan laughed. "Or climb that horrendous cliff for some scallops. By Shuni, what I wouldn't give for some of them right now!" she enthused, invoking the Goddess of Water. Her name was well known in Gredann.

"I can live without them or that cliff," Daeson countered wryly, causing her to chuckle again.

She was pleased she'd brought up some of the positive experiences of their past. Daeson looked at her more kindly and the air became companionable.

"We should all go to sleep. We need to get up early," Daeson announced, leaving the corona of the fire and heading to his tent.

He unzipped the door flap with unusual vigour, drawing Synjan's attention away from watching Aron secure the last of their food. When Daeson saw her looking, he gestured to the inside of the tent.

Synjan blinked at him. "What...?"

"I want you to sleep in the tent with me tonight," he declared.

An awkward silence arose, punctuated by the pops of the fire and something vulnerable nearby screaming as it was captured by a predator. The squeaks were swiftly muffled and Synjan turned to look at Aron, who broke eye contact to stare off into the distance. The grim line around Daeson's mouth had reappeared when she looked back at him.

Synjan stood and brushed off her pants before striding over and ducking into the tent. She sat cross-legged on the side she'd previously occupied and waited for him to join her, her heart pounding. He closed the tent door—not that it would prevent Aron from hearing every word they said—and sat opposite.

"Daeson... I'm not going to sleep in here with you tonight," she told him as gently as she was able.

"I didn't really expect you to, now that you've had sex with him," he replied curtly.

A cloak of mortification settled over her. Her cheeks burnt as she gaped at him. How did he know? She and Aron had been discreet when they'd returned... Daeson must've seen them at the waterhole? In the act. Her cheeks got hotter, the humiliation spreading through her whole body.

"I'm sorry you found out," she told him huskily, realising she couldn't tell him that she was sorry. She wasn't sorry it had happened. She also couldn't tell him truthfully that it had been a surprise or that it had flowed organically out of their grieving process; it had, but her attraction to Aron had been drawing her in his direction for much longer than just last night.

"So are you done with me now?"

Synjan blinked, fighting off a wave of sadness. "I'm not 'done with you'. We're still partners. We're just... not going to be lovers," she shrugged helplessly.

"I never asked that from you."

"I know," she winced. "I was pushing it on you. You must be relieved that—"

"Relieved is not the word I'd use."

"Okay, how are you feeling?" she asked, thinking it positive that he was willing to identify his emotions.

"Devastated. Betrayed."

The bottom dropped out of her insides. "B-because I had sex with Aron?"

"Because you're replacing me with Aron."

"How? We weren't lovers. You don't even want me like that!"

"How are so sure he wants you like that, that he's not just using you?"

His words gave her pause. She couldn't fathom what Daeson meant, since it clearly wasn't for sex. "Using me for... what?"

Daeson sighed impatiently, rolling his eyes. "Navigating."

Synjan raised her eyebrows. "He's been Wandering alone just fine without us. I know I make it easier but I'm pretty sure he's not interested in me for my talent."

Daeson wasn't to be dissuaded. "You're sacrificing our friendship for a bit of fun."

She felt like she was losing ground and she didn't even understand when the gambling had started, only that the stakes were very high. "Are we no longer friends?"

"When you phrase it like a question, I can't tell if it's true."

His words sliced through her, clean and savage. "Fuck you. I love you. You're my best friend," she told him stiffly.

His eyes closed and she watched the relief flood through him, lowering his shoulders and deflating the hostility that had kept his spine so straight. Clearly, he was scared but she couldn't respect the indirect method of his questioning. His talent for identifying and speaking the truth didn't mean he wouldn't play mind games. His wording reminded her of Nick and Omerri and she should have expected it. She'd never seen him as manipulative. Perhaps Aron was more insightful than she'd given him credit for.

"Once he's gone, we can go back to how we were."

Synjan marvelled at the extremes of his assumptions. He'd jumped from Aron replacing him to Aron being gone, rather than considering an arrangement somewhere in between. She got the feeling he wasn't doing it on purpose; he was expressing his desire and belief that Synjan would do what he expected.

"Daeson, stop that! You're manipulating me."

"What? How? No, I'm not," he blustered.

He'd said it, so it had to be his truth but she couldn't understand how that could be. He had the categorical outlook she associated with a child. "Yes, you are. I know you think Aron's going somewhere but you don't *know* that."

"C'mon, Synjan. Men like him don't hang around."

"Men like what?"

"Like him," he answered in a small voice.

Her lips pressed together as she made a connection for him. "You mean men that kill?"

"No. Roman didn't kill anyone."

"I'm pretty sure he has," she scoffed, "and he definitely would, to get what he wanted."

"To survive, he might. But I don't mean killers, I mean loners," Daeson clarified.

Understanding flushed her with shame. She oughtn't jump to such defensive conclusions. Roman had been a loner and Aron was, too. Daeson was probably right, though the thought of Aron leaving scared her. She pushed it out of her mind and brought the conversation back to its point.

"Look. Forget about Aron. What matters is what you said about us. We're never going back to how we were," she told him gently. "What I admired most in you was unachievable from the beginning."

"You're punishing me for what you thought?"

His truth had a way of cutting away the nonsense and she was ashamed of herself again. "I'm saying I wanted to be good because I thought of you as good but it's not that simple. I was coveting your innocence."

Daeson sighed his frustration. "I hate when you call me that. I'm not innocent just because I don't like violence," he scowled.

"True, but it's more about the fact that you and I were born on very different worlds, six years apart. I've come to realise the significance of our age gap. You don't understand why I am the way I am and I wasn't giving you the credit you deserved. We have little in common except for an appreciation of one another's talents and a friendship borne of proximity," she shrugged.

"People are different even when they're born on the same world. It's not being the same that makes us friends."

His salience gave her pause. "No... but our differences have become more apparent as we've travelled and they've divided us."

Daeson took a moment to think her words over. He looked concerned when he spoke. "Disagreeing is not dividing."

"Not dividing our friendship but our way of thinking is very different. You have a very... black and white way of seeing things. I've seen and done too much to believe in absolutes, I see shades of grey," she said, struggling to express herself.

"I don't have a choice but to speak in absolutes! I can barely say what I mean now because the words aren't exactly right. The more complicated something is, the less I can talk about it! Don't use that against me."

Synjan was astounded. She had never considered how deep the restrictions on his speech ran. She'd understood on an intellectual level that he hated this unnamed talent but now she saw how it held him prisoner. She finally understood on an emotional level that he didn't have the luxury of modifying his spoken responses to appease feelings or suit delicate situations. He could state the truth as he saw it or nothing at all. What she'd been labelling youth or inexperience was actually raw truth. He couldn't express himself any other way.

Appreciation for him and his complexity welled inside her. Even in his black and whites, there was no simplicity.

"You're right, and I'm really sorry for making assumptions or speaking for you. I've not given it enough thought. Tell me in *your* words why you feel we'll 'go back' to the way we were."

Daeson replied confidently. "Because of J'Bdyamn. We were on our own and we didn't argue. We talked a lot in this tent. We learnt about one another. It was nice. This place could've been like that."

She was saddened by his focus on the past. "Are you just going to ignore how things have changed since then?"

"What are you trying to tell me? Just say it."

"I feel like you're still not accepting me. I'm telling you how I've come to realise we're different but that's okay. We have to learn to embrace that and just... plant our feet and find our places for this ride we're on together because I think we'll do and see some amazing things. You're telling me you just want to go back to that time before you saw me kill a bunch of men. Back to when I was elevating you as the ideal person and letting you make all the decisions. It's not going to be like that."

His expression hardened and it sent a flutter of fear through her.

"You accuse me of being black and white yet you sit there simplifying what I want. You tell me that you let me make all the decisions, but *you* decided I had to Wander out of your world, *you* decided to Wander with me and *you* decided we were leaving Earth. I know we can't go back to who we were at the start but we can go back to how we treated one another. We treated each other better when we were strangers."

She pushed past her initial reaction of hurt to listen to

265

what he was saying. He was talking about respect and communication and she didn't communicate properly with him until J'Bdyamn. She understood now why he held that time as an example of how they should be. He wasn't even talking about Aron, just about *them*. Still, he resented her for making the decision to leave Earth? What other thoughts was he keeping to himself?

"That's a fair point. We need to talk more, I shouldn't cut you out of any decisions. Do you mean you wanted to stay on Earth?" she asked incredulously.

His voice softened when next he spoke, faltering on occasion as though he still didn't want to share this secret with her. "I wanted to talk about it but I didn't get a chance. It was overwhelming at the start... you wanted to keep moving because of the Hunter, so I went along with it. But... at the shopping place I decided I wanted to stay for a while because everyone was nice to us. I wanted to talk to you about it after we left there because it was loud and full of people."

His sadness defeated her. She really *had* done wrong by him. She owed him so much more. She leant across and hugged him as an apology, ashamed of her actions. If she *had* given him the chance to speak his mind, circumstances would be so much more pleasant right now. She sat back and spoke sincerely to him, her hand resting on his knee.

"I'm so, so sorry. I can't even fully explain what made me do it. I just acted on instinct and things went from bad to... catastrophic. It's a pretty accurate representation of my life before I Wandered and why I had to change it," she sighed, recalling the numerous failures she'd experienced in Ellis' employ. No. She was making changes, she had to remember that. She pulled her hand off Daeson's knee and sat up straighter, shaking off the mistakes of her past. "So. Let's be clear about what comes next," she smiled. "We'll both be glad to Wander out of this world. I'm still open to settling on a nice world but I'd prefer it to have fewer Authorities than Earth did. Do you think that's reasonable?"

"In the next world, it'll be just you and me?" Daeson asked, the hopefulness in his voice soured by the challenging look in his eyes.

Synjan licked her lips, trying to figure out how best to answer him. She was acutely aware that Aron was outside and would hear. Instinctively, she mapped and was dismayed to note that he'd moved even closer to the tent. Belatedly, she realised that Daeson would've felt her mapping the man he wanted to leave behind.

"I don't want Aron to leave," she answered truthfully, deciding to be blunt and cut off any objections Daeson might raise. "And it's more than the amazing sex. It's that he's an experienced Wanderer and we work well together. I think he's an asset." She invited Daeson's objections with a gesture, knowing he had them because of the awkward expression on his face. It melted into a pout as he spoke.

"You want me to travel with someone I don't like. You didn't want to do that for me with Roman."

Synjan was secretly pleased that he was wrong on that front. It didn't rival his, forced evacuation of Earth but it was along the same unspoken lines of intent.

"Actually, *he* didn't want to travel with *me*. I never got the chance to talk to you about it. I wouldn't have liked him but I know I'd have been able to travel with him. He was experienced and ruthless. I'd have managed." She'd co-operated with people like Roman her whole life. She believed that Daeson would've got sick of travelling with him long before she did. "Will you manage, with Aron?"

Daeson looked away. After a short moment, he looked back. His steady stare held a command she responded to. "I will. If that's what you want. It looks like he's what you want right now, anyway," he finished loftily.

She set her jaw, fighting off a flash of anger. These men were fond of questioning her loyalty, making her out to be fickle. Guilt swiftly followed anger because she *was* maddened by her desire for Aron. She couldn't risk discussing it with Daeson—not because of Big Ears listening outside—but because it was far worse than he thought. She wanted Aron in ways that scared her; she *wished* it was as simple as sex. She liked who she was when she was around him. She liked feeling worthwhile. Daeson had never made her feel that confident. She was hurt by his ruthless implication but also grateful he thought it was only about sex. The thought of choosing between the two of them would likely not go in Daeson's favour.

Synjan considered meeting his spiteful comment with one of her own but chose not to, for the sake of peace. "I do want that, yes. He's helped save your life once and mine twice, so civility is the least we owe him—for however long he chooses to hang around."

Her good intentions dissolved in the defiant flare of Daeson's eyes.

"She wouldn't have shot you."

Everything within her lurched and dropped sharply. *He*

would've let me die.

Daeson was so adamant in his view of Peri as the victim that he wouldn't have acted to stop her. Had Aron not been there, Synjan was sure she'd be dead. She'd frozen. Daeson hadn't moved. Peri would've shot her.

The equation was simple, yet Daeson refused to follow it to its obvious conclusion. Why? Would he have preferred mourning Synjan and travelling with Peri? She doubted it. Was it because he didn't want to be blamed as well?

"Daeson, she would have," Synjan told him firmly, pausing to allow him to register her truth. "You have to take responsibility for the part you played. You attacked Aron for saying she wouldn't have shot me, then ran off into the desert to avoid your feelings. To avoid everything. You tell me that men like him don't hang around, but who stopped her from shooting? Who stayed to help me bury her? Who was there when *I* fell apart? He was. And where were you?"

She felt like a hammer, bashing a nail. There was no way the nail would thank her for it.

"And why should I stay and help? You don't want me to blame you but it was your fault! You stole the gear! You stole her car! You put a gun in her face and stole her! Why are you saying I should accept you and your mistakes when you just want me to share the blame for your decisions? It seems that because Aron is helping you clean up your messes, you prefer him. You've told me many times that I've been your conscience but now your conscience is inconvenient because it's easier being with him. That doesn't make him better!"

Synjan rocked back, stunned by the vehemence of his

words. It felt like he'd been waiting a long time to say them to her. Although it made her heart race, she was glad to hear him letting it out. Arguing was so much better than running away.

"You're right. All of it. It *was* my fault," she agreed quietly. "But it's not blame I want to share with you. It's responsibility. I got us into a shit situation, I admit it. But we all decided to bring Peri to protect *you*. And when she lost control, you would've stood by and watched me die. I can't rely on you."

"Yes. I decided along with you not to leave Peri behind. I decided not to rescue her when she asked me to. I decided that my freedom was more important than her going back, if she even could," he admitted, pausing as she had, no doubt to be sure she'd heard him accept his part. "And no, you *can't* rely on me being a killer. You've praised me for it in the past. You've changed your mind about that but I haven't. I'm sure it's because of him. *He's* giving you permission to not feel guilty about taking lives." Daeson pointed to the door of the tent for emphasis, then dropped his hand. "I don't like that you've had to kill but at least you've felt guilty in the past. Your compassion is what makes you human."

Synjan felt indignant, angry that the changes Daeson saw in her were being attributed to Aron. He wouldn't even let her bear her own blame?

"Daeson, I will carry the guilt of Peri's death with me until the day I'm put in the ground," she told him, her voice trembling. "You have no right to tell me how I feel or attribute my feelings to another person's influence. What Aron has made me feel is that forgiveness is necessary.

And possible. I will *never* ask you to be a killer. I'll always shoulder that burden for you," she said, her voice thickening. She swallowed in order to keep speaking, blinking back tears. "But you better fucking take responsibility for *that* because what I ask of you is forgiveness. That won't come if you keep thinking of what we have as your role and my role. If we're a team, you need to step up and play your part."

Daeson was quiet, watching her eyes glisten. His hands twitched like he wanted to wipe her face or hug her but he rubbed his palms on his thighs instead. When he spoke, his tone mirrored hers.

"You should know by now that I can't play my part. I can't keep doing this. You want me to be someone I'm not. More like him, maybe. I don't know what you need but I know that I can't give it to you. I need to find a world to live in. This is not the life I want. You're the Wanderer. Not me. Find me a world to live in and then we can say goodbye."

His words caused her tears to run after all. She swiped at them, wanting to respond clearly, doing her best to get her breathing under control. She reached over and gripped his hand, squeezing it.

"Don't say that," she whispered brokenly. "I don't want to lose you. You're right when you say I've changed. This adventure isn't what it was at the start, when I told you I wanted to Wander indefinitely. It's *hard*. It's wearing on both of us. I don't see myself leaving you when we find that world. What I would ask of you, in the meantime, is just... open yourself up to change, too. You can't be the same person, not after everything we've been through. It's not how life works—we all grow up, eventually," she finished, dredging up an encouraging smile.

His expression was open until her last words, then it hardened again and he pushed her hand away from him.

"'We all grow up, eventually?' It sounds like you think I'm young and foolish because I disagree with you. How dare you talk down to me after everything we've just said! The only change I see in you is arrogance and hypocrisy. You think you're all about shades of grey but, by your own words, you said you wanted to be like me! Now I have to be more like *you*?"

Synjan pressed her lips together, resisting the urge to shout as her emotions rebounded back to anger. Why did he think change was so bad? It wouldn't kill him to be a bit more like her!

"Actually, I think you're young and foolish because you don't take responsibility for anything," she clarified waspishly. "And *I'm* being a hypocrite because I've realised that it was naive of me to envy your ignorance of life's harshness? That I was stupid to think I could turn the clock back? Fine. You say 'hypocrite', I say 'realisation'. I *do* want you to be more like me. I want you to change because change means growth. People change! People grow! I'm not talking down to you when I say that. I'm still growing and changing, too. If you think I'm treating you like a child, take a closer look at you, not me!"

Daeson stared evenly at her, apparently unmoved. "Don't tell me it's my fault you're treating me like a child. That's all you. You say 'six years apart' like it makes you older and wiser and you tell me to change because that's what people do, but I'm not going to change my values. I don't think I ever will—I certainly hope I never will. What about you? Have your values changed? Is that what's happened here? Or is it just that my values are now getting in your way?"

Synjan was stunned into silence. His insightful words were anything *but* childish. He'd touched on something she'd never considered. Any values she might claim had always been imposed upon her by Ellis. She'd never thought for herself; this journey was the first time she'd been allowed to.

No wonder she was doing such a terrible job.

Daeson was younger than her, yes, but that wasn't the point. He'd had *choice*. He'd grown up with a father that loved him, on a farm where he got to have input and make choices. Even when he was alone, he'd made the choice to sell and leave.

Ironically, the Portal had been the first time in his life choice was taken from him, yet the Portal had *given* Synjan that gift. Then she'd started imposing *her* choices on him. No wonder he was frustrated! If someone had come up to her and said, 'Hey, I think you should *choose* to take responsibility for these lives and their deaths,' would she accept? Not in all the worlds! So she couldn't resent him for resisting her. He wasn't immature so much as unaccustomed to being responsible for his own choices.

"You know... that could be a part of my problem," she admitted. "I'm not even sure what my values are."

"Maybe you should think about them before you lecture me," he advised coldly.

Synjan raised her eyebrows. So much for admitting a vulnerability to him. His condescension left her hollow. If she'd revealed her ignorance to Aron, the conversation would have gone in a different direction.

"I'll do that," she vowed, deciding grace was a better option. "Look, how about nobody sleeps in the tent tonight? Why don't you come out and sleep with Aron and I?"

Daeson pulled a face. "That makes no sense. You won't come in here but you want me out there?"

"Yes. You agreed you'd give Aron a chance and we're travelling together. We can all squeeze into the tent but it'd be a tight fit. I think it would be nice if we were all together. It'd be a nice gesture." *On your behalf.*

"I'll travel with him. I don't have to be nice to him."

Aron laughed outside the tent.

Synjan frowned in the direction of the laugh then looked back at Daeson. "Have it your way," she sighed. "Goodnight." She got up and kissed his cheek before unzipping the door and stepping out. She was mildly amused by Aron's surprised look as he scrambled to get up. He'd been sitting *very* close. He wouldn't have missed one word of their discussion.

The fire was burning down but they still had some foliage to sacrifice to it. Aron tossed on some more plants while Synjan sat nearby, mentally reviewing everything Daeson had said. The main thing she'd learnt was that she needed to communicate with him more, to let him know she valued his opinion. She had to give him the opportunity to make choices and, when that wasn't possible, to allow him to take responsibility in his own way.

She needed to make better choices.

When Aron sat down beside her, he was so close that she wanted to lean against him. She wasn't sure how he'd respond so she refrained, rubbing her face and staring into the growing flames instead.

"So how old is he?" Aron eventually asked.

"Eighteen."

"Huh, he doesn't look it, though he acts it."

Synjan smiled wearily, thinking that he really didn't but unwilling to argue any more tonight.

25

The Portal's Warning

SYNJAN POINTED OUT into the desert. "There it is!"
Hawke thought he heard teary relief in her voice.
He looked, most of him knowing that he would see
nothing, a portion of him hoping to see the Portal anyway.

Nothing. Just the same scrub-filled desert plains they'd
been travelling through. It had made for easier walking
than sand and they hadn't needed to dig so deep for water
but it had still worn him down. It felt like they'd been
travelling far longer than eleven days. The feeling of elastic
time was due to the extraordinary events and company he
was keeping; he was fit and healthy but had over a decade
of age on these two. Their energy seemed boundless.

The Healer hadn't wavered but he drank more than him
and Synjan combined. Apparently his talent wasn't
something he could turn off. It made sense, though it
annoyed Hawke throughout their journey, watching
Daeson guzzle their dwindling water supply. When they
got to Avaniero, he was going to demand a full body Heal

from the man-child, to get rid of the sunburn, the fatigue and the bites from all the insects; the flies and mosquitoes had discovered their own private oases in Hawke's and Synjan's warm blood. Either Daeson hadn't received any bites or he'd Healed them immediately.

As he put one foot in front of the other, Hawke thought about the repercussions Synjan and Daeson would face from this adventure. And him.

Their path circled back to Ellis, where it had begun and... wherever this was supposed to go. He'd fabricated a mission, dodged questions, forced orders and slaughtered a unit of trainees all in the name of a friend and a burning question. She'd answered him, he supposed. She'd told him that she left because she would've died if she hadn't— but that didn't feel like her whole story.

There was more of her to learn.

Hawke still didn't know how he was supposed to accomplish Kegan's wishes. Even if Kegs had a special ITR portal on Avaniero, where would the three of them portal to? Hawke could hardly arrive undetected at Oceangate with two Wanderer charges. Plus, he needed a solid plan to return to the Authorities, considering he'd be walking into an active investigation about the training squad. He'd have to trust Kegan would come through for him, like he had for his friend.

What was Ellis going to do to the two of them? Would he be like the typical angry father-figure, cuddling and then yelling? Would he go so far as to physically punish Synjan because he had a Healer handy? What if Hawke defected to him? Would that keep Synjan safe?

She took his hand and Hawke looked at her with a smile.

She was brimming with happiness and vitality, her cheeks pink and her eyes shining. It reminded him of how she'd been when he'd brought her to her peak two nights ago. It was charming to see it on her face in the daylight.

He noticed Daeson was holding her other hand but didn't look happy about it. Oh. They must be close to the Portal. It must be something amazing if it made her look like *that*.

"Why is it pulsing like that?!" Daeson yelled.

Hawke flinched away, instantly recalling the story about the three Navigators. The Wanderer Portal had defended itself against ill intentions by killing and blinding the Authorities around it with a pulse charge, along with the treacherous Navigators who'd led the enemy to it. What if the Portal could sense his deception? Would it strip him of his Shield? Or worse?

"Aron! What are you doing?!" Synjan screeched, her smile turning into an expression of horror. She lunged for him at the same instant Daeson reached out to nothing at all. Hawke watched the Healer's balance shift in Synjan's favour and saw him glance back, notice what had happened and attempt to pull Synjan forward. Daeson was quite obviously trying to dump him. A bolt of regret shot through him at the thought of losing

her

the pair of them after all he'd been through but Synjan yanked away from Daeson and grabbed Hawke instead.

His heart hammered as she held tightly onto his arm.

"What's wrong?" she screamed in his face. Her voice carried across the plains. He supposed she must be yelling over the noise of a Portal that only she could see and hear.

"He doesn't want to come with us! Leave him!" Daeson

yelled behind her.

"I want to come," Hawke said.

"What?!" Synjan turned her head and went on tiptoe, putting her ear closer to Hawke's mouth.

"I said, I want to come!" Hawke repeated, louder this time.

"Good. Then let's go!" she yelled, grinning at him and grabbing his hand.

"Is it still pulsing?" Hawke shouted at her, feeling like an idiot because the desert around them was deathly quiet. It was just them making all the noise.

"What?!" Synjan asked, reclaiming Daeson's hand. He looked both scared and furious—most of the latter directed Hawke's way. He'd unsuccessfully tried to leave Hawke behind and, in his place, Hawke would've done the same. He respected it even though he didn't like it.

Synjan squinted at him. Her head was cocked, waiting for him to repeat his question through a storm only two of them were privy to, while he stood in a void. Apart. Where he always was. A Wanderer among Authorities, an Authority amongst Wanderers. Belonging to no-one and nowhere.

Brita's voice floated from the depth of his memory.

Oh, Hawke, haven't you figured it out by now?

He hadn't. He thought about all the other questions he needed answered. What was one more risk? Brita's words had taken on a different meaning.

"Let's go!" Hawke roared, surrendering himself to *her*, to the Portal and to this bizarre adventure. Synjan smiled and swung their hands, emphasising their link. Daeson pressed his lips tightly together and reached forward.

Hawke felt his body being squeezed as though he'd been clutched by a giant hand. He cried out, fearful of what the Portal would do to him—before he knew no more.